© 2022 Anthony Thomson

All rights reserved. No part of this book may be reproduced or transmitted in any form or by any means, electronic or mechanical, including photocopying, or by any information storage or retrieval system, without permission in writing from the publisher.

Cover image: Devon Thomson
Cover layout: Rebekah Wetmore

Editor: Andrew Wetmore

ISBN: 978-1-990187-30-8
First edition September, 2022

2475 Perotte Road
Annapolis County, NS
B0S 1A0

moosehousepress.com
info@moosehousepress.com

We live and work in Mi'kma'ki, the ancestral and unceded territory of the Mi'kmaw people. This territory is covered by the "Treaties of Peace and Friendship" which Mi'kmaw and Wolastoqiyik (Maliseet) people first signed with the British Crown in 1725. The treaties did not deal with surrender of lands and resources but in fact recognized Mi'kmaq and Wolastoqiyik (Maliseet) title and established the rules for what was to be an ongoing relationship between nations. We are all Treaty people.

Use every man after his desert,
and who should 'scape whipping?
– *Hamlet*, Act II, sc. ii

For Heather
now, and always

This is a work of fiction. The author has created the characters, conversations, interactions, and events; and any resemblance of any character to any real person is coincidental.

Contents

1: Gravel Road Cops...9
2: GoodFare..17
3: Interrogation..24
4: Lord Byron..31
5: Student confidential..36
6: Grunge and Slacks...42
7: Two pizzas..47
8: Slim pickings..52
9: More than a paper cut-out...58
10: Symbols and doggerel..64
11: D. H. Nietzsche...70
12: Two colleagues..79
13: The Lockharts...87
14: Morgan's tale...97
15: Gould's neighbourhood...105
16: Warrantless search..113
17: Detachment sauna..125
18: Debates..136
19: Steaks and knives..146
20: Xavier and Janelle..151
21: Break and enter..159
22: Gerald and Darryl..164
23: Shadow of doubt...167
24: Pick and roll..172
25: Round one..177
26: At last..183
27: Departure..190
28: Ethics..198
29: Trials...204
30: Choices..211
    Acknowledgements..219
    About the author...223

Tony Thomson

1: Gravel Road Cops

Monday, 29 March 1999

Sweat greased my fingers squeezing the snub-nosed .38 cradled gently under my thigh. Bright reds and blues glared in all three rear-view mirrors. My left hand rested casually on top of the steering wheel. The driver's window was rolled down.

The cruiser's only occupant approached slowly, his right-hand hovering over his unfastened holster. He bent down to look in the window, his eyes widening in recognition.

I whipped out the revolver, pointed it at his chest and pulled the trigger twice. He hadn't even blinked.

He took one step back, then a second, one for each of the double taps from my empty revolver. If he'd said what his eyes were saying, it would have been drowned by the laughter from our early-morning audience, their police automatics safely away. Constable Paul Dobson's visible embarrassment over his screw-up matched the red from the cruiser's lights.

"What were you thinking, Dobson?" Andy Graham asked incredulously. "That he only had one arm?"

"It's only Wallace. What was I supposed to think?"

"Remind me not to call you for backup," Andy said, adding sulphur to Paul's wounded pride.

The simulated highway stop was the morning's last exercise. I was the outsider. Andy had invited me to join the early-morning training and had lent me the .38 for the live-ammunition target practice. He had followed the shoot with a brief talk about safely approaching a potentially dangerous traffic stop—or unsafely, as it turned out. We'd unloaded our sidearms and passed them around the circle for everyone's close inspection. Andy had assigned me to role-play the risky motorist. Good thing I'd aimed at Paul's bullet-proof vest and not under the bison insignia on his yellow-banded hat. That would have been way too personal.

Andy and I watched as the cops dispersed for their morning shifts. Paul fishtailed in the slippery gravel and didn't switch off his red and blues until he was well down the road. The fumes from his exhaust mingled in the nippy, spring air with the pungent smell of gunpowder lingering from the target drill.

"That didn't go well," I said.

"It went very well," Andy replied. "They'll remember it. Things aren't always what they seem."

"They're never what they seem."

"Don't go all professor on me. In my line of work, facts are all we have."

"Paul won't forget who was behind the .38."

"Everybody knew you had the revolver," Andy said offhandedly. "He didn't think you'd be so quick. He'll get over it. Ready for patrol?"

"Sure," I said, thankful for my flexible work hours at the college.

I'd accompanied Andy on my first shift in the county. He'd bought an extra-large, black coffee for me at the local Tim Horton's café—the Tango Hotel, in cop dialect—and headed out for what became an interminable evening. Driving along the bumpiest back roads in the county, he graphically translating the bilingual Royal Canadian Mounted Police acronym —RCMP-GRC: Gravel Road Cops. Before long, my bladder had forced me to plead for mercy. Andy's version of water torture for initiates.

We strolled over to his light-blue Crown Victoria, a ghost car assigned to Highway Patrol. Even with no police markings or light bar on top, the car is obvious on close inspection, with enough bulbs on the front and back to make a Christmas tree envious. It transforms in a flash from inconspicuous to emergency, partly for the safety of its driver and, it occurred to me, for its passenger. My seat isn't exactly riding shotgun. Even without a small cannon between the seats, the interior of a police cruiser is crammed with impressive technology, a cockpit even when the cop is a woman.

"You finish your hour of work yet?" Andy asked with what he probably meant as a wry smile. It was the usual greeting and a running joke.

"This time in the morning, I'd have to start lecturing at seven. University students don't wake up until noon."

They all knew I taught nine hours of classes a week at the college. In their minds, that was the extent of my work. For them, my so-called job is a worse boondoggle than teaching school, or a better one, depending on how you look at it.

My involvement with rural police forces in Nova Scotia was six years in, a spin-off from my graduate research on the gap between police policy and officers' actions. My final degree helped me land a job teaching criminal justice at Sterling University College, while the expertise had pried a modicum of respect from local police chiefs and detachment NCOs.

Developing a close relationship with ordinary constables had been trickier. They needed to trust my discretion, to know I don't report to their supervisors. Before long, some of the cops began inviting me into more complex investigations, appreciating my alternative eye. The mixed feelings I have about the criminal justice system remain private. It's often my primary antagonist.

Andy swung the car out of the firing range, cruising through the stop sign and heading along Highway One towards Halstead, the county seat and home of the college. Laid out during the horse and buggy era, the old main highway meanders through a dozen small towns strung along its east-west route like hooks on a jig. Giant Elms stretch along the road and line the longer driveways, bereft of concealing foliage this early in the spring. Gaping holes in the rows reveal where Dutch Elm rot had taken down some of the larger specimens and opened the properties to a passing view. Verandas slouch along the ground floors of the century-old farmhouses. Eyebrow windows on the top half-storeys scan the countryside for something out of place.

From this distance you couldn't see the crumbling shingles and chimneys, the rot in the casements and front steps, or smell the mould creeping from the perpetually-damp, rock-walled basements. Too many decorative, built-to-impress oak foyers opened to shadowy interiors and smouldering desperation. It isn't only personal experience making me wonder whether happy families were only apocryphal. Cops see behind too many of these facades.

This morning, not much seemed to be happening in any direction, including front and back, where Andy's attention was fixed. The only signs of mayhem were porcupines crushed in the centre of the highway and a few dead raccoons curled on the shoulder like they were taking a nap.

Andy looked every inch the 40 he had recently turned, with thinning brown hair grizzled around the ears. Squat and barrel-chested, he was a little less than the minimum recruitment height two decades ago. The detachment rumour was that Andy had spent the summer before his medical exam using a home-made contraption to stretch his ligaments. Being recruited is that important to most aspiring Mounties.

His career had not unfolded as expected. After twenty years in the

Tony Thomson

Force, Andy was still a Constable, one of several veterans in the detachment. In their eyes, they're the real cops, up to their nostrils in other people's shit lives. As the years go by without promotion, their morale sags along with their jowls. Most had joined the force when it was still possible without a university education or being more or less bilingual, which had become vaulting poles through the ranks. Veteran constables worried that women or visible minorities were becoming the new targets for token promotions.

Stopping on the shoulder, Andy took out a pair of tuning forks, gave each a sharp tap on the steering wheel and held their persistent hums to the fixed radar on the dash. Two numbers appeared in red, one calibrated for on-coming vehicles, the other simulating the patrol car's speed.

"Close enough," Andy said. He had once explained the complicated radar system, in his way: "Some asshole is going to take his speeding ticket to court and ask when I last checked my radar. So I'll be ready."

Almost every member of the public is an asshole. Not other cops, although they can sometimes be called worse things.

Andy set the radar to signal at 100 kilometres per hour, 20 over the limit. No point pulling anyone over under that. They'd be full of excuses you had to listen to, and the usual speed was closer to 90. He made a quick note of the time and the reading in his police notebook. Andy didn't believe in handing out warnings. "If I have to get out of the car," he'd explained, "they're getting a ticket." It wasn't always true.

As the cruiser gained speed, the fluttering swarm of gnats re-awakened in my stomach. On any shift you never know what will happen, even driving aimlessly through the rural countryside or circling around the small-town streets. The happenings occur randomly, some intensely etched, fodder for so much cop-to-cop dialogue and anecdote. Collisions on the highway, chases ending badly, alarms that turn out to be real, domestics, abused children—the harms possible in even the quietest police beat. Driving anywhere in the county, I come upon an otherwise nondescript intersection or pass an ordinary-looking house and a queasy memory surfaces, like fingers protruding from a loose grave.

None of them are my tragedies. I have no official responsibility to do anything. I'm usually a privileged observer, an almost-disembodied presence floating above the bedlam. Except the horror penetrates my senses. An intense configuration of visions and emotions are entangled in the multiple helices of my memory.

The police radio crackled out of its slumber. "Reported missing person, Painton, female, 19, five foot five, 120 pounds, blonde hair." A pause.

About Face

"Missing since Saturday. Time unconfirmed."

The initial description was hardly worth the airtime. You'd have to investigate half the college-aged women in Halstead.

For Andy, a missing-person call was none of his business, a morsel for the cops on Detachment duty, not Highway Patrol. Within a second, Paul Dobson answered dispatch and asked for directions. Brown-nosing, as usual.

I made a mental note to reach out to him for the scoop, hoping I hadn't permanently blown our rapport. I'll make amends with a bottle of his favourite rum.

Nova Scotia has its share of unsolved murdered-women cases, a few of them here in Sterling County. Missing-person files can be convoluted and often end tragically, although a few are wrapped quickly and simply. Last year, a Halstead woman reported her toddler missing. When a cop arrived, the kid popped out from the cushions piled on the sectional sofa.

"That missing 19-year-old is probably a college student," I said.

"Ah ha," Andy replied, acknowledging the obvious. "Nothing about what she was doing Saturday night. Probably out to the Bridgeside looking for a new boyfriend and still with him. If anything, it's just another 'my innocent daughter didn't come home last night' complaint."

I hoped Andy was right, although Saturday was two days ago. Late any weekend evening you can watch the parade of college-aged women sashaying along Main Street, dressed for a party at the Bridgeside, the only pub in town with a dance floor. If you were out early enough on Sunday, you could see a few stragglers heading home, hoping to avoid the stares of disapproving morning people. It's called the slut walk in the Baptist town, a word referring only to the women.

Andy turned left from Highway One on Trunk 11-A. It wends around a half-dozen family farms on the Valley floor then gradually ascends the South Mountain towards the hump of the long, narrow province.

Sterling County is sandwiched in the middle of Nova Scotia's Annapolis Valley between Kings and Annapolis Counties, like Saskatchewan in the Prairies. Low, wide ranges, known on the east coast as mountains, bound the wide, flat valley on either side. They are both under one thousand feet in elevation. In British Columbia, no one would notice them.

Andy's aim was fixed on suspended drivers. Like drunks, they roam the back roads out of the cross-hairs of the cops, the mountain's occupying force. Experienced cops recognize unlicensed drivers by sight or from their exhaust fumes as they accelerate away. Some of their beat-up trucks display Confederate flags in the back window, the owners proclaiming they're rebels.

I was admiring the view when Andy exclaimed, "Take a gander at that."

A Ford F-150 truck was using the downslope as a runway. It had gained only a few inches of altitude when it raced by us, its transfixed driver staring straight ahead.

Andy switched on the lights and made a three-point turn on the narrow road, leaving enough tread on the asphalt for some teenager to claim as his. I tightened my seat belt to near asphyxia.

Andy closed the gap hitting 140, slowed when we reached the curved flats near the bottom of the mountain and closed on the truck, which was still driving over the limit. The driver hadn't noticed the lights. A couple of wails from the siren caught his attention.

"Impaired," Andy growled. "This time of the day it's gotta be chronic."

The driver pulled over with his right tires on the gravel shoulder. Andy blocked the entire lane behind him. If the next driver was as blind as this one seemed to be, he'd be taken out by the chain reaction collision.

Andy wrote some details in his notebook and called dispatch. "I've got a 10-83, possible impaired, red Ford-150 truck, Alberta registration, Alpha Charlie Romeo, Five Eight Three." A few seconds pause. "Heading south on Trunk 11A, north of Pitch Lake Road."

Andy leisurely swung both legs out the door as if he had the whole day to cover the short distance. I followed Andy's lead, heading towards the passenger side of the truck. Bringing a drunk into the detachment for a Breathalyzer can stretch into the early afternoon. He left his hat in the car. Members were supposed to put them on in public. He wasn't in the mood to follow petty regulations. Besides, he'd told me, people stare at the insignia on the front of the hat and not in your eyes when you're talking to them.

Walking carefully toward the still-running vehicle, Andy rested his right hand on his holster and paused to glance behind the front seat. You never know what might be lying in plain sight and give grounds for a search. He was thinking a bottle, but he also made sure the driver was alone.

The wary approach had been the subject of this morning's training. Random car checks can be as dangerous for cops as domestics. *Rarely* doesn't matter: careless once is all it takes, especially for RCMP members patrolling alone.

From my point of view, the cautious expect-the-worst approach is too intimidating a style for a rural county. Almost everyone they stop is facing their first brush with the law, not the prime suspect in some serial murder case the pulled-over motorists think they've been mistaken for.

Andy looked puzzled as he took position just aft of the front door. The driver's window was still closed. The first thing a drunk will do when the lights come on is open all the windows, hoping to freshen the cabin air. You can nose even faint alcohol fumes, like the reek of a smoker's clothes after you've quit.

Andy tapped on the window and the driver rolled it down. I couldn't judge his reaction to the spill out.

The male driver appeared to be in his early 40s, broad-shouldered with large tattoos on his tanned forearms, a cropped, thin beard and straight black hair topped with an Edmonton Oilers' cap. He was wearing a hunter's red plaid shirt. He glanced at me through the passenger window just long enough to deliver an evil omen through dark, piercing eyes. He was grimacing a half smile when he turned back to Andy.

"Turn off the vehicle, please," Andy said, donning his professionalism if not his cap. "You were hitting the pedal pretty hard there." He leaned on the door and peered in, breaching standard protocol.

"I'm in an awful hurry," Plaid Shirt blurted, seeming more in shock than nervous, as if he'd awakened from a nightmare only to be plunged into another. "My mother's sick and she's home by herself. She just got out of hospital. I've got to put her in an old-folks home and just went to see about it, back there in Bridgewater. It took a long time, and she gets in a bad way by herself. And I just came back to Nova Scotia in time for my father's funeral."

Andy went through his formal 'give me your papers' routine.

"That guy looks weird," I said, back in the cruiser. "And he invented a pretty wild story. What didn't go wrong for him? I was wondering what he'd make up next."

"I believe him," Andy said. He hadn't made any move towards the roadside alert, the first breath test. Must not have been a whiff.

He filled out most of the Summary Offence Ticket while he waited for dispatch to check whether Plaid Shirt had any outstanding warrants. He didn't.

Andy exited the cruiser more adroitly than last time. "I have to give you a ticket," he said apologetically to the driver. "Going one-nineteen on this highway is way too fast for just a warning. The ticket is for exceeding posted speed limits, the lowest I can give you, so it could have been a lot worse."

Tony Thomson

He didn't give his usual lecture about the consequences of excessive speed. He'd seen enough to keep him from sleeping long into retirement, the details deeply recessed and private. Not part of any kind of talk.

"Thank you," the driver said, despite holding his ticket like a rotten valley apple. People around here usually thank the cops for their traffic ticket. Plaid Shirt wasn't from Alberta, I guessed. Like a fish too small for the fryer, he was happy to be released after being snared. Chronic traffic offenders disregard another ticket as just one more unjust aggravation, tossing it in the glove compartment to join the collection.

Andy resumed the patrol along Trunk 11-A, taking a left to Pitch Lake Road, just beyond where he'd spotted the Ford-150. No more out-of-province speeders or missing women reports. Suspicious traffic was in short supply on the mountain, probably thanks to someone with both ears to a police scanner. Warnings of an unmarked police car spread quickly through the rural telephone tree. When a ghost car's identity becomes too obvious, they send it to another posting. Churches use the same solution for abusive priests.

Just past the noon hour, Andy dropped me at Sterling College as requested, giving me plenty of time before my two afternoon classes. He would take the cruiser home at four, eat the usual dinner his wife had prepared, and settle down in front of the TV for another evening with a bottle for a companion, numbing his mind and dousing his grievances. His wife would read in the corner under a floor lamp before heading early to bed. Romance novels were her favourite.

I was eager to work my way into Dobson's missing person file. Maybe I'd need three bottles of dark Bacardi, two for him and one for me.

2: GoodFare

Entering through the back door of the Arts and Administration Building, I resumed the less remarkable part of my split life. I was usually happy to go into the college, even more now I lived alone. But this abrupt change of roles always left some lingering tightness in my core.

Andy hadn't stopped all morning for a break at a Tim's and there wasn't time to make my usual noon-hour basketball scrimmage. I entrusted my lunch and health to the Grab & Gag cafeteria in the A&A building —officially the Grab & Go. I couldn't tell how many hours the pizza had been sweating under the warming lamp. I hoped not long enough to confess its worst microbial sins to my olfactory police. I elected a mushroom and dried tomato veggie slice—self-smell-and-serve—with a small dark roast to smooth its way down.

Looking for a comfortable space away from the gaggling students, I saw Robert Teasdale signalling discreetly from a quiet corner table. Should I pretend not to notice? Would he feign not being offended?

Feeling ensnared, I weaved in his direction through the leg and sneaker obstacle course. With a straggly white goatee, pale skin, a head of tightly curled, silver hair, and light-coloured eyes, everything above Robert's neck practically disappeared when he stood in front of a white background. His beige shirt showcased his crimson tie, emblazoned with miniature College crests. Trying to be natty, as usual.

Of all the faculty in the department, only Robert had voted against hiring me. Not that I was supposed to know, but that kind of information permeates the college like dust from the chalk boards we still used. Robert thought they should have brought in another American. Or one who knew how to dress properly. That was a decade ago. Even so, my feelings about Robert aren't water under the bridge. They're more orange, low-tide, Bay-of-Fundy mud, still viscous and gummy if you find yourself wading in. Resentments die hard.

"Hey, Ian," Robert greeted me with what he hoped would be taken as a friendly come-and-sit. "Anything new?"

Vague generalities were all I owed him. "I just finished a stint on highway patrol. Not much happened," I added in hopeful discouragement. My answer nudged his thinking only slightly to a follow-up I'd hoped not to hear.

"You still doing that police thing? I thought you'd finished that years ago. Have you published anything yet?"

Robert was on the tenure and promotion committee, where he played the hard-nosed bad cop, one of those who kisses up and kicks down. His question had a disparaging edge I had to answer. "I use what I learn from my policing research all the time in my teaching. Stories add meat to the bones."

While I was delivering this takeaway, Robert's gaze had flitted to a group of women crowded around a nearby table. According to the scuttlebutt, women students complained about his attentiveness to more than their grades. It's no consolation being under the objectifying lens of the male leer to be told looking is safe because it substitutes for action. Too often it doesn't.

Robert's gaze finally swivelled back to my eyebrows. He thought he'd been subtle, but according to Mary, my ex-wife, women always know. Even from behind. Even if they don't show it.

"One of our women students has been reported missing," I told him.

"I hope she's not one of mine," Robert said quickly before superciliously continuing with his own thread. "Nobody gets promoted just for teaching, Ian. It's a popularity contest—you know, who's the most entertaining in front of the class. Student evaluations are a joke."

The conversation was going to no galaxy where I wanted to hitchhike. "You hope she's not one of your what, Robbie?"

"One of my students, of course," he replied with an edge, glaring at me while turning a shade more pink than white. He began stacking his disposable dishes and abruptly pushed back his chair.

"Well," I said, finishing what little of the slice I could, "I've got to prepare a new stand-up routine for today's class."

Robert walked away without responding to my passive aggression.

I took the stairs to the Social Sciences Department and my office refuge, thinking about how important humour is in a lecture. Most of mine is spur-of-the-moment, the riskiest type.

Part of my annoyance with Robert was professional. My police observations are participatory. Cops are real people with peculiarities and points of view I'd learned to appreciate. The more people invite you into their world and reveal their prejudices and foibles, the deeper the implied trust and the more insidious any violation of their versions of self.

What irritates me most during my semi-conscious sleeplessness is the fear of being inauthentic, that false imperative, as if you could ever be only a single, indivisible self instead of many selves depending on time, place, and who you're with. Playing Saint Peter at the Pearly Gates must be impossible and terrifying, having to divide complex humanity into saved sheep and damned goats. Overly conscious of the multiple faces I project, I'm authentic only in my inauthenticity.

Monday afternoon was a back-to-back teaching schedule. My introduction to human societies lecture was almost an hour away, followed by criminal justice. As I reviewed my yellowed, scribbled notes in my office, my stomach began complaining about the quantity and quality of its lunch.

When the phone rang, I didn't let it go to voice mail. The image of a missing young woman flitted in my head. I hoped it was Dobson with a better invitation than Andy's.

"Ian Wallace," I announced into the receiver,

"Hey! Can I get into that criminal law course next term the Registrar says is closed?"

The query was muffled, as though the College didn't pay enough money to the phone company. I understood the administration's intent. Make students commit to returning next fall before the summer deinstitutionalizes them. It was all about numbers and money.

But this call wasn't from a student. I knew that voice. I pictured Lauren Martin's dark, braided hair and expressive, hazel eyes, the features you notice first and can't forget.

"It's going to stay closed to you," I said. "The last thing I need in class is a bright Mountie who knows how the law actually works."

"You've had members in other courses," she complained.

"Yeah, and most of them passed despite my efforts. They're not popular in class because their military haircuts are too obvious. Students think they're narcs."

"And you think they aren't? I've heard you once assigned an essay on, 'Are Cops Pigs?'"

It occurred to me they could be boars or sows. That's not the way I saw Lauren. Far from it. "Once only, and that was the first time a member took the class. His answer was, 'Sure, some cops are pigs, but not me.'"

"They all say that. Listen, I have a file I need your help with."

"Can you say that again in case I misheard?"

"Are you sure I said it the first time? Can you spare some time this afternoon? After your classes?"

"I'm free now and it's lunch time," I said, hoping to go somewhere for an actual meal with Lauren.

"Sorry. What I have in mind won't be quick. We have a report about a missing young woman. I'm meeting with Sergeant Young next, then interviewing her parents. Oh, I have to go. Young is waving me in. See you about three-thirty, barring the unexpected."

I heard a dial tone buzzing in my ear. Lauren had hung up.

"Damn!" I said aloud.

Lauren must have been assigned to Dobson's investigation into the missing 19-year-old, the subject of the police radio call. Definitely a student at the College.

I presumed no one had found a body lying where it shouldn't be. Not yet. Death itself is seldom ambiguous, although the cause and circumstances can be, as thousands of crime novels suggest.

Lauren had opened my way into the case. Spending more time with Lauren would be a major bonus. She's the only woman I've casually dated since Mary made it both possible and necessary.

With my mind on the missed lunch opportunity and my newly aroused appetite, I wanted something more sustaining than the Grab and Gag. GoodFare, the local organic food outlet on Main Street, was just the ticket.

At the café door, I manoeuvred around Johnnie Walker, as he was known around town with more derision than affection. He'd told me his surname was Walton. When I tried to use it, he'd said with pride, 'I'm Johnnie Walker now.'

Every small town has an oddball character, conventionally either a sad but genuine fool or a Shakespearean one, wise under the wrinkles. You have to apply for the position with Town Council. Nova Scotia's not like England, where they pump out eccentrics by the beer barrel.

Johnnie was staring intently at the chalk menu on a sandwich board. It was placed to obstruct half the sidewalk in hopes of diverting traffic into the café. In his late fifties with thinning, grey hair, he wore coveralls and heavy work boots, although he had once told me he'd never done manual labour. He'd been a station clerk in Halstead when Nova Scotia had passenger trains. He still keeps an eye on the comings and goings of the townsfolk, usually while loitering around the Main Street Café, a less wholesome option than GoodFare.

"Hi, Johnnie," I said, navigating around both walkway obstacles. I'd offered the minimal politeness exhibited in a small town. It made me feel virtuous, although I hoped he hadn't heard an invitation to chat. The air clinging to Johnnie was still mostly sober.

Twin brothers who lived on the South Mountain owned the store. Not that you'd ever guess they were twins. They looked similar, but their personalities and presentations were California rain forest and Nova Scotia scrub. They took turns working the small café squeezed into a space at the back of the store along with a few tables scattered about. Soups, sandwiches, baked treats, and smoothies, all made from local produce, as advertised. The alternative community clientele made it a comfortable place for an occasional lunch.

When it was my turn at the counter, Larry, the California twin, said, "Whatch'a in for, Ian?" His dark, reddish hair and beard flowed straight down, rivalling the length of his blue-checkered apron.

"Hi, Larr. Crowded as usual, I see."

"Try coming back in an hour. There'll be nobody here."

"Why come then? You don't think I'm here for the food, do you?"

"Ha. Maybe I'll just skip you and serve Johnnie. He looks hungry."

"I'm not that hungry," Johnnie piped up. "My doctor told me I better start eating healthy, so here I am."

"Okay," I said to Larry. "I'm thinking a daily-special smoothie with an avocado and brie sandwich." Everything came with sprouts, even the coffee, but I wondered which local farmer grew the avocado.

I couldn't see a spare seat. A lunch in solitude beckoned outside.

Two picnic tables were jammed onto the small patch of mowed weeds next to the curb. The good weather was holding. Maybe we wouldn't be thrown back into winter before March was through.

Johnnie followed me out with soup and home-made bread. He headed for the other side of my table, within easy eavesdropping distance in case I started talking to myself. It looked as though he wanted to return more than my triple syllable greeting.

At best, he and I carried on a give-and-take relationship. He was touchy, though. I had to be alert not to cross his ever-shifting line.

"Saw you driving through town in that police car they think's invisible," he said. "Why don't they just give 'er up? Everybody knows what it really is."

"Yeah, but it works on the highway. The cops in Banff drive around in an unmarked car with a full rack of skis. Blending in with the tourists. Maybe here they should tie a deer on top."

"Only in season. Dead give-away otherwise. What did you do wrong this time?"

"Failed one of their kids, as usual," my standard reply. Some people took it seriously.

"The cops never do much around here, you know," Johnnie said.

I could sense his weather vane switching direction. Maybe I'd misjudged the blood alcohol reading.

"We're payin' for all this patrolling in their swanky, new cars and you still can't sleep through all the racket. Kids yelling and screaming at two in the morning like somebody's killin' 'em."

"It's a college town," I explained, knowing Johnnie could sometimes be reasonable. "Comes with the territory and keeps businesses afloat. Students bring a lot of bread and butter with them."

"They bring a lot of other things, too."

"Oh?" I asked, despite knowing better.

"You know what I mean. Young people nowadays bring trouble on themselves. You can't act the way they do, in public no less, without somethin' happening."

"They're young," I said, not quite ready to abandon the hope of less strident discourse. "You remember how that feels. You've told me about some of your wild times. Maybe they're even in love, in their minds, anyway. Students hit town in the heat of their budding adulthood and discover it's Baptistville. A town-and-gown truce is the most we can hope for."

"Age got nothing to do with it," Johnnie shot back. "There's plain decency and there's none of it. I'm just sayin' they're looking for trouble and gonna find it, too."

His face turned deeper red. My misapplied diplomacy had wound him tighter.

"The Lockharts are finding that out, all right," he said. "All Sunday afternoon Georgina was nosing around town, tryin' to find where her daughter was holed up. She wasn't stayin' behind in church, you can bet on that."

My brie and avocado turned into sprouts. Johnnie had provided a possible name and a face for the young woman reported missing. Melody Lockhart, a sophomore at the college, fit the reported description. She's a student of mine, one of the bright ones who sits near the front and gets my jokes. Only tuned-in students understand them.

I made a polite excuse to Johnnie and carried the remnants of my lunch inside, dumping what I could into the compost to rot in peace.

I searched my retinal memory, wondering when I'd last seen Melody in class. I couldn't be sure. She had seldom missed classes until a month or so ago. Lately, she's been coming to about half of them.

By the time I returned to the A&A, that blurry picture of her presence/absence had withdrawn behind my forehead.

Forcing my mind into the lecture rut of intro soc, as the students called the subject, I assembled the carefully numbered notes I'd scribbled last night. I want to appear on time. If any prof doesn't appear promptly within ten minutes students become fleeing geese alarmed by a starting pistol.

The basic point of my introductory lecture that afternoon was that each person sharing an experience with others interprets it differently, depending on their individual circumstances and interests. Ultimately, we all live in distinct realities.

The upcoming justice lecture asked whether the criminal system is designed to allow guilty people to go free, a quote from a judge I'd interviewed. He argued that setting the extraordinarily high standard of being proven guilty beyond a reasonable doubt minimized the tragic conviction of the innocent. It didn't always work out that way.

After concluding my two performances, I waited impatiently in my office for Lauren to arrive.

Melody had not attended the criminology class. I couldn't remember whether she had been in my justice lecture last week. But the notes I took during last Thursday's seminar indicated her absence.

The only pattern I could see in her seminar record over the winter term was an increase in absenteeism and a gradual decline in grades. I didn't know much else about her, not personally anyway, although she didn't seem the type to get into trouble. Assuming there *is* a type.

Experiencing time is never consistent with what the clock tells you. I looked at my watch so often it began to think it was under police surveillance.

When the phone did ring, it sounded like a 5 am alarm clock.

3: Interrogation

"Ian Wallace," I said into the mouthpiece, falling unconsciously into my wary, don't-bug-me tone.

"Good afternoon. It's Constable Martin," Lauren said, amused at my manner. "I'm glad you're in, Dr. Wallace. Can you please meet me in the hall outside the Registrar's office?"

"Sure. I'll close the shop and be right there."

Lauren was unrecognizable at first, although she was the only one standing in the hallway. She was in civvy clothes, her uniform keeping her hat company elsewhere. I wondered if she'd added an accessory shoulder holster under the stylish, deep-wine-coloured jacket. I was wearing my uniform: jeans and a sweatshirt.

"Hi Ian," she greeted me with a half-smile. "Let's sit here a minute." A few chairs waited patiently for seat warmers outside the closed door of the Registrar's office. "Do you know a student named Judith Melody Lockhart?"

"I don't know her as Judith." I hesitated before deciding to spin the little I knew. "Melody is 19 and still lives at home in Painton. She went missing last Saturday. Her mother, Georgina, spent Sunday after church looking for her, without any luck, but didn't report her missing until Monday morning. Dobson answered the call out of detachment, so it's his file. He must have requested your assistance. Since you're not in uniform, I assume you've been shifted temporarily to the General Investigative Section. I bet GIS is a relief, being in plain clothes on permanent day shift."

Having shot my entire bolt, I detected a slight, unreadable change in her expression. *Interesting.*

"Yeah." Lauren drew out the word. "I don't know much yet beyond her parents being worried about her."

"Normal. Not much to start with."

Lauren looked calmly into my eyes. "Her parents told me the only professor she talked about was you."

I squished around slightly in my suddenly less comfy seat, reinterpreting the subtle non-verbal. The police suspect the worst, and they're frequently right. I wasn't used to having suspicion aimed in my direction.

"Melody is one of the clever, quiet ones. She is beginning to volunteer answers, and takes notes on paper rather than playing with her laptop, which more of them do every term. I suppose you want to know the last time I saw her," I said with a resentful edge.

"Just so you know, I want your help on this file, but asking you was Sergeant Young's suggestion. 'The college part of it and remember he may be a person of interest,' is how he put it."

"At this stage, who isn't? Thanks for the vote of confidence."

"It's what I think that counts," Lauren replied with conviction.

"Sounds good, Lauren. Young might not see it that way."

"He's a stickler. HQ posted him here to stiffen the detachment's spine."

"Yeah, and I'm one of the weaker discs. He thinks civilians are useful only for civil matters like spying on cheating husbands, as long as it isn't him."

"We've proved him wrong before. First, help me with Melody's course timetable and the names of her teachers. And who her friends are and whether she has a steady boyfriend." She'd abandoned any formality pretense, but who am I to judge?

"Her timetable is easy. That's why we're here, and you want me to make the request by myself," I said, understanding she didn't want to make an official inquiry. They had kept the story out of the news so far. They probably had too little information to alert the public, and silence avoided unnecessary embarrassment. Confidentiality won't last long once the questions begin overflowing.

At the Registrar's counter, a receptionist I hadn't seen before, wearing a name tag that said 'Sally', acted as if she hadn't noticed me come in. Sally was probably about fifty, brown permed hair, dressed for any occasion that didn't include fun.

After a short wait to establish that it was her office and she controlled the conversation, she acknowledged my intrusion. I hadn't interrupted her.

"Hi Sally," I responded warmly to the query in her eyes. "Would you please print off a student information sheet for Judith Melody Lockhart?" using her new-to-me first name. "She's thinking about the double major option."

"Okay. When do you want it?" she asked, implying not soon.

"Well, actually, she is coming over later this afternoon. I need the information so I can advise her."

"All right, I'll see what I can do for you *this* time. Her parents and I go to the same church." Sally made it clear she was doing a favour for them, not for the likes of me.

She turned to her computer monitor, dredged the not-so-private information from the main frame in the computer centre, and directed it to her printer. She glanced at the information on her computer screen, waiting for her dot matrix machine to realize it had been summoned out of retirement.

"She'll be skipping class to meet you," she said, disapprovingly. "That apple fell a fair distance from the tree. Her father's a hard-working, God-fearing man. One of the best." In three sentences she had switched from disapproving to wistful, all the while peering at me reproachfully over the top of her glasses.

Sally retrieved the paper from the reluctant printer. "Here you go," she said offhandedly, although she wasn't finished admonishing me and my ilk. "Melody always went to church with her family. She suddenly quit after she started college. What do you people do to them?"

"Thanks, Sally. I think she'll be excellent in the programme. And good luck here. Your office does important work."

I brought the printout to Lauren, who had changed to civvies for the Lockhart interview and was now back in uniform. She perused it while sitting on the hallway chair. "This is far more information than I wanted."

"Let me help narrow it down," I said. "She's a scholarship student, although she comes across as brighter than some of the marks last fall suggest. Her current course load is at the bottom of the sheet: course number, title, teaching slot, classroom number, and instructor."

"Right. She's in two of your classes."

"They're both criminal justice. The first is a lecture class. The second is a seminar on Thursday afternoon. She didn't attend either of them last week," I concluded, having decided in the moment.

"Okay. So, she's also in Shakespeare with Connors, anthropology with Davenport, romanticism with Byron—is that his real name?—and modern drama with Benoit. That's a heavy load."

"Her next class is with John Byron in Room 134. It started at two-thirty." As Sally had noticed Melody would have to skip class to meet me.

"When does the class get out?"

"They're released precisely at four, so about twenty-five minutes."

"Is there somewhere quieter and more private we can talk?" Lauren said, glancing around. "I mean not in your office with those thin, hear-all walls."

"The library has some private study rooms. It's just down the wing on the right."

The library study rooms were designed for six people in a tutorial format. The rooms on either side of the cubicle we'd claimed as ours were vacant, keeping our talk private. Only about a quarter of the student body had discovered the library's existence.

I sat at the table in our commandeered space. Lauren shut the door and sat opposite me, withdrawing her black-covered notebook from the leather purse dangling from her shoulder.

"Thanks, Ian. This might sound formal, and I'll take some notes. Please don't take any questions personally."

I already was.

"Melody was absent last week. Has her attendance habit changed lately?" She began with an easy one.

"It's become increasingly spotty. The end of term workload makes most students panic. And five courses are a lot for even the best student. Professors assign readings as if their course is the only one a student is suffering through."

"When she's in class, does she sit with anyone?"

"She's usually in class before me. I don't think she sits or talks with anyone in particular. Students mark their seats early and usually sit in the same place. I don't remember her interacting with her row mates"

"Any friends you know of?"

"That's a harder question. Not that I can recall."

"What about a boyfriend? Do you see her with someone special?"

"Never. She seems the keep-to-yourself type. I'm sorry. I am trying to be helpful here."

"I know. Has she seemed out of sorts lately, more distracted or worried? Any changes in her behaviour?"

"Maybe a little less in the present," I replied, asking myself whether I'd noticed something or was reinterpreting the past. "It's hard to predict what impression she'll give on any day. Maybe that's what they learn in drama. She seems less modest in her presentation of self, but I've known her only since January."

"Do you see Melody outside of class?"

"Randomly in the corridors and cafeteria. She came to the office once. Nothing out of the ordinary—course related. She came across as self-conscious and reticent. Her writings are thoughtful and quirky, though. I appreciate that."

"That one time, did she talk at all about personal things?"

"No. Some students come for life-coaching advice although they always open with a gambit about the course material. I'm not the best guy to approach about their other problems."

"Who is?"

"None of the faculty in my department. I'd say the guidance counsellors, although there's one male psychologist I advise women to avoid."

"Good advice, I assume." Lauren closed her notebook and asked her wristwatch the exact time.

"We've got a few minutes," I said. "I've got some questions, too."

Lauren smiled wryly at me, signalling *of course you do*, and settled in her chair. "Shoot."

"Do her parents know about any boyfriends?"

"No. They think she doesn't have one. They'd be in Melody's don't-want-them-to-know category."

"What did they say about her friends at the college?"

"They know some old friends from high school, including a best friend she doesn't hang out with anymore. They couldn't think of anyone at the college."

"She'd have a laptop. Did you find it?"

"It wasn't on her desk in the bedroom. Her parents didn't want me prying, so I'll have to make it formal." She paused, then asked, "Do students have lockers?"

"Yes, over at the Student Centre. It would be tricky to get into without a warrant."

"That can be arranged."

Lauren made a notation in her black book, then looked at me. "You're wrong about a few things, Ian. Doing full-time investigative work is a long way off for me, for any female member in this county. You still hear all that crap about men being more rational and analytical than women. I'll have to work harder than any man to get a GIS assignment. The same goes for promotion. I'm prepared to put in the time and do the hard work."

"I hope you're right about that."

"You're also wrong about it being Dobson's file. It's mine now. He did jump on the call before I had a chance to respond. Then he interviewed Melody's parents, if you call a few minutes an interview."

"Dobson's not the right member for this file. He uses the vilest words for women he doesn't like. It makes me wonder as much about his sex life as his sexism."

"He's the worst verbally. Linda Clayson called me last night to tell me she'd convinced Corporal Smith to assign the file to me, instead," Lauren said.

"I'm glad Clayson is doing something for women members other than herself," I said, unable to hide my surprise. "The male cohort is going to love it."

"Linda's all right. She's due for promotion to corporal. She understands work relations in the detachment, in the Force, really. She's always been complimentary about my work."

"When Linda gets her corporal hooks, they'll transfer her to another detachment. Any positive assessments about your work won't come from her. Male supervisors don't recognize your abilities."

"She could have left me out of this file. I called Paul Dobson at home for a briefing. It was no personal favour. He'd already heard from Sergeant Young and hadn't bothered calling me first."

"Briefed you about....?"

"Almost nothing. Not much more than came from dispatch. I don't think Paul took the call seriously. That's why Linda wanted me on the file. We think Melody isn't one of those chronic runaways, escaping from a hard life and harsher parents, or a broken home. Paul says Melody Lockhart's not from any kind of difficult home."

"It's easy to think she comes from a stable and religious household," I suggested, remembering what Sally had said. "That may not be what's going on. Some families appear close and secure, but it turns out there's a tyrant trying to control everyone."

"Paul and Sergeant Young think she's just in a temporary, boyfriend rebellion phase. I'm trying to keep an open mind."

"Even Paul should see beyond the obvious."

"I don't think he looked at anything very hard," she said. "Just a simple example, the picture of Melody in his slim file was her Grade 12 graduation shot, in full coiffure and make-up. Her parent's choice, I'd bet on it. No woman looks like her grad photo. Of course, a prom shot would be worse."

"What else did you learn from Melody's parents?"

"That you're wrong about Melody living at home."

"Was I right about anything important?"

"Sorry for deflating that imitation Sherlock you tried to impress me with. Melody moved into an apartment last September. She was supposed to meet her mother last Saturday afternoon at the coffee shop on Main Street and go for a quiet walk. It was Melody's idea. She needed to talk about something important. Her mother couldn't tell whether she was frightened or excited. Melody didn't show up. That's when her mother began to worry. When Melody didn't go to church on Sunday, she tried to find her. You got that part right, Ian," she added, kindly.

"Great."

"Do they go to your church?" she asked, topping the question with a light dollop of sarcasm.

"I join that herd only once in a blue moon, when there's a wedding or funeral I can't avoid."

"So, you'll be in church soon. We've got a blue moon on Wednesday."

"But no funeral, I hope."

"Me, too. I'm really asking where you came across any information at all."

I answered Lauren's direct question by summarizing my small-town gossip sessions with Johnnie Walker and Sally. Details always lead me to more questions.

"Does Melody have roommates?" I asked.

"No, she lives alone in one of those old downtown houses they rent to students by the room."

"Probably alone," I said, thinking two people have been known to share the same room long-term, especially its horizontal furniture. When Mary and I first became serious, my apartment didn't see me for a week.

"The other tenants in the house are bound to know something useful," Lauren said, "such as her recent habits and who visits her."

"I'm not even sure Melody is missing as much as being missed," I suggested.

"I see what you're getting at. We have too little information to try adding it up. I plan to talk to her housemates this evening."

"Where do we meet?"

Lauren's hesitation was brief. "I'll come by your apartment. We'll interview them together."

"Excellent. I'll be waiting. What's next?"

She stood up. "It's time we had an audience with Lord Byron."

I was happy to see the usual-to-me Lauren.

4: Lord Byron

We set out for Byron's Romanticism class. The wing with the Arts classrooms was not far along the corridor. Students were already emerging through a few of the escape hatches, yawning and glassy-eyed. When 'class is officially over' silently announces its arrival, students flood out, the ones who took early naps leaving first.

The door labelled 134 was still in its do-not-disturb position.

John is the closest person I have to a college friend, someone you still like despite knowing them well. He had gone to university in the late '60s. All that was left of his youthful radicalism was a thin beard, long, unkempt hair which he'd trimmed to just below his ears, and some hippy ideas he clung to tenaciously with no one interested in sharing them. He played basketball as the English schoolboy he was, strictly within the rules, sportsmanship above all, competitive only with himself, and no macho trash talk. He'd rather lose with his sense of honour intact than win with a whiff of unfairness. I hated being his teammate.

Students began gushing out of the classroom, joining the milling throng. John Byron was still standing in front of the desk, conversing with a few stragglers, all young women. Taking the Romantics seriously can be as dangerous for love-obsessed co-eds as electronic zappers for mosquitoes.

I followed Lauren as she moved conspicuously inside the door. John glanced our way, peering through his thick, round, metal-frame glasses. He knew I wasn't trying to hurry him. It was a little early for the changing of the guard and, anyway, I wasn't due next in that room.

When John finally began packing his things, the residue from the class took the hint and dissolved whisperingly away. Lauren reached behind and closed the door to keep the next wave of students at bay.

"So, what's happening, Ian," John said, directing his raised eyebrow question at me.

Before I had a chance to make introductions, Lauren said, "Professor Byron, I want to talk to you about one of your students, Melody Lockhart." She pulled her police badge from an outside pocket of her purse.

"Surely she's not in some kind of trouble?" he said, glancing in surprise at the symbol of dangerous officialdom.

"Not that we know of. We're hoping to talk with her but can't seem to track her down."

"Are you saying she's Missing?" The capital 'M' was his.

"Not exactly. We don't know where to find her." Lauren was trying to maintain her balance on the swaying PR tightrope after letting one end slip. "Can we talk somewhere, more privately?"

The door was beginning to bulge from the weight of students waxing against it, denied the exercise of their right of entry.

"Will my office do?" John asked.

"Certainly," Lauren said agreeably, before I could suggest the library.

I trailed along, the third wheel. I wondered whether Byron's picture was posted on the GIS suspect wall, assuming they had started a new rogue's gallery. I imagined mine pinioned there.

In his office, John took the seat behind his desk, looking at Lauren while maintaining a comfortable distance from the cop and her sidekick.

She began with the query that lay lightest on her mind. "Is Byron your actual last name? I'm just curious. You teach the Romantics, after all," she explained with an ironic smile. *I have a degree of my own*, her subtext implied. *We're not so different.*

John returned the smile and withdrew a stock reply from his cliché drawer. "It's worse than that. Both my parents were literature professors and they named me after the usual three English Romantics. John's my middle name. My first is Percy. I hate it. There's a reason he's referred to only as Shelley. You're here to talk about Ms. Lockhart, however."

"Of course," Lauren said. "We're not certain when she was last seen, and we have few clues about what might have happened to her."

"Are you suspecting foul play?" John asked. "What an absurd euphemism that is. It makes some of the worst things imaginable sound like a game."

"We're nowhere near that conclusion," Lauren said. "Nothing points directly to harm. At this stage, we're just trying to learn what we can about Melody. When I spoke to her parents, they said you're the only professor she talks about."

I'd heard that line before. Lauren's questions followed a similar trajectory to the ones she'd tried on me. I began to feel better about my interrogation.

"Melody's taken classes from me in each of her three years. Last year, it was nineteenth-century literature and now the Romantics."

"Was she in class last Friday?"

"No. And she just missed her fourth class in a row today."

"Has Melody seemed more distracted this term, or worried about something?"

"She's certainly a different person this year. Melody has always been hard-working and gets deeply into the readings. You can see it in her essays. When I first knew her, she was quiet. Timid is a better word. Sometime last fall, she started to come out of her shell. I think getting interested in drama had a lot to do with it. This term, she's gotten into a whole other universe of Romanticism."

"Do you mean Nature? The Love Ideal? Eroticism?" Lauren wondered.

"You left out the way I approach the subject, which is social and political. Even Karl Marx started out as a Romantic. Melody didn't take to my version. In the beginning, she was drawn to what the word romance has shrunk to in popular culture."

"Drawn to your triple namesakes?"

"She was, but I'm sure it was more than buttering up, if that's what you mean. What I'm getting at is that, with some exceptions, they present the gentle side of Romanticism. It also has a darker, more dangerous edge. Her recent ideas reflect that point of view."

"You mean in her writing. What about her behaviour or how she acts?"

"Melody is a country girl and dressed the part in plain, everyday clothes. Last term, she dyed her hair black and began wearing sombre colours. Now, since just before spring break, she's gone blonde, sports brighter, more flamboyant blouses, and always has a long Isadora Duncan type scarf. She started skipping classes about the same time. It made me wonder whom she saw when she looked in a mirror."

Byron seemed a lot more observant than I'd expected.

"So, you get to know your students quite well. That's admirable in a professor," Lauren commented, not willing to single out Melody from the pack as I suspected Lord Byron had.

"Well, Melody is quite bright, you know," John said, pleased by her compliment. "The Romantics spoke to her, at least the temperate, ethereal ones. Something else has her attention now."

"Or perhaps someone else. We need to talk to her friends," Lauren said. "Who comes to mind for us to talk with first?"

"I can't think of a single one," John said flatly. "Drama would be the place to start."

So far, John had added a thicker layer of veneer to our cardboard cut-out impression of Melody. I was hoping for a little more 3-D.

"You taught Melody in each of her three years at the College," I said, when it looked like Lauren was ready to leave. "She started out as a psych major and switched to Comparative Literature. We're trying to get a more detailed picture of her and hoping you can help."

"Students take psychology because they think it'll help them understand why they're so screwed up. Once they discover the subject is mostly about rats or brains, they drop it for something with more humanity."

"What makes you think Melody was screwed up?" Lauren jumped in before I could ask.

"Aren't they all?" John said. "Melody, more so. She's lonely, insecure, different, searching for something and doesn't know what. She's spiritual. Not that business they feed her in church. She's mystical, more like Blake. I was the one who advised her to move into our honours programme."

"Melody changed her behaviour, but what about her ideas?" My follow-up.

"Studying literature changes anyone's thinking if they take it seriously. You could tell by her writing. She isn't the same dreamy, unhappy loner who sat in the front row."

"Did the thought ever cross your mind Melody might be self-destructive?" Lauren asked.

"Oh, no," John exclaimed, with more emotion than he'd displayed so far. "She's no Young Werther, if you know what I mean, although suicides do occur in college. And Melody was going through something emotionally difficult earlier this term. I don't know what."

All three of us sat quietly, thinking our own thoughts. Lauren broke the momentary silence.

"Well, you've given us something to ponder. Thanks, Dr. Byron. We might have more questions later if you wouldn't mind."

"Not at all. My pleasure." He meant it.

As we headed for the door, he still wore the same self-satisfied smirk he'd plastered on his face after spitting out Werther. *Academics*, I scoffed silently, excluding myself.

"I hate interviewing academics," Lauren said when we were out of earshot. "They're so long-winded and pompous."

"Exactly."

"I have to get back to the detachment," she said. "I'll make arrangements to meet the other tenants in Melody's rooming house. That will mean contacting the landlord."

"You'll have to invent some innocuous reason for talking with them."

"Right. And that high school friend of Melody's, Christy something, is going to one of the Halifax universities. I'll call her parents and get a number for her. I don't think she'll be all that helpful. It's a lead I have to follow."

"Please ask her about Melody's church-going habits."

"Okay," Lauren said, implying by her tone it wasn't going to be top of the conversation. "Oh, and I want to know whether Melody has a locker. If she does, I'll get a warrant."

"You're not going to be able to keep the cone of silence on this case, you know."

"I'll talk it over with the Sergeant when I get back. It'll mean organizing a press conference, maybe tomorrow morning, assuming the file isn't closed. Melody's parents will be included."

"I'm looking forward to meeting them," I said.

"Some time tomorrow afternoon, following the news conference, back in their house. For all we know, they're the only ones who are hurting."

I began to wonder what else I could ask, and a good idea occurred to me. Lauren's better timing beat me to it.

"Let's have pizza tonight. We need to talk. I'll drive over for you."

"I missed having lunch with you," I replied.

"Me too."

"By the way," I said. "Since this story is about to hit the tabloids, you should let Bill Paxton know before tomorrow. You'll have to involve the Director of Campus Police, and sooner is better. Bill will want to be present for a locker break-in."

"I'll call him soon," Lauren agreed. She headed for her cruiser, which she'd left in one of the A&A visitors' parking spots, not bothering to put any money in the meter. The campus police could only fantasize about giving it a ticket.

Departmental assistants/student confidantes know more about a student's personal life than any faculty member. Back on the second floor of the A&A building, I walked to the hallowed penthouse wing housing the Comparative Literature Department, top dog in Arts.

5: Student confidential

The Department Head's office was closed, as I'd hoped. Trish Stuart was at her desk in her tiny office. She had been with the department longer than most staff have been at the College. She modelled the maternal, someone-to-trust type, married only to her job. They are called secretaries to justify their woeful pay, although they run their departments behind the scenes. Career-oriented faculty see staff as their personal human resources, using them for their own advantage. Maybe I wasn't so different.

"Hi Ian," Trish greeted me. "Patrick is out this afternoon."

"Actually, Trish, I thought you could help me." I can be patronizing, although that's not how I characterize myself. Who would?

"I'll certainly do my best."

"You know the students in your department better than anyone."

"Well, I wouldn't say that. Sometimes better than their parents, though."

"I'd bet on that. Melody Lockhart came to talk with me about declaring a social sciences double major."

"Maybe you should talk to Pat. He does the academic advising." Trish looked disappointed.

"You do plenty of advising, too. That's not why I'm here. Melody's marks are first rate. But when she came to see me last week, she looked distracted and worried, upset about something. She said she was fine. That's not how it looked. Do you know if she's okay? I can't think of any student to ask."

"Melody's always been a little distracted. I haven't talked to her for a while."

Trish appeared to be weighing her options, deciding what to lead, what to hold back, and what to secrete about her person. "She's got it pretty rough at home," she finally said. "What I can't understand is what took her so long to move out."

"What made it so bad?"

"Her father is overbearing, at her all the time. I don't think she can breathe without his permission. He's committed to the Church of God Almighty."

"I heard she'd stopped going to church."

"Who could blame her? I was shocked she'd started going again a couple of months ago, although not every Sunday. At least it's the United Church this time, the one with a hint of liberalism. She did start reading her Bible again."

"Sounds like a dutiful daughter."

"Not exactly. From what she tells me, she has a totally new view on the Bible. Her father wouldn't recognize it." She didn't suggest it was anyone's fault.

"How did she get to college in the first place?" I asked.

"All her teachers insisted Melody belonged here."

"How is she making out?"

"She likes her classes a lot, but you're asking about her social life. She doesn't talk about it much. When she comes in here for a chat, she's always lonely. I can't think of a single close friend. She has decided she hates being called Melody, by the way, and asked me to use her first name, Judith."

"I'll remember that. Has she come to talk lately?"

"No. I wish she would."

Amen to that. Aloud I said, "You don't know any of Melody's friends. Does that go for her boyfriend, too?"

Trish shifted her gaze from my general direction to the door and the hallway beyond. "It goes for men in general, and not just her father."

There was a dose of bitter green in her reply. Trish's friendly demeanour was slipping. "I'm surprised Melody didn't talk to me about switching her classes," she said in a guarded tone. "Look, Ian, I've got work to do. I don't know what any of this has to do with being a double major."

"Thanks a million, Trish. I only wanted to know what's troubling her."

My sense of Melody Lockhart felt less sketchy. A cold, hard father is as bad for a daughter as an absent one. Worse, perhaps. If he's not constantly there in the heavy flesh, you can at least dream about him being a better one.

Heading home, I began the routine trek through the hallway maze to the psychology wing. I felt like a well-conditioned rat no longer conscious of the changes in direction, caught in some covert psychology experiment.

Finding my way to the pellet reward of an exit-only door, I struck the push bar with my hip and emerged into the slanting late-afternoon sun. The photographer's-angle lighting brought out in relief the detailed features of the old vocational building, its decorative secrets unmasked only momentarily by the sun's spotlight until it sank fractionally lower.

I walked along Main and turned left at Bridge Street, where Trunk 11A begins or ends, depending on where you're from. The bridge overlooks Pitch River, running at full tilt in the spring when the flow is heaviest. The river courses parallel to Main, leaves town like most of the local youth, and dumps its silt into the Annapolis River. No trace of the fifty-foot Bay of Fundy tide is discernible this far inland.

The Bridgeside Pub is the last building before you cross the river from downtown. Occasionally, I'd detour inside for a beer before returning to my lonely apartment, sometimes joining Barry Davenport, our resident anthropologist. I spied his old Land Rover in the pub parking lot. He spent so much time at the pub, it seemed to be his second office, maybe his preferred one.

The pub's dim interior took some pupil adjustment. A small foot-high stage stood at the back wall with a dance floor in front. Booths were arrayed along both sides. A few out-of-work men lounged in front of their drinks.

Barry was sitting in one of the booths with two men in their forties who sported long, straggly hair and beards, and wore tattered denim vests covered with paraphernalia related to an outlaw motorcycle club the Hell's Angels had absorbed. But not this sad pair, apparently. I never knew what to expect from Barry, but it hardly seemed possible he was doing local research.

Barry got up when he saw me and led the way to one of the empty booths. He had a beer glass in each hand and a worn, leather briefcase he hugged tightly under his arm. It almost never left his grasp because it holds the only copy of a new, typed manuscript he's secretive about. He says it's growing into a book-length expansion of an article he'd recently published. He'd proudly distributed reprints of the article during the last department meeting. His specialty is the revival of ancient tribal rituals in the modern world.

I declined the drink Barry offered because of the upcoming meeting with Melody's roommates. He ordered two whisky chasers. I couldn't tell how much he'd already had.

Barry and I had been on competitively collegial terms since we'd hired him, though we seldom shared the same opinions or beliefs. In this supposedly higher learning environment, I debated ideas only with him.

Tall, with light-coloured hair and well-tanned, Barry had the broad shoulders and athletic build of a football linebacker.

He acted as though he came from money, his apparel subtly announcing expensive casual, not something I would have noticed until Mary refocused my eye. Barry sported a Rolex on his wrist. He'd once bragged it was suitable for scuba diving when he'd noticed me staring at it. I'd been pondering whether it was a knock-off.

He was in his late-30s, a few years my junior. People wondered whether he was still short of the big three-0. Something about the tightness of his skin around the eyes and the slight stiffness near his mouth made me suspect a minor plastic rejuvenation. Not something I would swear to or ask him about. First impressions aside, it doesn't take long to discover Barry's abrasive egoism or his right-wing politics.

"You've had a distracting day," Barry said, after I slouched into the wooden booth across from him.

"I spent the morning on highway patrol," I said. "A young woman from the College was reported missing."

The waiter delivered the two shots. Barry downed one immediately.

"Hmm," he muttered. "That's news? Tuition keeps them boarding at home, even if they hate it. Before long, things you couldn't imagine in this full-church, futureless town drive them out of the house."

I noticed the Australian undertone in his speech, which he'd acquired in Adelaide. "The student is Melody Lockhart. Do you know her?"

"Not a name I recall from marking papers. Just another unmemorable student. Did anything worthwhile come up this morning?"

"We patrolled along Pitch Lake looking for suspended drivers. All we found was a crazy speeder from Alberta."

"Pitch Lake," he said. "That's where I've got property on the water. You remember the cottage, the one you and Mary visited once, before the wife took off."

He meant June, his ex, not mine, although either might fit the context. Barry had remained single since June left him five years ago; probably why he spent so much time in the pub.

I sighed. "That's recent history for me."

"We're both better off this way. But why are you still wearing that owned-by-someone ring?"

"It wards off unwanted women, like garlic for vampires."

"Isn't a vamp or two exactly what we need?"

"I don't feel the same as you do about moving on. The separation was Mary's idea. But we managed a fair split and keep on pretty good terms."

The two misfits clinging to their motorcycle club identities stopped at the booth.

"See you next week, Barry," the burlier of the pair said. "We'll keep you supplied."

I suspected he didn't mean with information.

As he passed the waitress, he made breast-grabbing gestures with his fingers. She ignored him.

"They call themselves the 13th Tribe," Barry said. "None of them have two clues about the meaning behind the name or any of the insignia they wear. But that's enough about work."

He took a long drink of his draft Guinness and listened to the rumble of two Harleys pulling out of the parking lot. He downed his second whisky.

"Does keeping on good terms mean you get along with your ex's live-in boyfriend?" Barry's timbre had shifted perceptibly.

"We just keep out of each other's way."

"He had kept out of your way for quite some time before you found out."

My chin felt his left-right jabs. I'd once used his padded office chair at the college as a confessional. Everyone needs to unburden themselves sometimes. He was using what I'd said to needle me.

I ratcheted my irritation to the defensive, counter-punch stage. "You and I both know June didn't run away from you without good reasons."

"Relationships fall apart in all kinds of ways, for all kinds of causes," Barry said, slipping into his distant, expert lecture mode.

"You'd know all of them from personal experience," I said, pushing myself away from the booth and his company. Popping into the Bridgeside had been a mistake. My discussions with Barry often ended acrimoniously. He says I'm overly sensitive.

I followed the route the bikers had taken towards the front door, offering a friendly smile to the server on the way out. She ignored me, too.

My digs occupied the ground floor of an old house converted to an affordable-for-me triplex on Livingstone Street, just a couple of blocks south of the river. South Halstead—Soha for short—was the equivalent of living on the other side of the tracks. A few dormant perennials on either side of the walkway strangled each other up the trellises, eager to renew their struggle for light and carbon dioxide.

I dropped my sneakers in the front closet at the end of the oak foyer. It was a recent renovation, along with the bathroom behind it. According to my elderly neighbours, these conveniences had replaced a wide oak staircase with an ornately carved newel post. Local carpenters had undertaken the disembowelling,

My pizza date with Lauren seemed a long way off. A little leftover Madras curry was in the fridge. I couldn't remember how long I'd kept it waiting. When I eyeballed the curry, nothing seemed to be peering back, so I popped it into the microwave to remove the chill.

I plunked the curry bowl on my serpentine-shaped, applewood desk. I'd paid exorbitantly to have it custom built by a local woodworker Barry had recommended. He'd been so pleased with his creation that he'd carved his name, 'Gerald Balcolm', on the bottom of the right-hand pedestal.

Lauren had said she wanted to talk during our dinner. She meant discussing the case. I hoped it would also be about us. The curry had not satiated my appetite.

Feeling at loose beginnings, I searched for a good read to pass the time. Raymond Chandler's classic mystery, *The Lady in the Lake*, beckoned from my fiction shelf. The main characters in this hard-boiled genre contrast sharply with my variable-density public shell and soft-boiled interior.

Chandler's lady lived in pre-World-War-Two Los Angeles, peopled by the useless rich, gangsters and their molls, corrupt businessmen, and cops on all their payrolls. It was a world away from daily reality in Sterling County. But the book conjured in my mind a mournful vision of Melody's bloated body slowly gassing to the surface in some nearby lake. Was it prophetic or only another fiction? The image was only in my head, but I couldn't wipe it out. Stubbornly refusing to disappear, it had become part of the disordered ambiguity of my reality.

Putting the book aside, I summarized on paper what I knew about Melody Lockhart. I wrote less than a page, only slightly better than Dobson's thin file. How much of what I believed to be true about Melody was fact? I was a long way from understanding her and knowing what had happened.

Livingstone Street was still quiet when I went to the window for the fourth time to look out for Lauren. I mused about what we might learn from Melody's house mates. Lauren wouldn't have had time to get a search warrant, but we'd be alert for any justifiable cause for a warrantless one.

Tony Thomson

6: Grunge and Slacks

When Lauren finally arrived in the marked, low-profile cruiser—one with RCMP insignia and no light bar on top—she was disappointingly back in uniform. I'd done nothing special to prepare for supper unless you counted the shower and shave, the deodorant, and the careful selection of my favourite black shirt and white tie.

"Should I be seen with the likes of you?" Lauren asked. "Halstead's conspiracy theorists will have proof the mafia and RCMP are in cahoots."

"All one of them, and that's me."

Lauren turned the cruiser off Main to Maple Street, where Melody's rooming house loomed on the right. Like many of the century houses in Halstead, it had been scooped from empty-nested seniors for a fraction of its value by pipsqueak, local contractors aspiring to be slum landlords.

"Two of Melody's housemates are expecting us," Lauren said. "They should know a lot about who she sees and what she does."

I was happy she had said *us*, for more than one reason.

The main door to the rooming house was unlocked. Her room was on the second floor. Tenants were temporary, the grime and rancid smell of the place permanent. You could nose the droppings ground permanently into the fraying red indoor-outdoor carpet that covered the floors and tumbled down the steps, the glue giving way everywhere.

Lauren knocked assertively on Number Five. I couldn't suppress the premonition Melody was in danger, not just a runaway enjoying a secluded hideaway with a boyfriend. I visualized her answering the door sleepily and saying, 'Hello.' I'd be through with the file, but she would be safe.

Lauren's reveille call startled only the bluebottles buzzing angrily within. She knocked again and announced her presence officially and that she merely wanted to make sure Melody was all right. She pushed the door and found it locked. "Damn," she said, pushing harder, as though she was imagining the worst of scenes.

Two young women joined us in the hallway. "She's not home," the more forward of the pair said. She was dressed appropriately in alternative grunge.

"Hi. I'm Constable Martin." Lauren displayed her badge. If someone takes more than a quick glance at it, you begin to wonder about them.

"I'm Rachel," she said. "You called me."

"This is Dr. Wallace, from the college. He's helping me this evening."

That about summed it up.

"You must be Piper." Lauren addressed housemate number two, who wore a conventional sweater and slacks. Piper nodded.

"We're trying to locate Melody," Lauren said, sharing her attentive gaze equally between both women.

"We haven't heard a thing from her room for days," Rachel replied. "We thought she'd gone home for a visit. She's been doing that a lot lately. At least she says she does. But her mother showed up here on Sunday, looking for her. Did something happen to Melody?"

"She's probably not in any trouble," Lauren said, her tone smoothing the choppy waters she'd stirred up in their minds. "Her parents are worried about her, that's all. When was the last time you saw her?"

"Not since Thursday night," Rachel said.

Lauren looked directly at Piper, who pinched her eyebrows, adding little to Rachel's reply. "Did you ever see Melody with a boyfriend, maybe here in the house, maybe outside?"

Rachel's face appeared strained, like she was stretching her memory on a rack.

"Maybe at the Bridgeside?" I said.

"Nah, she never goes there." Rachel's tone implied *That's impossible.*

She glanced quickly at Piper, who disproved my theory she was mute by adding, "She's quite plain, really, shy and quiet, the shrinking type."

"Not somebody any of the college guys I know would want," Rachel said.

"When she first moved in," Piper said, "we thought she'd never have a boyfriend. When it looked like she found one, or she thought she had, it didn't last long." Then, more hesitantly, as if gossiping with the untrustworthy, "But we think someone was in her room Thursday night."

"Yeah," Rachel added, redirecting the attention. "We both heard her talking to someone, quiet like. We're pretty sure it wasn't a girl." She paused for breath and Piper took over.

"She raised the volume of her music, so we couldn't hear—if you can call what she listens to music."

"Did either of you see this visitor?" Lauren said.

They shared an involuntary glance. Piper had become the tacit spokesperson. "No, and we didn't hear anyone come or go. Melody sometimes goes out through the window and down the fire escape. Maybe that's what *he* did, too."

"What time did you hear Melody talking to someone?" Lauren asked, her black notebook waiting impatiently for more shorthand.

"It was after nine," Rachel said. She glanced at me. "Piper and I, like, study together. And that's about the time we went down to the kitchen for a snack."

"We think she might be staying with her boyfriend," Lauren said. "You told us she thought she had one. What did you mean?"

"We never saw her with anyone," Rachel said. "For a while, though, she was all happy like, even friendly. And then she suddenly became all weepy and sad. You could tell she'd been dumped. We thought she was gonna move home."

"When did the break-up happen?" I asked.

"Sometime in the middle of January, I think," Piper said.

"Can you tell us anything else about that boyfriend, or who was with her last Thursday?" Lauren said.

Both girls shook their heads.

Lauren looked in my direction, gesturing with her head that we could leave. I pretended not to notice. "What kind of person would you say Melody is, Piper?"

I waited with more patience than the fidgeting Lauren while Piper formulated her opinion.

The excluded Rachel waded into the void. "She's laced some tight, and she dresses weird, like she's a hippy or something. At least she does now. Her room smells funny, too."

"Can you describe the smell?" Lauren asked quickly, not concealing the concern she felt.

"Like what they burn in church."

Incense. Another thought had been tugging at me. "Piper, you said Melody had poor taste in music. What does she listen to?"

Lauren lifted her eyebrows. They would have knocked off her hat if she'd been wearing one.

"Yes, quite unusual. She used to play jazz and light classical," Piper said. "Then she switched to Hungarian, gypsy-style dances and exotic instrumental pieces—I'm a music major, voice," she said. "Lately, Melody's been into old-style singers, dull, monotone chords with no range and long lyrics. Nothing lively, with rhythm or a decent melody."

She paused, looking surprised by her last word, and looked at Rachel, "Do you remember the time we overheard her trying to sing in the washroom, something about some hotel in Chelsea? Something quite rude?"

"No, I don't," Rachel said, unhelpfully.

"Well, that's what I mean when I say she's strange."

"Well, thanks, you two," Lauren said before I could pry any further. She handed Piper her card. "You've helped a lot. Please call me if you think of anything to add."

"You did a good job confirming that boyfriend lead with Grunge and Slacks back there," I said once we were outside.

Lauren's eyes were narrow and anxious as she led the way around back of the house to the three-storey wooden fire escape, built to the aesthetics of the fire code. We climbed to the second floor. The curtains inside Melody's closed window were parted.

Lauren peered into the room.

"Anything?"

"Nothing troubling. There's a small wardrobe instead of a closet. The bed is made."

"So no body," I said lightly.

"I got worried when they said the room smelled funny," Lauren said. "I can slip in easily, but I think it's best to wait for the warrant tomorrow."

I remembered about Christy Something as we drove downtown. "Did you manage to call Melody's old school chum in Halifax?"

"Yes. I didn't think she'd be much help and she wasn't. They lost touch in their first year and Melody didn't have a single boyfriend in high school."

"Did she say anything about Melody's church-going?"

Lauren paused before replying. "Of course I asked. Melody was a regular attendee when she was in high school. Christy never went. Melody stopped believing after she started college. Their friendship ended anyway."

"Did Christy mention how religious Melody had been?"

"Pretty deep, I gather. Christy went one Sunday when they were in high school, just to see what it was like. She said the preaching was all about the devil and sins of the flesh. Some people started to vibrate."

"Is that the word she used?"

"The exact one. Apparently, no one vibrated more than Melody. She went to the front. The preacher touched her forehead and she fainted dead away in front of the whole assembly."

Lauren glanced over at me. "It sounds wild, doesn't it? The questions you asked about religion and music are interesting and all, but our focus should be on the man she was with last Thursday night. That's the important question."

"Precisely," I said, agreeably. "I think we get closer to the answer by knowing who Melody is or who she might think she is."

"Well, your approach has been helpful before. Maybe if she committed suicide, we'd need to understand her. But I think she's in danger, and not of her own making. Time is short."

"Even so, I don't want to ignore the 'who she is' question," I said placatingly. "We can do both. It may pay off in the end."

7: Two pizzas

We headed to The Italian, which specializes in thin crusts, a tomato-basil sauce claiming to be authentic, and a wider-than-Halstead-average range of toppings. Lauren wanted thick, chewy bread under pineapple and ham. I ordered black olives, feta cheese and bacon strips. We sat at a table in a private corner with no sustenance other than conversation.

"The press briefing is scheduled for nine tomorrow morning outside the detachment," Lauren said. "I'll pick up the Lockharts beforehand."

"You've talked to them once. Do you think they'll shed more light on what happened to their daughter?"

"Her mother said she doesn't know much about Melody's life after she left home and seems quite bewildered about what's happened to her daughter. I didn't talk to her father yet."

"I'm bewildered, too," I said. "Melody's an enigma."

"With luck, we'll identify the man in her room last week after we search it. I've arranged to pick up warrants at the courthouse after the press briefing."

"Warrants?"

"Melody does have a college locker. Campus security will join us for the search before noon tomorrow. The third warrant is for her room at her parents' place."

When the pizzas arrived, Lauren looked hungrily at mine. We split them.

She had shared some of her life story during one of our early dates. Her first posting was in the British Columbia Delta. The transition to big city policing was difficult for a small-town girl from Saskatchewan who thought she could make a difference. The community was troubled and difficult to police. Male members were worse.

Lauren's easy to get along with. She's personable and friendly, a demeanour in a woman that brings its share of problems with men. None of the personal problems she faces in the detachment are her responsibility. Male members accidentally-on-purpose rub against her, make lewd jokes, leave suggestive cartoons on her desk, complain her bullet-proof vest flattens her chest, want intimate details about her sex life, and proposition her while pretending they're only kidding.

Lauren never complains about the persistent abuse. If she brought a complaint up the ladder, it would become *her* problem. 'Members are always razzing each other,' her supervisor would tell her. 'You've got to learn to suck it up. It isn't personal.' Of course, it was deeply personal. If she complained, male constables would call her a fucking rat.

I understand her strategy. She pretends to ignore the harassment or twists the verbal trash and fires it back at the men. This approach keeps her career afloat at the cost of perpetuating the abuse, making it all one long running joke.

Lauren's long-term plan is to outwork them and conclude her files efficiently and successfully. 'My abilities will earn the respect of my NCOs,' she said once. 'Promotion may come later than sooner, but it will come.' I kept my doubts about her optimism to myself.

From the Delta detachment, Lauren transferred north to Fort Norman, on the Mackenzie River. It can be a rough place to police, especially when drinking is involved, but the experience was unforgettable. She longed for a five-pound Arctic char grilled over an outdoor fire. Better than salmon.

She learned a lot about the limits of policing and her own. It was doubly hard being the first female in the detachment. She became the members' chief game when they weren't chasing the local girls. Her gender helped build rapport among the women in the community, who have a lot of authority in daily life.

Fort Norman was a lonely place, especially in winter. Lauren got close to one of the more amenable members and moved in with him. He was originally from Nova Scotia but liked the northern lifestyle so much he stayed there when Lauren transferred east in 1966 to push her career forward. The transfer to Nova Scotia helped her feel close to her boyfriend, who she had hoped would follow her. He hadn't. So far.

I handle my feelings about Lauren in my usual cautious, self-protective way even though they aren't ambiguous. I'm drawn to Lauren and had sensed something reciprocal during our lightweight, off-duty dates. Had my ego misread the signals? When the male ego is attracted to someone, it magnifies the slightest friendly gesture into assuming the feeling is mutual.

Lauren looked at me over the remnants of my pizza. I wondered what she'd been thinking during my reverie. She reached back and freed her braid from its restraint. Her hair cascaded down her shoulders, silky and soft, just right for touching. So much youth and vitality.

She looked in my eyes and said, "You're looking quite handsome, by the way."

"Thanks," I said beaming with surprise.

I could tell she was disappointed, as though I hadn't said what she hoped or expected to hear. She sat, silent and sad, looking around and not at me.

You look great, too! would have been much better than thanks—a programmed reply which had escaped unthinkingly. It could have been worse. *But I'm not* had flashed behind my eyebrows. When you feel unworthy, you say things that confirm it.

"I have to go to the loo," I announced suddenly.

Lauren's gloom trailed after me like the sole of my shoe was dragging toilet paper back into the washroom. I stood at the sink and stared into the large, bright mirror long enough to see the furrows around my eyes and forehead grow deeper and the effect of gravity on my cheeks become more pronounced. The reflection in the mirror felt compelled to respond: *What's with this ennui, Ian Wallace? You're losing her. Do something.*

Suddenly afraid the loo might become a Dear John, I rushed out, hoping Lauren hadn't left a brief *see you later* note. She hadn't, which said more about her than me.

"Sorry, Lauren. I was upset about what I said and didn't say to you just now, and why."

"Well, we weren't planning to have dinner, *per se*. We're just here to eat."

The *we're still friends* line seemed the rehearsed result of her own ruminations.

Lauren's tone changed, though, when she added, "What did you mean to say?"

"That you always look lovely to me."

She smiled and looked down at her uniform, amusement breaking through the chill. "I came straight to get you after shift. But really, all this gear has got to be a turn off."

"That's not the way male members see their uniform, especially in red serge."

"They appreciate the reaction they get. But men don't fall all over themselves when they see a woman in uniform."

"That's not what I think about when I look at you."

We were both silent for a moment, chewing on our own thoughts and feelings.

"I'm not sure the timing's right," Lauren confided quietly. "That's what I wanted to talk about."

"The timing is however we want it to be. I'm nervous about things, too."

"It's not that simple. For example, you still wear your wedding ring. I know you split with your ex only six months ago. The rule of thumb is to wait a year and not jump into something complicated or not wholehearted."

"My marriage died well before that. Nothing can restore that ancient painting. I feel whole-hearted about this."

"Maybe you can't get beyond the wish to get back with your wife."

"Ex-wife. That's what the year wait is supposed to be about. You also need a reason to move on, and I have one now. The timing for what we can have doesn't come with a statute of limitations."

"I enjoy the time we spend together. You make me laugh with your odd way of looking at things, and I care for you."

I could see it in her face, along with something else behind it, waiting to emerge.

"After Fort Norman, I don't want to get involved with another member. Workplace relationships aren't healthy for either person. And outside the police community, the uniform and everything that goes with it is a major barrier to intimacy. So, pickings are slim. That's true around here, too." She looked me in the eye after that one. I was happy she felt comfortable needling me.

"That's not much of an endorsement, but I'll take it."

"It's not that simple. That's what I mean about timing. My career is my focus right now. I'm the lead investigator in this case. I'm not sure where it's going. Either way, it will be an important step for me."

"You can have a career and a civvy intimate. Maybe it's the only kind you can have. And I happen to be more than available."

"It's hard for a member to have a private life, especially in a small town. That's one of the reasons members socialize with each other. We're under layers of public scrutiny you wouldn't believe. And it's a lot harder for a woman, with the survival of the double standard that's so persistent, it seems almost instinctual."

"Some instincts work in our favour," I said, raising my eyebrows.

"Be serious for a minute, Ian," she said with what I interpreted as genuine exasperation.

"I can be serious and unthinking at the same time, in the best of moments. You should try it."

"I appreciate that, I do. I'm not sure how I feel about us. I'm not ready to just fall into something, not without thinking it through and what it means about the future, my future."

Not our future.

With that hanging over me, we left the restaurant and drove silently toward my apartment. Disappointment with our conversation elbowed aside my hopes. I felt confused about Lauren's signals. She hadn't consigned the complications to hell. Our separate internal debates continued.

When she pulled the police cruiser onto Livingstone Street and parked outside my house, I leaned over and gave her an affectionate kiss on the cheek. She smiled warmly and squeezed my hand.

On the sidewalk, I looked back. Lauren was glancing around and not looking at me. Was she wondering if anyone noticed the public display of affection?

I turned for company to the evening news. The antique record player in the corner, now a liquor cabinet in disguise, clambered for my attention. I imagined sipping the scotch concealed inside. It wouldn't keep me awake, whereas ruminating over what I knew about the missing Melody Lockhart, let alone what Lauren had just said, would for sure induce insomnia.

I took the Raymond Chandler novel and the whisky to bed, hoping to keep my nightcap and worries within reasonable limits.

Among mysteries, I like least the multiple-plausible-suspect versions where it's necessary to juggle enough characters almost to the end before allowing the least conspicuous to fall. I preferred the why-and-how dunit to the who. It's difficult to separate fiction from living and remembering and telling other people about it.

My skimpy, one-page summary about Melody Lockhart should grow exponentially tomorrow.

Tony Thomson

8: Slim pickings

Tuesday, 30 March

Up at six forty-five and out ten minutes later for a run. It wasn't false virtue. I couldn't sleep, only partly because of the brief, localized downpour at the night's darkest hour. Lauren and Melody had competed for my nighttime ruminations.

I took the trail along the south side of the river away from the college, grunting acknowledgement to other early self-flagellators. The college women's soccer team steamed past, mist rising from the tops of their exposed heads. The morning was spring chilly. Half the run would be over before my body thanked me for wearing only shorts and a T-shirt.

Making one foot chase the other was easier when my mind was occupied. I wondered whether I was on the path Melody had planned to stroll with her mother and what might have been on her mind. I could only imagine their dialogue.

As I turned about and headed home, what she might have revealed became increasingly dire in my imagination. There were far too many missing integers, variables, and operators to solve Melody's equation. Knowing more about her would add some additional mathematical expressions, although simple explanations are usually best.

I parked my car in an all-day zone near the detachment, not presuming to occupy a visitor's space behind it. Five years ago, the back door was always unlocked, but a new RCMP policy had erased my easy detachment access. Nothing local had caused the changes. A violent incident had occurred in another province, but the RCMP unfolds any change in safety procedures nation-wide, regardless of local circumstances.

The rear entrance was now locked, admittance by invitation only. The front foyer had become a small, enclosed cave with a hard, wooden bench, a bullet-proof glass window with an intercom, and a locked door. The intimidating security undermined the ideology of community-based policing the brass had been trying to sell.

A handful of people were waiting in a clump outside the detachment for the press conference. Linda Clayson, the dedicated media specialist, was planning a short announcement, statements from Melody's parents, Philip and Georgina Lockhart, and time for just a few questions from the press. The media was in the dark about the topic of the conference. 'They'll be slithering around on their own soon enough,' Linda had confided to Lauren. The local news hounds become a hindrance when you're trying to build a case out of the public eye.

Wandering around front to mix with the crowd, I recognized most of the small coven of part-time snoops from various local media outlets. Most of their information comes from official announcements, just as the authorities have concocted it. They reprint press releases almost verbatim. A fringe of curious onlookers hoped something was finally happening around here.

In between the press and the front door, a reed-thin floor microphone stood sentinel, staring at its tripod feet while valiantly holding at bay the mini-mob armed with papers and pencils. They looked more like accountants than reporters.

I stood near Slim Starr, the only professional among the lot. Slim covered the county beat for the Halifax daily. According to the operating definitions in a small town, nobody needs investigative journalism. That's for big city problems. Local media outlets don't have time or money for reporters' hands to be stained digging into the red Valley soil, which rarely has actual blood in it.

Slim was about my age, with a closely trimmed beard beginning to change colour around the fringes. He covered the brown hair hanging just over his ears with a Montreal Expos cap he probably wore to bed. With a fishbone gray blazer over an open-necked flannel shirt, he looked like a cross between an academic and a regular guy, wanting to appear to fit into as many worlds as possible.

"What brings you out this early morning?" he asked me.

"I heard this has something to do with the college," I said vaguely.

The entourage emerged from the fortress, Linda followed by Melody's parents and Lauren. Sergeant Young must have had urgent business elsewhere.

The sandman residue dropped from the reporters' eyes. Georgina appeared nervous, Philip stoical and unblinking.

Sticking with her plan, Linda kept the briefing true to the meaning of the word. Her minimalist version concluded with, "If anyone has any information that may help us locate Melody, please call the detachment or Crime Stoppers."

Georgina was due next, with Philip limbering up on the sidelines. She looked matronly in a floral-patterned dress under a mid-length openwork, beige sweater. A light green bandana stretched over her head, covering the tips of her horn-rimmed glasses.

When she spoke, Georgina's voice was firmer than I'd anticipated. She had written her words, wanting to make sure she said everything. She paused occasionally struggling for courage to continue.

"Thank you for your help, Constable Clayson. We just want Melody to be safe and we're praying she will return to us. She had some difficult times. I know that better than anyone. I've tried with all my heart to protect her....She's going to university now and doing really well. She's even got her own place. I'm so proud of the young woman she is becoming.... Melody has a strong spirit, a will to live and live happily that I always knew was there. I see such a bright future for her....Please don't take her away from us, or us from her. Let her come back home."

Georgina stepped back, standing slightly behind her husband, the emotional toll palpable in her bearing. She had spoken slowly and deliberately, bent by an overwhelming force, addressing an anonymous other, not speaking directly to her daughter. I wondered whether she had more than an inkling where Melody is.

Philip Lockhart shuffled forward empty handed and adjusted the mike for his height while making sure the tripod feet still had someone looking down at them. He wore a dark suit and white shirt, a tie limply askew in front. No amount of life rehearsal had prepared him for public speaking.

"As my wife said, we are praying to God Almighty that our daughter comes back home. We will forgive her and protect her, as we always have. Please, God, guide her home." With a final gesture of his hand, he launched his plea to the seagulls.

Only his brevity had been merciful. I heard only the echo of the Church of God Almighty.

What an incredible name. Whose churches were all the others? Somebody must have decided they'd gotten to the bottom of all that speculation.

Philip's reference fired one of Tennessee Williams's lines along a seldom-used neuron: 'The truth is at the bottom of a bottomless well.' Barry Davenport, the cultural anthropology expert, says Williams means infinity, ultimately God. Infinity is an important concept if you don't deify it.

I turned quietly to Slim, "What a switch. I wonder how many hours Philip stayed awake thinking of the least helpful thing to say."

"You should be a reporter, Ian. You're more cynical than I am."

Linda's secular voice, superimposing the real world on the imaginary, brought the jumble in my head into line She was inviting questions from the assembly and caught an easy one:

"I'm sorry for what you are going through, Mr. and Mrs. Lockhart," Kerry from the *Weekly Mail* began. "Corporal Clayson, do the police think Melody has been the victim of foul play?"

"At the moment, we have no reason to suspect Melody has been the victim of any deliberate harm. Our inquiry into this matter is at an early stage."

"Do you think she's run away from home?" The voice came from behind. It seemed a logical question to me if it meant *away from her father*.

"Our inquiry is just beginning and we're following all possibilities," Linda said

A few more queries generated different versions of Linda's political, no-information reply, until she said, "Now, we have time for one more question," generously extending the session beyond what was warranted.

It was obvious they were getting only tepid air from the police. Slim's hand shot up anyway. The fellow reporters deferred to the recognized professional among them.

"Does the RCMP think last night's outbuilding fire on a property along Pitch Lake Road was a case of arson?"

It caught me by surprise, not Linda. "We are investigating the cause of the fire with the assistance of the Fire Marshall. We have no definitive answer as to its origins. Thank you for the questions and to all of you for coming. We hope to resolve both inquiries in short order."

People had begun to disperse before Linda had finished talking. Former university students, I expect.

Hurrying after Slim, I drew abreast. "What's this about a fire at Pitch Lake?"

"Why do we bother to write the news when nobody reads it? A shed near the end of the lake caught fire and caused an explosion last night, probably a propane tank. Everything became smoke and ashes."

"Everything?"

"Well, the shed and everything inside it. They'd built it on the beach, near only water and grass, so the fire didn't spread to the woods or the house."

"That was a lucky break."

"Yeah. The woods are still plenty wet, and it happened just after that downpour last night. The fire department keeps an old pumper on the mountain. That helped, too."

Slim had once written an article referring to Valley Volunteer Fire Departments as boys' clubs wasting community money on expensive toys. I resisted reminding him of it.

"What makes you think it might be arson?"

"The Deputy Chief at the scene said it looked suspicious."

"Isn't that a remote spot for a pyromaniac's bonfire?" I asked.

"Maybe. Several people across the lake called it in. They heard the boom before they saw the flames. Too loud for thunder. I'll follow that story, although the lost teenager one is likely bigger."

"Clayson said they don't suspect foul play."

"They always say that. Secrecy is congenital among cops. Of course, there's always white slavery. That would be interesting," Slim said flippantly, opening his car door.

A reporter's point of view.

As he drove away, I wondered where Slim's beak was leading him. He'd investigated human trafficking in Halifax, young girls often in their mid-teens who ended up in brothels in Toronto. Nothing so far indicates the metro-based gang activity had spread to the Valley.

When Mary and I had read Slim's article, I'd objected to the term white slavery. Mary had disagreed. 'Lots of things that happen to women are types of slavery,' she had said.

I negotiated my entry to the detachment with the guard-post clerk. Lauren was at a desk, obscured by piles of loose papers threatening to disperse randomly in all directions, like some cases I'd been privy to. Detailed written reports provide the primary means for holding police accountable. Public complaints work, too, but they aren't common around here. Rural police have higher approval ratings than hometown hockey teams.

"Time to go," Lauren said, happy to postpone the paperwork tedium. "I have to swear information for my three warrants."

"I was surprised by Mrs. Lockhart's pleas at the press conference. She may know more than she let on."

"I thought they were both odd, in different ways. I've arranged to go to their house about four this afternoon. There's a lot to do before we see them, though."

The old Sterling County Courthouse was built from dull, brown bricks framed by soot-discoloured granite, originally carved from a large quarry despoiling the North Mountain. The courthouse was the most substantial building in the downtown, if you ignored the churches. Lauren parked in the police-only zone in front and we took the stairs to the second floor.

She had arranged to meet a local Justice of the Peace, who didn't look old enough to be one of the original New England Planters, although I had to look twice to be sure. The Bible on which Lauren lightly placed her palm had been around almost that long.

The JP reached slowly into a bottom drawer where he kept his more flexible rubber stamps and made the impending invasion of privacy a legality. "Poor Mrs. Lockhart was on the radio news at eleven," he said, offering a stained-tooth smile of sympathy by association. "It's a shame."

"She's having a hard time. Thanks for these. They'll help us find her daughter."

At least the local radio station had been on the ball when they interviewed Mrs. Lockhart. I thought about what else she might have revealed. Excessive speculation is an academic disorder.

"We'll meet with campus security, break the lock, and bag anything useful," Lauren said on our way across town.

Melody's locker was in for a rude awakening. I hoped we weren't.

Tony Thomson

9: More than a paper cut-out

Bill Paxton, Director of Campus Security, had an office on the third floor of the Student Centre. When the RCMP had Hoovered his small-town police department into the RCMP, most of the cops got rolled into the national police machine, changing the blue stripes on their pants to yellow.

Except for Bill, the town police chief. He retired at fifty and applied in a pique to the college to augment his meagre pension with a juicy nine-to-five plum. On the policing status totem pole, the campus species is carved near the bottom, just above security guards. Private investigators and other interlopers, like me, are buried in the dirt at the base of the pole.

Bill was waiting in his office for his week's excitement to begin. Lauren greeted him with the cordiality inter-agency cooperation required. He was a large, heavy-set man with a pronounced paunch, a greying, military-style brush cut, and dark-rimmed glasses. Like most of his generation of small-town police officers, he'd been hired at a time when it didn't matter if you could spell truck as long as you could lift one. This unfavourable image clings to small-town cops even though they often rival the RCMP in formal training or outweigh them in experience. Most RCMP members still talk about them with contempt when they're not around to hear.

Bill briefly scanned Lauren's warrant with just enough attention to appear professional. He glanced at me and handed it back. He'd probably noticed I wasn't named on the document. From the corner of his office, he retrieved a metre-long bolt cutter, its well-ground edges showing it was not merely an office ornament.

"You'll need one of them empty containers," he said, pointing to a stack of banker's boxes by the door.

I hoisted one aloft. Lauren and I followed Bill, who led the way downstairs carrying a clip board. A Nikon F5 was slung around his neck.

Lockers lined both sides of the corridor connecting the Student Centre with the A&A building. Bill stopped at locker 169, checked it with his list of renters, and took a photo of the front and sides. He stopped short of yanking the locker out from the wall and shooting it from the back. His bolt cutter turned the lock into waste metal with one crunch. I wouldn't want most people's fingers in there.

The hinges didn't creak when Bill opened the door. The fumes wafting out were no worse than would have come from any locker shut away from air circulation.

Before we handled anything, Bill took candid camera photos of the inside, a private existence we had suddenly invaded. Lauren and I craned our necks in anticipation like archaeologists opening an Egyptian tomb.

Other than a course timetable taped to the flaking, vomit-green paint, Melody hadn't stuck a single photo, calendar, or to-do list on the inside of her locker. Even graffiti was conspicuous by its absence.

A warm, hand-knit sweater hung on the left-hand hook. A few stationery items rested on the locker shelf. Beneath a pair of comfortable indoor shoes, three binders and a jumble of papers and paperback books lay on the bottom of the locker.

Bill reached in with his bolt cutter/Swiss Army tool, lifted the sweater off its hook and dropped it in the banker's box. It didn't disintegrate into ancient, desert dust.

Lauren had fewer qualms about contaminating evidence, confident in the discretion of her thin, plastic gloves. The sneakers stashed only stale air in their toe spaces. She dropped them into the banker's box along with Melody's pen and pencil collection and a three-hole punch. That left three binders and the books and papers, which Bill helpfully plopped into the box.

Removing the stack uncovered an item of interest. No one touched it at first, as though we were avoiding the bad luck that curses all tomb raiders.

After Bill took its photo from several angles, Lauren used her Bic pen to slowly pry apart the edges of the folded tinfoil. "Ecstasy," she and Bill said almost simultaneously when the capsules were exposed to the air and the Nikon F5.

"Probably," Lauren corrected them both. "But we'll have it analyzed."

My cut-out image of Melody was gaining a surprising depth.

Bill methodically compiled a list of the locker contents and gave a copy to Lauren. She sealed and labelled the container using the packing tape and marker she had brought, and thanked Bill for his help.

I took on the role of a sepoy and carried the box with its grave cargo out to the low-profile cruiser.

Back in the detachment, Lauren filled out more forms detailing the contents of the container. The RCMP had invented triple-entry accounting. Lauren was in charge of the exhibits for her file. It was important to document the continuity of custody any time someone handled them. If the investigation spiralled into a bigger case, some other member would be assigned comptroller of goods.

Lauren unsealed the banker's box and opened the thickest binder. I fished for another and caught Melody's class notes on Romanticism and cultural anthropology. I had time only to browse the contents before we went to search Melody's rented room.

She was a compulsive note taker, at least in John Byron's class. Glancing at the marginal jottings and doodles, I could see no initials traced into the paper or conjoined with M.L. in love hearts about to be pierced by Cupid's arrow.

Her professors' initials appeared often, followed by dated lecture notes. Melody had annotated them with abbreviations to mark common themes and tropes to help organize her essay writing.

The most common marginal note was WTP—Will to Power when she had first used it—which she had frequently written in red or underlined. She quoted the philosopher Nietzsche, who believed that the superior few among us exert their will over lesser people for their own advantage. I was surprised to discover Melody's interest in the mad German philosopher, whose doctrine was elitist and misogynistic.

I skipped further ahead in the binder to her skimpier notes from Davenport's anthropology class. Barry had ranged unsystematically through a variety of cultural beliefs and practices, but primarily African. He had judged them according to their distance from Christianity. Nothing sprang from any of the pages to give a clue about anyone who might play the role of Romeo in Melody's life.

"Judging from her course notes," Lauren said, breaking into my thoughts, "Melody works harder in Shakespeare than criminal justice. Do you concentrate on criminal law? She's written a lot of notes about sexual assault."

"It's an important topic that raises issues about law, policing, prosecution, and sentencing. The whole legal gamut. Especially the delicate problem of what consent means and the difference between the old crime of rape and the new definition of sexual assault."

"Everyone should know about consent, the men more than the women," Lauren said.

"I finished lecturing on that topic a couple of weeks ago. I also discuss moral issues like euthanasia, abortion, and incest. Students find them more interesting than how to define a break and enter."

"Anyone would." She closed the binder she was holding. "Our appointment with Melody's landlord is coming up. Corporal Meade will join us there."

Jake Meade was an old-school forensics expert. He'd said he liked working in the Ident section because it's clear-cut. The evidence is there, or it isn't. It's never that simple, but Ident severs his work from direct, personal contact with victims and suspects, which makes policing such a human profession, for better or worse.

Once we had locked the exhibits securely into their new lodgings, we drove to Melody's rooming house on Maple Street. A man in a striped suit waited by the front doorstep. Lord of the manor. He stood impatiently with his hands on his hips.

"It's about time you showed up," he said.

"We're on police business time," Lauren said dismissively. She went through her badge and warrant routine.

The landlord unlocked the front door—no open access this morning—and went ahead of us into the building. Once upstairs, he unlocked Melody's door.

"We'll take it from here," Lauren said.

"Knock your socks off," he said and thumped his way downstairs, muttering loud enough for Lauren to hear, "Friggin' women cops."

Melody's room was small and sparsely furnished, with a single bed and a night table, a dresser, a writing desk and chair, a small bookcase with a microwave on top, and a wardrobe in lieu of a closet. It looked exactly like a student's rented room except that Melody was unusually neat. Her bed was made and obviously unslept in. Clothing wasn't strewn randomly about the room.

The desk did triple duty as a lunch counter and music stand for her CD player. A half-consumed bag of Humpty Dumpty potato chips flirted on the desk with two dirty glasses, which a couple of super-sized houseflies guarded territorially. A red plastic milk crate housing her CDs and cassettes was under the desk next to a six-pack of Keith's with two unopened bottles and two empties. I saw no sign of the other two bottles or of Melody's laptop.

Lauren covered her hands in plastic gloves and passed a pair to me, an invitation to touch things. She headed to the wardrobe. "You start with the dresser."

Searching other people's private spaces always creeps me out. The grubby feelings I carry home from these intrusions don't wash away in the shower because scruples don't dissolve that easily. Going through Melody's personal things felt worse because I knew her.

The only playthings on Melody's dresser were a few Steiff stuffed animals. The top drawer held a few plates, some cutlery and glasses, salt and pepper, and a few other kitchen things. The drawer below it was about half full of her clothes. Dark, sombre outfits mingled with much flashier and, I assumed, newer wear. When I lifted them out to search underneath, they hung limp and lifeless in my hand. I tried to imagine them filled with Melody's quiet curiosity and insight. The third drawer overflowed with old-fashioned skirts and blouses. It was hard to close again because the clothing refused to be stuffed back inside.

Her bottom drawer held some towels and wash cloths, slips and underwear, and two bathing suits. One was a flowered single piece with an attached skirt. The other, a black bikini with a thong as an excuse for a back. Her clothing choices were incongruous, like they belonged to two different people. Maybe three. Melody had certainly outgrown her childhood.

I tried to leave her drawers as I'd found them, thinking she would want to find them that way.

I saw nothing except dust behind the dresser or anywhere else on the floor.

"I didn't find anything in the wardrobe to help us identify Melody's Thursday-night visitor," Lauren said. "I hope we have better luck with the night table."

She looked first in the small drawer under the lamp and doily. "Interesting," she said, raising her eyebrows at me.

I peered over her shoulder and saw Melody's birth control pills. She looked at me, holding the recognizable, day-by-day container.

"Melody has missed taking them since Thursday morning."

No one we knew had seen her since. I suppressed the smart-aleck line that had come spontaneously, as they do. *Georgina and Philip might be in for a surprise when she came home.* I hoped the image of her homecoming was a wish for her safety.

I focused my attention on the red milk crate. On the top was a collection of Leonard Cohen CDs with Liszt's "Hungarian Rhapsodies" mixed in, as upstairs tenant Piper had said. Cohen's "New Skin for the Old Ceremony" was awaiting its encore performance in the Sony CD player. Melody's collection included American blues and Billie Holiday, as well as the romantically dubbed Savage Garden and the ofttimes woebegone

Alanis Morrisette. I wondered whether Melody was an infatuation junkie.

Among the literary works on her bookshelf, I found a Bible with Melody Lockhart neatly printed on the title page in a child's calligraphy. The book opened to a page in *Ephesians*, where Melody had heavily underlined the passage

> In Him we were also chosen as God's own, having been pre-destined according to the plan of Him who works out everything by the counsel of His will.

I wasn't surprised to find that Melody had written "God's Will to Power" in the margin.

We heard a knock on the door. When Lauren opened it, Corporal Meade brushed past her and proceeded to open his kit. Lauren caught his attention.

"I want fingerprints from the glasses, the chair, the beer bottles, the CD player, the desk chair, and around the door and rear exit window."

Meade barely nodded and got to work.

Lauren bagged the Bible along with the birth control pills and a few other items of interest, including Melody's hairbrush. The room appeared to be drug-free.

We shifted the bed to look underneath, removed the sheets, and flipped the mattress. It was wide enough for two only in the coziest of yoga contortions. I did some token straightening. Neither of us thought her twin bed was innocent.

Tony Thomson

10: Symbols and doggerel

Lauren glanced at me as I sat in the passenger seat of her cruiser. "I'm taking some of the exhibits we found in Melody's apartment and locker over to Ident in New Minas. And I'll consult with GIS for advice with the file. Do you want to come?"

It was a tempting offer. I'd had some of my most memorable shifts with both RCMP sections. Just not tempting enough. "I'm anxious to get back to Melody's binders. They might reveal her intimate feelings." That thought gave my scruples a pause, but only momentarily.

"She might have written them with a certain somebody in mind. That would be useful," Lauren said, continuing along her boyfriend thread. "The New Minas trip shouldn't take long. I want to go back to the college and get a lead on some real friends before we meet her parents. Somebody knows something. Can I meet you at your office, about two?"

"Sure."

Lauren parked at the rear of the detachment, unlocked the back door, and retrieved the box holding Melody's binders from the evidence locker. "You can find some stale coffee and soggy doughnuts in the members-only lounge," she said.

I smiled at the gentle teasing. *When Lauren gets back from New Minas, she'll ask whether I've identified Melody's lover*. I hoped to learn more about her than the two kinds of pills she had undoubtedly hidden from her parents.

I carried the box into an empty interview room and unsealed it. Leaving aside her class notes, I thumbed through the third and thinnest binder, which seemed the most interesting because Melody had kept her own scribblings in it. She had copied a collection of poems, aphorisms, quotations, and song lyrics that had spoken meaningfully to her, beginning with Robert Herrick's "To the Virgins to Make Much of Time." I wondered who helped her gather her first, passionate rosebuds.

Melody had placed her own poems at the end of the binder, with dates and her initials, the love-sick doggerel of adolescence. Her poetry was dreamier and less physical than Herrick's.

Her first composition was a two-stanza poem written in January 1998 during her sophomore year, while she was still living at home:

> Steel, oh heart, to memory's vines,
>   Orphaned 'ere love was born.
> Bury the sorrows of former times,
>   No fateful memories mourn.
> Destroy the past as it has you,
>   Erect no future pains.
> Release thy soul and bid adieu,
>   Forsake convention's chains.

That was the year Melody had switched from psychology to comparative literature and abandoned the holy road. Although the poem spoke about dark times, it didn't hint at anything beyond commonplace, youthful rebellion.

The poems from her second year and the beginning of her third were strewn with thys and thees and similar antiquities, insipid imitations of the old Romantics. Most of her poems were cries of longing, the paralyzing infatuation of a congenitally-timid, deeply self-conscious, and seriously repressed young woman. Melody's early poems were mostly about the bliss of imagined love, the essential, sublime experience, rosebuds of the mind and not the body. None of them touched on the latter. I pictured her vibrating and fainting in the church of fundamentalism.

Morrisette's lyric "Infatuation Junkie" didn't capture the deep-down desires Melody was trying to put into words. No signs of any temporary highs surfaced from her lovesick poems, only an overwhelming despair and a mounting sense of unworthiness. She had exchanged her childhood fetters for the mental ball and chain of unrequited love.

By the end of her second year, intimations of suicide had begun to elbow their way into Melody's imagery. Almost every year, one of our students drowned their sorrows in the ultimate way. Maybe John Byron was wrong, and Melody did have a self-destruction complex.

But she had survived her sophomore jinx. She'd stopped writing poetry last November, or at least handwriting it. I wondered again where her laptop was hiding and whether she'd typed her back-window man's name in a bold, confident font.

Who had helped Melody convert her original desires of the mind into the so-called sins of the flesh? She doesn't use the pill to ward off a modern-day immaculate conception.

Although Melody's late adolescent dreams began with an illusory obsession, sometime last fall, in her junior year, she had singled someone out from the pack, the idealized but animate being she exalted in her love poems. It would make sense to keep her parents in the dark if he were someone they wouldn't approve of. That didn't narrow the field much.

The college was the likeliest place for Melody to have met the one and only, as she was longing to. It's an improbable place for finding a kindred spirit with her sensibilities. The student intellectual culture is practically nonexistent, if that phrase makes any sense. I pictured Melody as a desperate loner, drifting aimlessly until someone's irresistible gravity drew her in.

I turned back to the beginning of the binder, where Melody had compiled a selection of quotations, mostly from literary sources drawn from her course readings. Unlike her poetry, it wasn't clear when she had begun or stopped writing them. Melody had annotated the collection with initials. In the margins of some she had written her ubiquitous WTP. This acronym may be the most likely clue for understanding what the words meant to her. Deciphering her thinking shouldn't be difficult.

Her first sources revealed little of Melody beyond a desire to please her professors. Things became more interesting when she got to D. H. Lawrence, starting with his longing to escape from a stifling, malevolent society. It had probably inspired her poem about breaking convention's chains. I would bet that the society Melody had in mind was her family, at least her father.

Her later Lawrence quotations were all physically rather than spiritually focused. The next two were

> A woman has to live her life, or live to repent not having lived it—D.H.L.
> It's all this cold-hearted f****** that is death and idiocy—D.H.L.

The asterisks were Melody's. She hadn't added her signature WTP in the margin. Instead, beneath "cold-hearted" she had written in red and underlined the letters PL! I wondered whether it was an initial standing for her father, Philip. What fucking did she mean?

She had followed the D.H. section with quotations from the play *Marat/Sade* which emphasized the Marquis de Sade's obsession with sensuality and extreme pleasure. She had added the marginal notation

XB, likely referenced her drama teacher, Xavier Benoit. The only other set of obvious initials in her binders had been her teachers'.

Next came a regendered quotation: "If [woman] is made for pleasure, let [her] take [her] fill—H. Ibsen." I hadn't expected to find the feminist twist. On the margins, Melody had written in large letters: "Live in desire, disorder and danger, or not at all."

The vehemence of the bold statement took me by surprise. The aphorism was unattributed and likely Melody's. Alongside it was the usual WTP. In this context, it may have meant "Will to Pleasure." Melody had moved on from contemplating a life of imagination to one of feelings.

Tennyson came next: "Better to have loved and lost than never to have loved at all." Underneath, Melody had written in red, "Better to have loved whole hog, at least for a while. Perhaps only for a while—ML." I assumed they were her initials. Once again, the acronym WTP appeared in the margin.

Looking more closely, as one must, I noticed that Melody had lengthened the right side of the P in the WTP abbreviation, transforming it into a misshapen A. That letter could designate many things, including someone's initial. Thereafter, she had used A more frequently than P in her notations.

Further along, it looked as if Melody had used her red pen so often, it was running out of ink. But it wasn't a drying out Bic. She had used white globs of liquid paper to blot out the right side of several As, changing the characters to misshapen Fs.

WTF.

I first read it as What the Fuck. F could be another single initial. Or she might have meant Will to Fuck. Was she adjusting her formula from adolescent to X-rated, consistent with the evolution of her desires?

On the top of the next page, Melody had used coloured ink to draw unexploded fireworks ascending toward a crescent moon. If it was New Year's Day, she hadn't made a list of resolutions to breach, not in so many words.

I turned the page, to see WTA with WTF written underneath it, all enclosed in a red square. I was willing to bet the A was an initial and the F was what one might expect.

Interestingly, some time afterwards, Melody had drawn several large and deep X marks through the box, practically obliterating the A. I didn't need to be a professor of symbology, if they existed, to interpret the meaning. Her first sexual experience hadn't been pleasure, regardless of her will.

Beneath the box Melody had written, "Only when something is experienced does it become real", with 'experienced' struck through with another harsh X.

Then there was the name "Rosetta!" followed by <u>Two Women</u>, the title of a De Sica film. It had been one of the College Film Society's fall semester screenings. The two women who were central to the plot, a mother and her daughter, Rosetta, were gang raped in Italy during the Second World War.

Underneath was a new annotation, "Power <u>of</u> A." It was the same initial she had tried valiantly to obliterate after her fireworks night. The whole section suggested a violent abuse of power.

I tried to collect my thoughts. Melody had created an unusual form of personal diary. Reading it had helped me develop a picture of her last six months. It had begun in the fall with an unbearable infatuation, probably with A. It had progressed to a relationship, which became sexually charged until it was consummated suddenly and disastrously. Grunge and Slacks had witnessed Melody's despair, although what they had interpreted as the bitterness of being dumped had been much crueller.

According to John Byron, Melody had endured another suicide interlude after what, I believed, must have been a sexual assault. Not long thereafter, however, she began to dress flamboyantly and act with more confidence. Rosetta had learned that her sexuality could be a form of power. Perhaps Melody had come to the same conclusion.

Melody had included two final entries in that section of her binder, the first of which was anonymous:

> Desire's embers alight, unquenched,
>   By scent, by touch, by passion wrenched.
> Silken silence, enwrapped, unfree,
>   Awaiting to be seen with Thee.

I suspected it was another of Melody's compositions. After downgrading her One and Only to her First, she was enduring the punishment of having to be silent about her new relationship.

For her final inscription, Melody had simply written her first given name, Judith, which she had asked Darlene, her departmental confidante, to use.

It was time to move out of Melody's head into the real world. *What a lot of mental gymnastics for a single initial, A!*

But that wasn't my deeper purpose. I now had a much more robust picture of who Melody was and what she had gone through. What's happening to her now is a culmination of all that went before.

I left the evidence box with Corporal Smith to be secured. Lauren wouldn't be impressed by the single letter I had identified. I needed a name, and I knew where to look next.

Tony Thomson

11: D. H. Nietzsche

It was just 12:30, the half hour with no classes at the college. Using a phone on an unoccupied desk in the detachment, I called the college switchboard and asked for Professor Benoit, the drama and film teacher in the Humanities Department and one of Melody's current crop. When I explained my purpose, he agreed to see me right away.

Xavier had been with the college since it became a university. About two decades ago. He wasn't Acadian French. Originally from Isle aux Morts, a fishing outport on Newfoundland's southern French Shore, Xavier played the Gallic dandy at the college in an ascot, goatee, and beret, a role for which he had auditioned and selected himself. He ran the college drama club, choosing any genre of play as long as it was French.

This year's production was Peter Weiss's *Marat/Sade*, a daunting directorial undertaking set in Paris during the French Revolution. I am sure Xavier had an explanation why the playwright being German could be excused.

As usual, his door was open. His office was unrivalled in its massive clutter, reflecting less posturing than hoarding. It looked like an archive dumping room, with heaps of recently-donated, uncategorized documents. Xavier had crammed his wall-to-wall bookshelf with double rows of books to save space. On every other flat surface in his office, including most of the floor, he had piled journals, loose files, and papers, topped by books for paperweights.

Maybe he wanted us to believe that creativity and chaos were closely linked. Inspirations appear suddenly, in bursts of internal atomic energy, out of the mess. Organization and planning were for pedants, like me.

"What are you going to do with all this stuff when you retire next year?" I said as a greeting.

"When I'm *forced* to retire," Xavier said. "It's age discrimination, you realize. It's against the *Charter*. I'm going to challenge it."

"Maybe it'll help if we say how much you're needed around here."

"So kind. I don't think I'll ever go willingly. The thing is, I'm only old from the eyes down. Ah, that's not right," he said after a moment. "I'm only aging from my eyes down to my waist." He raised and lowered his eyebrows several times, demonstrating they still worked, too.

"Old age is a state of mind, Xavier."

"I hear you're roaming around with that cute Mountie again," he said in what I thought was a thicker French accent than usual. By cute he meant a woman, a word that's never an expletive in his vocabulary.

"She's on Melody's case," I replied. "If it was Paul Dobson, I'd be spending time with him."

Xavier knew Paul, a fellow Newfie. "Lucky for you it isn't him."

Once the obligatory small talk was out of the way, Xavier wanted to know everything about Melody's disappearance. I had practised a short spiel on the way over. He listened attentively, but I was more interested in what he might know.

"The problem is, we're drawing zeroes when it comes to finding any of Melody's friends or her lovers," I said, using a term he might identify with.

"The concept 'lover' hardly applies to Melody. She's a one-woman play without dialogue. I invited her to join the drama club and introduced her to some of the members, especially the men, hoping the company would help lift her out of herself. She started to watch rehearsals and worked backstage. My students are close and, dare I say, tolerant of eccentricities."

"They tolerate you," I said. *Venerate is more accurate.* "How well do you know Melody?"

"You know me, Ian. I'm attracted to any woman. But I'm partial to the flamboyant, someone with the spirit of life and adventure who can push me in a new direction. That's not Melody, although I noticed that she showed some new spark this term. I haven't seen her recently. It's drama. You notice when people are absent."

"I have one possible lead and I hope you can help with it. Melody seemed to be attracted to a man with the initial A. Does that bring anyone to mind?"

"First name or last name?"

"I don't know."

"Melody was friendly with Aaron Campbell, but that's not unusual. He's very popular, and not only among the girls in drama. An excellent actor. But I can't say anything about how involved she was with Aaron. I doubt it went very far."

"Do you know where I could find him?"

"You can usually find the drama crew in the cafeteria during the lunch break. If Aaron isn't there, you should ask Joanie Peters. Students know more about each other's lives than any of us. I mention Joanie because she's the social centre of the club. I'll come down and introduce you. I doubt she'd be taking criminal justice."

Wherever Joanie sat, she'd be at the centre. The drama crowd occupied a noisy table, enjoying more laughter among themselves than an audience ever rewarded them for their comedies. Joanie's long, bleach-blonde hair framed a face featuring dark brown eyebrows. She was happy to see Xavier and invited him to join them. We'd have to sit on the table.

"Thanks Joanie," Xavier said. "I see everyone is ready for class. This is Ian Wallace, from Social Sciences. He's helping the police find Melody Lockhart. Could you spare some time to talk with him?"

"Sure," Joanie said obligingly. "I hope she's okay. We were just talking about her."

"That's nice," I said. "But let's go somewhere quieter. How about one of the benches in the garden outside?"

"Okay," Joanie said reluctantly.

The small garden outside the A&A wasn't yet in bloom except for a handful of purple and yellow crocuses, which had awakened early from their van Winkle winter. I sat on a bench opposite hers.

"Thanks for talking with me. The police don't think anything's happened to Melody. They think she's with a boyfriend somewhere, but can't identify him. I know that she had a boyfriend earlier in the term until they had a hard breakup."

"That's not true," Joanie said. "At least about breaking up with a boyfriend. She's a sad sack, you know. Xavier tried to get her involved in drama but she'd be hopeless on stage. All she did was sit around, mooning over Aaron like a lost puppy."

"Could he tell she was interested?"

"Everyone likes Aaron, but Melody was just so *obvious*. He was never actually, like, *into* Melody. He did try to be nice to her for a while. He told me all about it. Any breakup was just in her crazy mind."

"Why crazy?"

"When Aaron said he wasn't interested in her, she threw a fit, started crying and tried to hit him. He had to get away from her."

"Did everyone know about this?"

"No, he only told me. He and I are going out now. We really hit it off in rehearsal."

Rehearsal for what? I wondered.

"I'd like to meet him. Do you know where he's likely to be?"

"He won't know much about Melody."

"I get that Aaron and Melody were never a thing, but he might think of something if I ask the right questions. Xavier thought he could help."

After a short pause, Joanie said, "He said he'd be home, running his lines over lunch. He's playing de Sade in, you know, *Marat/Sade*? It's a really challenging role. I'm glad he's not playing Marat, though. I'd have to stab him!" Joanie giggled. "He has an apartment over on Elm Street, just off campus."

"Thanks. I hope things work out the best for you two." *And that the mention of a stabbing isn't prophetic.*

I glanced back as I headed for Main Street and the phone booth on the corner. Joanie was still sitting on the bench, admiring the optimistic crocuses. She was probably rehearsing "Joanie Campbell" to herself.

No one had torn the phone book out of the booth. I consulted the Halstead section and found that one of two A. Campbells lived at 13 Elm Street. The second lived at a much posher address. He was the most expensive dentist in town.

A telephone call would be counter-productive. Elm was a short stroll east off Main. I walked briskly in that direction, hoping I didn't have too obvious a glob of gum underneath my fake detective's shoe.

This was going to be a difficult interview. I'd built a picture of Melody's hateful encounter with the young Mr. Campbell and its aftermath. I didn't want to confront him right away. He'd be bound to deny any wrongdoing. I hoped to confirm the truth, not just hear his version of it.

I thought about discussing the case with Mary. My judgment about relationships is usually less accurate than what she calls her intuition. But that was inappropriate now that she no longer had an unofficial spousal exemption.

Aaron lived in another old, converted house near the College end of Elm, a duplex divided into upstairs and downstairs flats. It looked to be in good repair, with freshly painted white shingles and dark green trim.

Two mailboxes faced me on the veranda. The one beside the grand entrance advertised the occupant as A. Campbell.

I could hear music vibrating through the door as I knocked alternately with the slow beat. I didn't hear de Sade practising a soliloquy.

Aaron answered the authoritative knock and looked at me as if I were a vacuum cleaner salesman. With reddish, wavy hair, piercing blue eyes, and ruddy skin, he looked the Scot his surname suggested. His sleeveless shirt did little to conceal the build he'd worked hard to acquire, more for looks than strength, I figured. I recognized a Leonard Cohen tune playing from somewhere inside.

"Hi Aaron," I said brightly. "Dr. Benoit said I'd find you home."

He looked neither surprised nor wary, perhaps trying on inscrutable. "So?"

"I'm Dr. Wallace, from the college. Working with the police. We're looking for information about Melody Lockhart."

"She's not here," he said, lacing his reply with a knot of antagonism. I was glad I'd said Benoit and not Joanie, although that mightn't have been such a bad thing for her.

"Nobody thinks she's with you. Our problem is she doesn't seem to be anywhere, and she has no close friends we can ask. We're trying to talk to anyone who knew her, even a little bit. Dr. Benoit said you could help us."

He looked at me warily but invited me in. He closed only the screen door behind me.

His flat was much fancier than mine, including the furnishings.

"I know Melody a little bit," he said.

I chose to sit on a pressed back oak chair that didn't have a cushion. Aaron turned off the record player, cutting off Cohen in mid-moan, and sat in the middle of his soft, comfortable sofa.

"We know a little about Melody," I said, hoping the pronoun made my inquiry seem more official than casual. "The kind of music she listens to, the books she reads, how she feels about her family, that kind of thing. The more we can figure out her personality, the more likely we'll know where she went and, we hope, who she's with."

"Well, I can't help you with that," he said. "She's never had a real boyfriend."

"Never? That's something we didn't know." I began to feel pessimistic about my first approach to the interview. "I liked the Cohen you were playing, by the way, 'Last Year's Man.' *Songs of Love and Hate* is one of my favourite albums. It's nice to hear it on vinyl again, too. It's so much clearer. Melody has quite a collection of Cohen CDs in her room over on Maple Street. We've searched it and her college locker this morning."

"Yeah, she only has CDs. Vinyl is the right way to listen to good music; you know, something with meaning in it."

"I hear you're playing de Sade in this year's play. There's a lot of meaning in that play. Is Melody part of the cast?"

"Not a chance. She quit coming to the drama club."

"Dr. Benoit said she would benefit from being part of it, that she might come out of her shell. He said he asked you to help her feel a little more comfortable in the club."

I hoped I hadn't stretched too far the supple fabrication of Xavier's intention. I wanted Aaron to think I knew more than I was letting on and, more importantly, less than I knew about other things. I had also suggested a socially acceptable reason for his interest in Melody. So far, he'd been reluctant to reveal much. When you don't want to speak truth to a police officer or, in this case, someone masquerading as one, it's useful to play out a few small details, the better to protect the ones you want undisturbed.

"Yeah, Xavier did say something like that. At first, she was afraid to talk to me, something to do with her crazy father."

"Oh, for sure. Did you hear him at the press conference we arranged? What an ass!"

"Yeah, on the radio. Him and her mother. What performances."

Aaron settled back in his sofa. Philip Lockhart was a mutually despised target. "Melody wanted to get as far from him as she could," he said.

"You sound a little sorry for her. That makes sense. Did you talk with her?"

"Sure. Xavier had asked me to, and I did feel sorry for her. She's smart, you know."

I wondered whether intelligence was anywhere on his list of important attributes in a woman. "Saying Melody's smart means something coming from a man who's about to play the Marquis de Sade. That's a complex, ambitious role."

"It sure is. And de Sade's the real hero of the play, not that pussy, Marat."

"There's something interestingly Nietzschean about de Sade."

"The other way around. De Sade came first." Aaron said, becoming more animated. He enjoyed correcting a professor. "But Nietzsche said it best."

"Will to Power," I asserted.

"Absolutely, but so much more." Aaron leaned forward, volubly ratcheting his enthusiasm. "The will to life itself. It's about the transvaluation of values. Pride, greed, lust, gluttony are all humanly necessary and therefore good. Creativity has been crushed too long in the iron cage of

Christian morality. The true genius is always seen as evil, but no progress is possible without violating conventions. 'There is no ought anymore,' Nietzsche said. 'Everything is permitted.'"

"I get it, Aaron. I hadn't thought of all that. But according to John Byron, Melody is deeply into the Romantics."

"Byron doesn't have two clues about what Romanticism really means. He's doesn't even understand the poets he's supposedly named after. Melody fell hard for the romance, the soap opera and fluff."

He summoned himself from the sofa for better oration. I hoped I was an appreciative audience. "Romanticism isn't about that silly nonsense called romantic love. It's a wilful, passionate immersion in the most emotionally powerful and dangerous experiences we can have. Nietzsche's the great nineteenth-century Romantic, not that frail Shelley."

"Melody was bright, you said. Did she agree with your ideas?"

"Totally. I thought she was really coming around. Nietzsche realized it's not about thinking. It's about doing, about experience." He was pacing within the narrow circle of his own mind.

"You thought she was coming around?"

"Fear of real passion and full-bodied experience was exactly Melody's problem."

Not yours, I assumed. "I think you're wrong about Nietzsche," I said aloud. "He was a flagrant misogynist. He feared what he saw as women's power over men. For him, men should treat women as objects to dominate."

"He wasn't wrong, but Nietzsche was too involved with that power thing. And way too Victorian, even though he was German. Nietzsche didn't understand pleasure, especially sexual pleasure. Sexuality is our most creative expression of egoism and instinct, the true mark of human nature. Women want it as much as men do, you know. Maybe more. It's instinctual, in the blood. They're just so screwed up by conventions, by Christian morality. Just to *think* about it is sinful. That's Melody all over. But Jesus, did she want it."

"How did you know?"

"For women like Melody, thinking gets in the way of doing. Her body knew what she wanted. It's a lot wiser than the mind."

"You understood what her body craved even when her mind told her no."

"Exactly."

"Yeah," I said, standing up from my uncomfortable chair and staring Mr. Campbell in the face. "You're a regular D. H. Nietzsche. Men like you have finally figured out what women want. And they want you. And if they don't know it, you'll prove it no matter what it takes. You're the irresistible superman, that big illusion you have of yourself when you prey on women."

"Right." Aaron drew out the word slowly and sat back on the sofa, visibly composing his thoughts. "Once things started to get genuinely romantic, a little bit sensual, Melody bolted like a deer and went running back to her daddy." Now his soliloquy sounded rehearsed.

"You're not saying what really happened," I said. "You're trying to suck me into the lies you tell yourself."

Aaron looked at me, realizing his audience of one had been egging him on. "What do you mean?"

"Judging from her writings, you went way past first base, all the way home and beyond. Your role was far worse than some fantasy seduction."

"That's just in her imagination," Aaron said defensively. "I tried, that's all. She was scared to death to be touched. Nobody will believe anything she wrote about me because nothing happened."

"Maybe Joanie will."

"Not when I tell her you're a prick. That you came here accusing me of, of rape or something."

"That's not a word I brought into the conversation."

"Listen, Jack, I've got work to do and you're wasting my time. You better clear out. Now."

I've had that effect on people before. "Sure. Maybe the uniformed cops can get more out of you down at the detachment. They'll be next."

I saw myself out of Campbell's flat, leaving the door ajar for him to slam behind me.

He was the bigger prick. I had a good idea what he had done with Melody and what he'd told Joanie he'd done. She's next, another notch for the would-be Lothario, Squirmy Campbell.

I hoped the R word had made Campbell nervous, too afraid to complain to the detachment about my approach. Even so, in his mind he had merely consummated his seductiveness. Melody appeared to be ready, even desirous. But she was young and inexperienced. At some point, she resisted. How you surmount that last barrier of resistance makes all the difference, not just morally, but in the law.

Date rape may be a campus epidemic, but in this case, trying to convince a jury there had been no real consent would be tough. The defence would raise a reasonable doubt about Campbell's state of mind, that he genuinely believed he had consent. It would be up to the prosecutor to prove he had no such honest belief. There wouldn't be much evidence to bring into court on Melody's behalf when we found her, assuming she would be willing to put herself though all that public suffering and humiliation.

She seemed a peculiar target for Campbell, who could probably string along more than one woman at a time. What prestige could he claim by bedding Melody? She'd represent barely a footnote in his résumé.

Joanie was a more likely victim.

After all I'd seen and heard, I mostly believed Campbell's claim he didn't know what had become of Melody. The serial womanizer had moved on to a new unfortunate. I should have strung him along further in case he had an inkling about who her new Casanova might be. You're always curious about your last one's new partner.

Maybe Lauren will squeeze a name out of his greasy pores if she sweats him a little in the plain, white box of the interview room.

12: Two colleagues

I'd ignored Lauren's invitation to dine on Monday's leftover doughnuts and coffee. After the press conference, I didn't want to face any questions about Melody in the GoodFare. The college cafeteria was my best option. I selected a Mediterranean wrap for lunch and carried it upstairs, ignoring everyone's eyes.

Nothing to do before Lauren arrived except mull and munch. I was waiting to see the Lockharts and explore the sizable family fissures I'd learned about from the press conference and my talk with the Literature Department secretary.

I wasn't in a fit mood to prepare tomorrow's lectures, which I doubted I'd deliver. I felt the blue flu leaching down from my forehead, although pretending to be sick wouldn't be avoiding work. I'd still be on the case.

Reaching for the phone, I called Slim Starr at the *Halifax Herald* to find out more about the fire he was checking into. He was out of the office, investigating his lead. I left a request for a call-back to my home phone.

Lauren came by about twenty to two, in her uniform. "Plans have changed," she said. "I've arranged to see Cathy Clarke. She's working from her home over on Oakland Road."

Cathy was a psychologist and not one of Melody's current professors. Oakland Road was one of Halstead's upscale neighbourhoods.

"What did you learn from Ident?" I asked as we drove along Main Street.

"Corporal Meade found a few prints other than those he identified as Melody's. The only ones on the beer bottles were hers. He found a poor-quality partial of an unidentified print on one of the glasses. No second print like it anywhere else—on the chairs, the door frame, the windowsill. He brought the glass into New Minas and they're trying some tricks they hope will bring out the print. Jake found lots of hair from Melody's hairbrush, blond with dark roots and black ones, both dyed. I'm reasonably sure they're hers."

I filled Lauren in on Aaron Campbell and what I leaned from him.

"He's a piece of work," I concluded. "He raped Melody."

"Are you sure?" Lauren said, aghast.

"He didn't admit it, but it's consistent with what I read in her binder, and how Campbell acted and what he said."

"That's really tragic. But you think Campbell isn't responsible for her disappearance?"

"So far. You'll want to interview him."

Lauren turned off Main Street to Oakland Road.

"Whose idea was bringing in Cathy Clarke?" I said.

"Corporal King suggested I consult her about the file."

Cathy Clarke taught a class called The Homicidal Brain. Much too general a title, in my opinion. Homicides are more common among intimates than random strangers, and no brain structure has been found to explain that. Violence bursts out suddenly among people densely immersed in family ties, the way divers' lungs explode when they surface too quickly from the depths. Love and hate are wound together in complex patterns.

Cathy specialized in mass and serial murders. Brain science might have a place if you weren't looking for a so-called natural-born killer. You can't detect a murderous instinct in the brain of a newborn. They're an atypical breed, despite what TV and the movies say. For Hollywood, there's one on every street corner, like there used to be gas stations or variety stores.

We parked on the street in front of Cathy's house, a brown one-and-a-half story with a big gabled window above a large front porch covered by an extension of the roof. Her antique, red VW Bug was parked in the driveway. She had hand-painted *Goliath* on the rear engine bonnet. I liked that display of character.

Lauren walked past the driveway along the side of the house. "Cathy said she'd be in the backyard."

Cathy stopped gardening as we appeared. The yard was surrounded by a brown, wooden fence, with a large garden plot in the centre, recently tilled.

She was short and trim, with sandy hair tied tightly back and large, round pink glasses. She stood by a well-supplied compost pile she had uncovered from its protective plastic dome. She stabbed her garden fork into the pile when she saw us coming around the corner. Some water vapour escaped from the rotting vegetation.

"From what you explained on the phone, we have a missing person," Cathy said to Lauren, without preliminaries. "I can suggest only a few ideas. Usually, I have much more to go on."

"Melody Lockhart was a timid loner," Lauren said. "We're only beginning to learn about her."

"As you had said. First, I wondered whether she was a suicide. I doubt that's what happened. Suicides seldom just disappear. They want the people they blame to discover the evidence."

Cathy placed one foot on the garden fork and pushed it further into the soft refuse. She turned it over and mixed it with some leaves and twigs. "Other aspects of her case make suicide unlikely. She was apparently out from under her parents' roof and had a lot going for her academically. You thought she showed signs of coming out of her self-protective cocoon. That suggests she might be a runaway. Maybe there's a boyfriend to sneak away with. You also suggested something problematic in her upbringing."

A tangle of earthworms oozed from the soil she had turned over. They writhed in the sunlight and tried to rebury themselves.

"We've had our share of family abuse in the Valley, including sexual abuse," I said, reminding Cathy of the fact as well as of my existence.

"Of course," she said. "The Sterling case was a spin-off from the hillbilly sex scandal in King's County. The other involved a stepfather. Melody's family doesn't fit either of these types."

Looking directly at me, she said, "As I recall, you were on the wrong side in both of those cases."

"We all agreed about what was done and who did it. Legal Aid asked me to write an opinion about an appropriate, rehabilitative sentence."

"How did that work out?" Cathy replied, nettling me while concentrating on her compost. Some more heavy digging unleashed a compacted stench.

"But Ian's point," Cathy continued, "is whether Melody was a victim of abuse as a child, perhaps even incest."

"If she was molested," Lauren asked, "isn't she a greater threat now she's out of her father's control? It would be a dangerous family secret he wouldn't want exposed."

"Yes. That's an angle to consider. But I don't think the incest scenario is likely."

"That's why we came to see you," Lauren said. "So far, we have only one lead. Ian found out that Melody had a boyfriend."

"Two boyfriends," I said. "Melody's first was a drama major. Now it seems she has a new love interest. I'm working on an identity."

Lauren's forehead wrinkled in surprise. I hadn't gotten to that part yet when we talked earlier.

Cathy exposed more compost. "Not enough for drawing any conclusions," she said dismissively, "although it's too soon to rule anyone out. Given her authoritative father, I suggest she was either repulsed by or attracted to dominating males—probably either of the extremes at different times."

She gazed at two entwined, squirming worms and said, clinically, "Excessive egoism and self-deprecation are two faces of the same coin. Both are rooted in self-obsession. But, contrary to what you might think, Ian, I don't believe she was the victim of some deranged multiple killer, not that bucolic places like Halstead are immune."

"Or that ordinary-looking people might not be harbouring a Mr. Hyde in their laboratories," I added, stretching Cathy's point.

"In my class about mass murderers, I show pictures of Paul Bernardo and Karla Homolka and ask who they think they are. They typically identify them as celebrities. Serial murderers can be handsome and charming. Think of Ted Bundy. But usually they aren't like that."

"Exactly," Lauren nodded. "We need to keep this investigation on the ground."

"Of course," Cathy said, resting her hand on the fork. "I suspect you'll find an intimate relationship turned violent, with the act done in a fit and covered in a rush. If I'm right, the victim's body will be discovered before long in some shallow grave. You just need an idea where to look. Please keep me informed of the progress of your investigation and when I can next be of assistance, especially if you identify a prime suspect."

Lauren thanked Cathy for her help. She returned to off-gassing her compost.

I'd found her professional attitude clinical and off-putting, like she was talking about a forensics sample and not a person. I wondered how much money the RCMP had forked out for the consultation.

We were left with two of Melody's teachers to interview: Barry Davenport and Rosemary Connors—Shakespeare. Barry had agreed to meet us in his college office.

"Tell me something about this one," Lauren said.

"Barry isn't just the academic star in my department," I said. "He's an entire constellation. None of us comes close to his long list of specialized publications. On the rare occasions he attends college events, he enters the room with the glow of the smartest person present."

"I take it he's smart," Lauren said, deadpan.

"He graduated from a small college in Illinois and finished a PhD at the University of Adelaide. I have no idea what brought him to Nova Scotia. They say in Ontario that Sterling College is stuck in the middle of sticks and woods. Barry shows no signs of being committed to the place. He disappears from the province when classes are over and occasionally when they aren't."

We took the slug-paced A&A elevator one creaky floor to the top of the building. It ground to a standstill and the doors reluctantly opened.

A ray of dusty light spilled out of the open door at the far end of the corridor—Barry Davenport's domain. Particles of dust flitted about above the square of carpet the flickering sunlight lit up.

I tapped lightly on the door, and then we marched in.

Barry had been reaching for the phone, but he switched his attention to our arrival. "Come on in."

He offered Lauren the single, comfy reading chair below the north-facing row of windows. A fan strained to coax enough draft through the one open window to make the space breathable.

I stood in front of his bookshelf. Many of his books were hidden behind an array of photographs of himself. Photos showed him scuba diving or hiking in exotic places, usually accompanied by a belle of the week. He had even gleefully posed with a slaughtered giraffe. Other pictures were local and showed him skiing at Martock, surfing at Lawrencetown Beach, posing in front of a speedboat in Queensport, sailing a sloop off Chester.

Barry looked directly at Lauren and said, "Ian told me Melody Lockhart is missing. She takes my anthropology class, as you've undoubtedly learned. How can I help?"

"We think she might be with a recent boyfriend, although we don't have more than a hint of a name," Lauren said.

"I'm sorry, Constable. I don't pay much attention to the social life of my students. I'm interested only in their academics. I remember Melody, though. She's shy and mousy, quite unremarkable."

For faculty members like Barry, students were a nuisance to pack off as soon as possible so he could get back to his research, what the job was all about. In one of our chats, Barry had referred to his students as slope heads.

"Has Melody been attending class regularly?" Lauren said.

"I can't say."

"We have one person of interest," I said. "Aaron Campbell had an intense but short encounter with Melody."

"I know Aaron considerably better. He's one of the few male students in the college who thinks he has something to say."

"Aaron seems completely taken in by Nietzsche. Is he on your syllabus?" I asked.

"Of course. Nietzsche is the nineteenth-century anti-Christ. Students in this college hadn't heard his name until they took my course. They're astounded anyone would overturn the moral values they were taught since birth, whether they're Christians or atheists."

"Why would Melody fall for someone like that?" Lauren said, looking in turn at me and Barry.

"Oh, he's quite charismatic. An actor, I believe. He's the opposite of Ian, here," he said, still looking only at Lauren. "Ian's too passive to chase after anyone. Women despise weaklings, timidity, femininity in men."

He nodded his head in my general direction. "He's terrified of being trapped by a wilful woman, as you appear to be, especially when you're in uniform. The minute some woman who appears strong shows some interest in him, which must be a rare thing anyway, Ian runs as fast as he can in the other direction."

"The hell I do!" I exclaimed, not as much insulted as stung by something that might have a glimmer of truth.

"Ian's attracted to women like you. They never feel the same toward him. Women want active men who take the lead in the courtship ritual. Even now, when women are trying so hard to be like men, down deep they want to be dominated."

Barry glared at Lauren. Leered would be more accurate. "As for Ian here, he's still miserably mooning over his ex-wife and wouldn't know the difference between a seduction and an invitation to tea. He should take lessons from Campbell."

"Following that idea and thinking about Campbell," Lauren said quickly, appearing to ignore the tirade while cutting off my response, "how forcefully would he carry out what you're calling a seduction?"

"That I couldn't say. I just know his type."

I bet you do.

"Campbell is treacherous, like all his clan," Barry continued. "Smarter than the average Britisher."

"His 'clan' is treacherous?" Lauren asked blankly.

"The toady Campbell clan did civilization a favour when they massacred those Scottish Highlanders," Barry said, still talking directly to Lauren. "Like all Britishers, Aaron's an intellectual poseur. So is Ian, here. As for Melody, I expect you know more about her than I do."

Both Lauren and I were taken aback by his vehemence. We glanced at each other, each hoping the other had the next bright idea.

Barry turned back to his portable typewriter and placed his bejewelled fingers on the keys. Cops weren't in his bailiwick. "I've just got to finish this," he said, throwing the excuse over his left shoulder for good luck.

Lauren recovered first, modelling equanimity. "We've hit a dead end, Dr. Davenport," she said. "Please call the detachment if you can think of anything that might help."

Barry had given our cue to leave none too subtly.

Once we were back in the dazzling daylight, I felt compelled to say, "Davenport's not wrong about the marriage break-up eating at me, but I'm not as dense as he lets on. He just picks away at my scabs."

"Men like him think they're irresistible to women. Frankly, he gives me the shudders. Does he always talk that way? I haven't heard some of those terms for a long time."

"Barry comes across as right-wing, especially when he's riled up or been drinking. Recently he's become blunt instead of cautious."

"The way he talked about you was infuriating. It felt terrible swallowing what I wanted to say. It just seemed inopportune."

"You were right to, Lauren. I'm sorry I blurted out what I did because it made him more aggressive. He says things to ruffle me. I take shots back. I didn't want this talk to be about me. I hated it being about us."

"I'm glad you defended yourself."

"Let's just forget it," I said.

"Okay." She glanced at her watch. "Professor Connors can wait for tomorrow. Mrs. Lockhart expects me about four. She said she'd told her husband when I planned to arrive. We should go over now without calling in advance, before Philip gets home."

"Copy that," I said. "Mrs. Lockhart won't be expecting me, though."

"No. Just make yourself inconspicuous."

"As easy as being Giant MacAskill."

"I'd say Paul Bunyan's Blue Ox if you hadn't suffered enough today."

"Thanks for that mercy. If I'm interfering at the Lockharts', just give a signal and I'll wait outside."

"Okay. But when Philip Lockhart gets home, come back in with him."

"Copy that."

"And stop saying that."

I resisted the impulse to add a third. Of the two of us, she was the only one armed.

Lauren followed the college loop back to the street, passing the sciences wing, a collage of monochrome concrete slabs that looked like a giant's Lego blocks. This specimen of architectural brutalism had been the first of the 1970s additions to Sterling Community College, when it had received the status of a university, becoming identity-insecure in the process.

Lauren directed her cruiser towards controlled-access Highway 101, which cut a wide swath through farmland. As flat and straight as a prairie road and only two lanes, official speed limit one hundred kilometres an hour, the 101 was engineered for collisions. The pair of bold yellow lines in the middle is the only highway twinning, a virtual barrier doing little to prevent traffic from straying into the opposing lane. Head-ons are hard to survive.

When you leave the provincial capital, Halifax, on the 101, a prominent tourist sign names it the Harvest Highway. In the detachment it's called Organ Harvest Highway.

13: The Lockharts

As the cruiser settled into its not too fast, not too slow speed, Lauren spied a one-eyed Buick in her rear-view mirror. The driver pulled out to pass, slowly but deliberately.

Lauren slacked her speed and stared directly at him as he went by. He returned the gaze.

She made a snap decision and turned on the lights after he pulled in front. Stopping a car for a dead headlight is entirely discretionary. The near-sighted Buick had been travelling a respectable 110.

The driver pulled onto the shoulder as soon as the lights came on. Lauren stopped behind, halfway out in the lane and said into the mic, "I've got a 10-11, roadside stop, headlight, silver Buick Park Avenue, Beta Tango Echo, Two Nine Zero." She paused briefly. "101 heading west, just past kilometre 160."

Putting on her hat, Lauren approached the Buick according to the Manual. She looked warily through the back window and then stood just behind the driver's door with her holster unsnapped. His window was already down. I followed on the safe side of the cruiser and leaned down to look in the passenger window. The driver obligingly rolled that one down, too.

He was about 30, well-built, blond hair, cleft chin, someone my ex would have called handsome, a category that didn't include me. She was the expert. If beauty is in the eye of the beholder, we search longingly in that eye for our own reflection.

"Hello, officers," he said, suppressing a salute. He greeted Lauren as if he were charming the ladies on his way into church.

He reached into the glove compartment for his documents, which he found easily, and into his wallet. He didn't ask why he was being detained.

Lauren enlightened him anyway: "Your left headlight is out."

"I see."

Lauren hadn't changed her position. "I want to see your driver's license, registration, and insurance," she ordered matter-of-factly. They were already in the Chin's hand.

She inspected the documents. "This car isn't registered to you."

"It's my father's. I've borrowed it," Cleft Chin said. "So?"

"Where's your car?"

"It's in a car wash for a full detailing."

I followed Lauren back to the cruiser. Dispatch reported Cleft Chin had nothing in the computer information system she could use against him. She wrote two summary offence tickets, one for the headlight and one for exceeding posted speed limits.

The driver threw them on the passenger seat, said, "Thanks," sarcastically, and pulled away with only a token amount of gravel spray.

"He looked pretty clean-cut to me," I said. "You were by the book with him." Cops tell you they trust their instincts. They remember the few occasions when something that didn't feel right panned out.

"He looks like trouble. I don't trust him," Lauren said heatedly. "That polite shit was just a scam. He's been through plenty of stops and is way too comfortable handing over his documents."

"I didn't like him either," I said, although my grounds were significantly different.

Underneath his smiling compliance, Cleft Chin had committed one of the seven deadly sins: contempt of cop.

"I wanted to search his trunk," she said, "but there's no reasonable and probable cause. And it's not his car."

One of the drawbacks of researching people is that your presence changes their behaviour. From a cop's point of view, I wasn't a brother cop, someone who would be trusted to lie under oath if she had invented an excuse for a search.

I wondered whether the talk with Cathy Clarke had made Lauren suspicious about what Cleft Chin might have been up to. The stop wouldn't disappear quickly from her mind because she'd left business unfinished.

Lauren took the Painton exit to Highway One. The Lockharts lived in an old farmhouse on the north side of the old highway, made invisible from the road by a thick clump of alders. A single opening through the trees led to the bottom of a heart-shaped gravel driveway that curved towards the unpainted house and merged at the rear. The physical layout of a place doesn't always reflect its moral reality.

On either side of the driveway, the gently sloping land promised no more than a summer crop of hay. The Lockharts had truncated the farmstead to less than a hobby.

The front door of the house was five feet off the ground, a feature that is often called a mother-in-law door. The veranda had collapsed of decrepitude years before. The Lockharts hadn't replaced their front steps. According to country manners, people used the back door.

Lauren pulled the cruiser behind the house. The crunch of loose gravel grinding into the tires announced our arrival. Ours was the only vehicle in sight.

"We've heard hints about a buried family secret," Lauren said. "Maybe that's what Melody had wanted to talk to her mother about."

"It wouldn't have been a pleasant conversation for either of them."

We were welcomed in the manner customary to rural Nova Scotia. Two barking mongrels took their post on either side of the car. My greeter was a large mix with visible shepherd lineage. On Lauren's side, a hyper black and white longhair, part sheepdog, growled menacingly.

Lauren tapped on her horn and waited for Mrs. Lockhart to appear at the back door and corral the hounds. They left muddy prints on each car door in case we needed to identify them later.

"The dogs keep the coyotes away," Mrs. Lockhart said apologetically.

Maybe not all of them, I thought. *Some might be already inside.* She looked older than I remembered from the press conference, over sixty, still wearing the same floral dress minus the sweater and bandana.

"Hello, Georgina," Lauren said warmly. "This is Dr. Wallace from the college. He's helping us find your daughter."

"Thank you, Dr. Wallace," she said. "I just don't know what to do."

"We're here to help," Lauren said sympathetically.

Georgina led us inside, through a shed attached to the house. Cut and split hardwood was stacked along the back wall, high at the left, dwindling to a few sticks on the right. A second, interior door led to the summer kitchen dominated by a wood stove with a baking oven and cooking surface. Some dilapidated wooden furniture stood around forlornly, waiting their fate in the fire. She let the guard dogs loose, and they settled down near the stove, soaking up the last heat from the oven. They had acquiesced to our intrusion, for now.

A third door led into the main kitchen and the twentieth century, where electricity lightened the room. We followed Georgina like ducklings through the kitchen and the adjoining dining room to a central foyer, dominated by a six-foot striking clock, older than the house. The foyer opened to the living room on the opposite side. The floors were laid with wide pine boards, painted dark brown.

The living room looked like an antique shop that had just enjoyed a run on its better pieces. I may have been wrong about the century. The faded Persian-style rug, the run-of-the-mill overstuffed cloth chairs and sofas, the deadly-to-dust ornately carved tables, and the sideboard covered in lace doilies and over-sized lamps gave that impression.

A faux leather lounge chair sat directly between the two front windows, where it faced a large TV on the opposite side of the room. I could almost see a Lord and Master sign on the throne chair.

We sidled in, squeezing among the artifacts. Mrs. Lockhart sat in one of the padded armchairs. And Lauren accepted her invitation to sit in a nearby love seat.

I looked around for the least conspicuous chair. *I should have brought sunglasses to hide behind.* I settled in a Victorian settee with a decorative oak centre on its rigid back. It had been designed to make courting as uncomfortable as possible for Victorian couples.

"I'll put on a pot of tea," Georgina said. Country manners despite our mission. "I've also got some brown bread that still has a little warmth in it. I'm not expecting Philip to come home until four. Should I give him a call?"

"Tea would be nice, Georgina, but please don't bother to call. There are some things I want to ask you first."

"Won't take five minutes, and please call me Georgie," she said, already halfway to the kitchen.

Lauren got up quickly and walked over to the mantle. I was equally curious.

The Lockharts had arranged a gallery of photos around a family portrait. Philip stood at the centre hovering over Georgina, who sat in a wooden chair in front of him. She held a toddler on her lap. Two women, probably in their later teens, stood to Philip's left. I couldn't tell which one was Melody. On Philip's right was a boy, who looked somewhat younger than the girls.

On one side of the group portrait were four almost indistinguishable pictures of tightly swaddled babies. On the other we saw two high school graduation shots, a third of a girl about the same age dressed in Sunday clothes, and a space where Melody's grad shot had likely been.

"Interesting looking family," Lauren observed. "I'll ask Georgina about who's who before I get to anything heavy."

The pendulum clock played the half-hour Westminster tune.

"Time isn't on our side," Lauren said.

I'd returned to my seat of presumed invisibility before Georgina returned. She held a teapot covered with a knitted tea cozy in one hand and balanced a tray on the other. "It just has to steep for a few minutes. Help yourself to some bread." She placed the tray on a table near Lauren. It was piled with thick slices of crusty brown bread, a small pot with butter, and another with a berry preserve. She reached into a sideboard and took four decorative teacups with saucers from its dark interior.

"I was looking at the photos," Lauren said. "Four is a nice size for a family."

"Isn't it? That's Melody on my lap. What a sweet baby she was. God, I hope she's all right. She was a little bit of a surprise, an autumn baby they called her. I spoiled her. Couldn't help it. That's Brian there, with his sisters Morgan and Ashley on the other side. Ashley's the oldest."

"She can't be that old," Lauren said in mock surprise.

"Ashley is 37! I can hardly believe it. Melody is only 19." Georgina looked at the darkest corner of the room. "Melody is her middle name. Philip wanted to call her Priscilla. It's Biblical but I still hated it. When I filled out the birth certificate, I wrote in Judith."

"Do all four children still live nearby?"

"Ashley lives in Toronto. And Brian moved to Newfoundland, where he works on the drilling rigs. Melody stayed in Halstead after she graduated high school. So did Morgan. She's married to such a lovely man. The only grandchildren Philip and I see regularly are hers."

"Having family close by is really important," Lauren said.

"I helped Ashley and Morgan after each of their births. I just got back from Toronto Friday night. We have a new grandson, and Ashley has her hands full with him. But I wish I'd been here when Melody needed me."

"All your kids need you. They need you to do the right thing by them," Lauren said.

"Melody calls me almost every Sunday. I'm so worried about her."

"I was touched by what you said at the press conference," Lauren said. "We're received lots of tips at the detachment and we're following each of them. We're hopeful Melody will be home soon. Do you have any idea what might have happened or where she is?"

Georgina didn't answer. Instead, she looked directly at me.

"Excuse me, Mrs. Lockhart. I think I should wait outside."

I returned to the kitchen, opened the door to the summer kitchen long enough for one bark, and closed it without going through. I re-crossed the room and lingered quietly in the door-space leading to the dining room.

Georgina was speaking and I had to strain to hear: "Philip says it's important to keep family affairs to ourselves. He's very private that way. 'Nothing can come from family gossip except more pain for everyone,' he says."

"He's not here, Georgie. Say what you want. Put Melody first."

"Some things are just too hurtful to talk about. We're all in this together."

"The long-term pain of keeping things hidden is much worse."

"I know. Christians are supposed to be honest, but what if the truth hurts someone you love?"

"Not telling the truth is worse, especially for Melody."

"I don't want people to find out, for her sake."

"People know, Georgie. They always know, even when you think they don't. Even when they pretend they don't."

"Do you think so?"

"I'm certain."

"Oh my."

There was a pause.

"I should have said something a long time ago."

"What's done is done, Georgie. It's what you do now that counts."

"But it's too late!" Georgina said, soft sobs constricting her speech.

"Why is it too late?" Lauren's tone, for the first time, registered alarm. "Has Philip done something?"

"Yes. He called her the spawn of Satan when she was old enough to understand the words but not why he used them."

"Did he *do* something to Melody?"

"No. It's what he didn't do. He was against it from the start. He never really loved Melody. And I wanted her so badly."

"I don't understand, Mrs. Lockhart."

"Melody is my baby, and I love her as much as any of my children. But she's adopted. We kept it from her, pretending she was ours. Now I'm terrified she's found out. I'm sure that's what she was going to tell me last Saturday. I think she's gone off looking for her birth father and might be with him now. That's who I was thinking about when I wrote out what I said this morning."

A brief lull in the conversation was punctuated by the hall clock going through three-quarters of its full song and dance, still too early for any Big Ben bongs.

"Oh," Georgina exclaimed. "Philip will be home soon."

"Would you please tell us who Melody's birth parents are?" Lauren asked, gently.

"No," Georgina said flatly. "The adoption was arranged through the church. The pastor agreed to keep the whole thing private."

We could all hear the revving of a car hurrying along the left driveway artery and pulling behind the house. I went to the door leading to the summer kitchen and the hounds, and pried it open a smidgen.

Philip wasted no time coming in, the cruiser a vivid 'the police are already here' signpost. He stepped into the kitchen breathing hard, surprised to see someone waiting who didn't look like a cop. I could see the two dogs through the doorway. They hadn't made a sound or lifted their ears.

I stepped to the doorway, facing Philip. "Good afternoon, Mr. Lockhart. I'm Dr. Wallace, working with the RCMP as they try to find Melody. My partner, Constable Martin, is in the living room with Mrs. Lockhart."

"You could have waited for me," he said, brushing past me. I followed him inside.

Georgina and Lauren were standing under the central chandelier, between Philip's armchair and the TV. The teacups and bread lay untouched on the tray. I couldn't tell whether Georgina's or Philip's face was the more flushed. Georgina looked fearful.

Philip struggled with his anger. His wife hadn't eaten an apple from the tree of knowledge about good and evil. She'd baked a pie with it and given away a slice.

Georgina said nothing. Philip glanced over at the tray, perhaps wondering how large the piece of pie had been. "Some things should be kept private," he said to Georgina. "They're too hurtful to talk about."

"I had to tell them Melody was adopted, Philip. I should have said that to the police. And now she's probably gone somewhere trying to find who her birth parents are."

"How did Melody find out? You didn't tell her, did you?"

"No, no. I don't know how she found out."

"It was probably that sister of hers, who doesn't go to Church," Philip said.

The spiritual twine he used to bind his life together had no elasticity. And the everyday flux of living tests even the most resilient bonds.

We hadn't entered a domestic dispute as much as reignited one. Lauren interrupted the spat. "I need to search Melody's room, Mr. Lockhart. This is your house. Would you please show me the way?"

"I suppose you have a warrant," Philip said.

"Yes, we do, if you want to see it."

"Don't bother," he shrugged. "We should all go upstairs." He looked pointedly at Georgina.

"You go ahead, Philip. I'll take the tea back to the kitchen and join you."

Philip led Lauren and me to the foyer and up the central staircase. Melody's room was at the back, on the right.

"We're looking for anything that might help us learn what Melody might have done and who she might be with," Lauren said, surveying the room. "We're particularly anxious to find her laptop. Perhaps her diary."

"She doesn't keep a diary. Diaries are self-indulgent and full of sinful thoughts," Philip said. "None of our daughters kept any such thing."

Georgina joined us and stood just behind me as we crowded around Melody's door. "She hasn't slept in here for months," she said, "since she left home. I've kept her room the same, waiting for her to come back."

I wondered whether Philip had also left Melody's room untouched. He wouldn't need a warrant to hide anything suspicious.

The room was plain except for the peculiar, multi-coloured quilt on her bed. It was hand-sewn from dozens of padded octagonal pieces. Her mother's labour of love. There were no pictures, posters, or photos in the room. It wasn't dusty or strung with cobwebs. Georgina wasn't Mrs. Havisham.

Lauren entered the room. Philip watched her intensely, filling most of the doorway. If she wasn't self-conscious, I certainly was.

She looked everywhere Melody might have stowed her laptop and inside drawers she couldn't have, including her night table. Nary a computer, a disc, even a CD or cassette tape. And no diary or calendar. The closest she had to one, I assumed, was the binder I had tried to dissect.

"Can you think of anywhere else in the house we can search for her laptop, Mr. Lockhart?"

"No, I don't. When she lived at home, she only used it in her room. Try that apartment I'm paying for."

Just before Philip turned to lead the way downstairs, Georgina slipped a piece of paper into my hand. I pocketed it and raised my eyebrows sympathetically.

When we were back in the main kitchen, Lauren said, "We need to talk with Morgan, Mr. Lockhart. She's the only other family member who still lives in Halstead."

Philip looked dizzily at her, like the room he was in was beginning to spin out of his control.

"You should leave Morgan out of it. The whole family knew Melody was adopted. Every one of us swore to keep it a secret, from Melody most of all. Even Brian, who was only thirteen. Morgan doesn't know any more than we do."

"We have to follow every lead," Lauren replied.

"Why? You know she's not a missing person," he said. "She's just gone off on some ridiculous chase."

He turned to his wife. "Bringing in the police was a mistake. We should have handled it ourselves."

She didn't reply.

Philip turned back to Lauren. "I'll call Sergeant Young at the detachment. Georgina is the one who reported her missing. We'll let him know we're no longer worried about her. I don't know why they assigned a female to this case. That young constable who came here first was more professional. Our business is done."

Philip showed us the way to the summer kitchen and shut the inner door without following us through. I rested my hand on one of the old wooden press-backed chairs, thinking of pictures of lion tamers I'd seen. The dogs stared menacingly at us and the shepherd-mix let out a low growl, but neither of them arose from the floor. They'd heard their master's angry voice on the other side of the door. That was the most help we'd gotten from Philip.

We drove down the driveway not feeling the household love it was meant to simulate. Once through the gap to Highway One, I reached into my pocket for the note Georgina had surreptitiously handed me. I half wondered whether she had written 'Help!'

"I don't think we should have left Georgina there," Lauren said. "I couldn't invent a pretext that could pry her loose, not one she'd be able to follow or Philip wouldn't veto. We'll have to check back later this evening."

"Good idea," I said. I unfolded the piece of paper and looked at it. "Georgina was trying her best. She wrote out Morgan's last name and phone number on this and then slipped it to me. Morgan Conrad."

"That saves us some time," Lauren said. "I'll need more information than I have to convince Sergeant Young we are dealing with more than a bullying husband and father, or worse."

She called Dispatch and requested an address for Mrs. Morgan Conrad in Halstead. "I don't want to call her. We'll just drop in. Her father has probably already warned her we're coming. She's independent-minded, though, enough to stop going to their church. His call will just raise her hackles."

"That should help us. What do you make of what we just heard, Lauren? It wasn't what I expected."

"Me neither. I'm not ready to rule out molestation, even incest."

"He's a worse patriarch than I had imagined, and that's saying something."

"Physical abuse is also possible," Lauren said, "which is why I'm concerned about Georgina. Men with his mentality think that women and children are property."

"What did you make of Philip's 'spawn of the devil' remark?" Lauren said.

"That caught me off guard, too. Maybe he'd meant the devil had tempted him, so it wasn't his fault, blame the seductress. But spawn suggests an offspring. Following along that line of reasoning, Melody may be his daughter. If so, Ashley is probably the victim or the first one. She's the daughter who moved out of town, as far from her father as she could get."

"So, at every moment, Melody would remind Philip of his sin—or Ashley's, looking at it from his point of view," Lauren said. "Ashley would want to get away from Georgina, too. Mothers know what's going on under their roof."

"Yeah. But they're terrified or just turn a blind eye, pretending it doesn't exist because they wouldn't be able to face themselves if they knew but did nothing about it."

The shadows were getting noticeably longer as we followed Dispatch's directions to Morgan's house. She was probably preparing supper and might not welcome our visit.

Lauren parked the cruiser in her driveway. Any time a cruiser is parked outside a house in a small town, half the population knows about it an hour later.

14: Morgan's tale

Morgan Conrad lived in a middle-status neighbourhood a little south of Highway One. Similar to most new houses in town, the front was dominated by a double garage, a design that allowed for minimum lot and maximum house. The front was brick and mortar. On both sides, the exterior switched to vinyl siding. The design is meant to impress viewers face-on.

Two cars were parked in front, a sedan and a minivan, the compulsory mobility consumption of suburban families.

Lauren rang the visitor alarm. The only sound from inside was the muffled squealing of young children. Morgan's husband eventually answered the door with a child clamped to each leg, two daughters, about four and six. He looked at the pair of us as the bearers of unwelcome news, like Mormons going door to door, even though I'd left my white shirt and dark tie at home.

"Hello, Mr. Conrad. I'm Constable Martin from the RCMP. This is Ian Wallace, from the college. We're sorry to come at such an inconvenient time. It's important. We need to speak with your wife about her sister Melody."

"Has she been found?" he asked anxiously.

"Not yet. We're hoping you can help us," Lauren said, addressing the request to Morgan, who had joined her husband at the door.

The younger daughter detached herself from her father and stood in front of her mother. Morgan wore a denim apron over t-shirt and jeans. Her brown hair ended with a flip below her shoulders. She looked like an older version of Melody.

"Paddy, I want to go out with the officers for a while. I'm not sure how long. There's a stew on the stove and some Irish dumplings ready to go in. I'm sorry to leave you with it, but I can't talk in front of the children."

She hung up her apron and turned to Lauren. "We knew you'd be coming over. My father gave me the warning. We should find somewhere outside to talk."

"I really appreciate that, Morgan. We didn't find your father very helpful."

"I'm not surprised. Just give me a minute."

Morgan changed slippers for boots, put on a coat and scarf, and hung her leather purse over her shoulder. We walked to the cruiser. I took the felon's position in the back seat.

"I don't want to talk in the car," Morgan said. "I'm not sure where to go. Maybe the school playground. They have some benches which aren't uncomfortable."

It had been warm for early spring. The air temperature was tethered to the sun and both were sliding below the western horizon.

Morgan settled at the end of a bench, looking resigned. Lauren sat beside her. Some room remained at the other end. So I sat there.

"Thanks for speaking with us," Lauren began. "Your mother told us Melody was adopted. But she wasn't able to tell us much about the circumstances except that it was arranged through the church and kept quiet. We don't know who her parents were or what happened."

"Mom's not going to say much in front of Dad. The adoption wasn't arranged through the church."

Morgan was quiet for a short while. We waited.

"I'm Melody's mother. You've probably guessed that. More than once I've been called a Goler's daughter—you know, that hillbilly incest family over in Kings County. It wasn't the same at all but, in lots of ways, it was just as bad. I made sure Paddy knew all about what happened before we got married. I don't know what I'd have done without him. He saved me, really. He helped me find myself, become somebody. I work in the local library and I'm a potter. Moist clay in your hands feels so natural, so good. It starts out just a lump. Then you imagine what it could become and make it exactly what you wanted. I'm getting good at it, even earning some money. A friend sells my work in her craft shop."

She paused. The evening breeze rustled the branches.

"After I married Paddy, I decided to put all my family history in a metal box, lock it and bury it in the backyard. I wanted to never think about it again. It worked for a while. We moved into a new house, had four kids. We're trying to give them a normal and happy upbringing. Now, things are getting complicated."

"What do you mean, complicated?" Lauren said.

"No one ever told Melody about the secret of her birth. It was simpler that way and kept peace in the family. Then Melody's father moved back to Sterling County. I had to let her know before she found out from him.

She didn't want to believe it at first, until she realized I meant every word. We've always been close. When Ashley left, I was her only sister, even though I was 16 years older, more like her aunt. I felt a lot closer than that."

Morgan needed a little more priming. "What happened when Melody found out?" Lauren said.

"I want to tell you my story, but I really have to start at the beginning. I want you to understand. My father was a hard man. Is a hard man. I don't hate him, exactly, even though I hate many things about him. We lived in Windsor for the first half of my life. He worked as a plumber, doing odd jobs. He was extremely moody, up and down, sad or angry. He worked only irregularly, so we had some tough times. Mom doesn't talk about them.

"Eventually, he found the Church of God Almighty. I guess it was good for him, in a way. But life at home became worse. Disciplined is not the right word. Regimented. He wanted to make sure we were among the elect, at least that's what he said. He didn't spare the rod, in the most degrading way. It gave him so much power over us.

"Ashley and I went to church. Dad forbade us to be friends with anyone outside the congregation. We weren't sheltered. That sounds like being protected from a storm, as though the danger comes from outside. We were barricaded in, living with the hurricane. Oh my," she sighed. "If I hadn't given up smoking, I'd light one right now."

She inhaled some of the cool evening air, taking long breaths. It sounded like a story she'd told herself many times over, lying awake at night or in the early dawn before the clock radio begins telling its own tales.

"Ashley started sneaking out of the house at night. She went pretty wild. It wasn't long before she was pregnant, at 17. Her boyfriend was a couple of years older and just as crazy. His name was Brandon. He was good looking and funny. He knew how to be charming. My father hated him and wanted to disown his daughter. Mom took her worries to the pastor, who convinced them to arrange a hasty marriage. Ashley agreed. I wish she hadn't."

Morgan had another long drag of imaginary nicotine, holding her breath like smoke from a joint before expelling.

"Things started to go downhill about halfway through Ashley's pregnancy. Brandon started drinking more, staying out late at the Bridgeside. They argued a lot and he threatened her. Ashley asked him why he even married her. That's when he hit her for the first time, in the stomach. She thought she was going to lose the baby. She didn't say a word about it to me or Mom. That was just the way things were."

"Women in abusive marriages think it's their fault," Lauren said quietly. "They put on a public front to save face."

"After Brandon Junior was born," Morgan said, "Mom wanted to see her grandson. She convinced Dad to let them come for visits, usually on Sundays after he had another anti-pride inoculation. Any family troubles were kept private. Dad insisted on it.

"Things just got worse for Ashley after the baby was born. 'It isn't fair,' Brandon said. 'I was trapped into this stupid marriage. I'm too young to be tied down by an ugly, overweight wife and that brat she claims is mine.' I didn't learn any of this until afterwards."

"After what, Morgan?"

"They'd come over to the house for dinner. It was the only time I saw my sister and her family. I was 15. I didn't know anything. I barely knew how babies were made. And I liked him. Brandon, I mean. I look back on it as a teenage crush. He was nice to me. He made me feel pretty and special, and he carried on with me, especially when we were alone. After dinner, he'd go outside to chop wood. He'd take off his shirt when the weather was good and I'd peek at him through the window. I ducked out of sight when he saw me. He was used to heavy work and tanned so naturally. I thought of him as my bronze Adonis. He asked me to call him Antonio, the nickname he preferred."

She looked down at her feet. "It seems hard to believe now. My father said I led him on. I wasn't leading him anywhere I wanted to go or knew anything about."

Morgan was staring at the treetops at the edge of the playground, not talking to anyone except herself.

"One Sunday I wasn't feeling well, and Mom let me stay home from church. Brandon left early and came over to the house, to see how I was, or so he said. He was alone."

Only Morgan could interrupt this minute of silence.

"You know what happened next. Right there, on the kitchen table. He gave me a kiss when he left. I remembered the horror of that kiss for the longest time. I don't know why, but it seemed the cruellest thing he did. I was in absolute shock. All I wanted to do was go upstairs and crawl into bed, but I had to clean myself. I used the tub, sobbing the whole time. I couldn't tell anyone. My God, I felt sinful, like it was my fault. My sister will always hate me, I thought. Dad will kick me out of the house. I could hear the preacher droning in my head, condemning me as a whore. I wished I were dead."

Lauren, who had taken her hand, said, "I'm so sorry, Morgan. Did you do anything about it?"

"I did go on. But, no, I didn't *do* anything. I was in bed for the whole of the next day but couldn't think of any convincing lie. I only got up when Mom said she'd have to take me to the clinic and see what was wrong. The doctor was bound to tell my parents. So, I went back to school, tried to act normal, to pretend it was all a bad dream.

"Then, my period stopped, and I was sick in the morning. Mom knew the signs. When we were alone, she asked me outright whether I was still a virgin. I thought to tell her, *it depends on what you mean*, but of course, it doesn't. You are or you aren't. I had to tell her who did it and how. Mom cried harder than I did. That night, she told Dad. He flew into a rage. I knew he would. 'What did you think was going to happen with your shameless flirting?' he said. 'You reap what you sow.' It wasn't the pastor who called me the names I imagined.

"Mom tried to bring him down off the rooftop. She'd had a lot of practice. They agreed to keep me out of school and arranged for me to live in Halifax with one of Mom's sisters. That's where I gave birth to Melody."

"Your mom wanted to keep your daughter and raise her as her own," Lauren said.

"I'm supposed to say that something good came out of something evil. That wasn't how I felt at the time. I just wanted my life back. Mom said an adoption was out of the question. She was still young enough to make it seem one of her own. I was thankful for that. We moved out of Windsor and came here to Halstead. I hoped it would stay in the past."

"It wouldn't stay buried in the backyard," Lauren said gently, "and now Melody's father is back. Did he come specifically to look for you?"

"No, I don't think so. He's from around here, originally."

"When did you see him, Morgan?" Lauren asked.

"It was about a week and a half ago. I saw a truck from Alberta parked just down the street from our house with a man in it, staring at me. He drove past, looking at me the whole way. He had a beard, but I knew who it was. I felt the Prairie winter clinging to his truck.

"Then I remembered something my friend Kate had said, the one that sells my work in her shop. There's a sign in the window advertising Morgan's Pottery and a picture of me sitting at my wheel. A man came in and said he wanted to order a special piece for his wife made by the potter in the picture. Kate gave him my card with my phone number. It doesn't have my last name on it, but he found me. Now I'm really worried."

"What will happen, Morgan?"

"Everything is going to come out. I'll have to live it all over again, this time in public. And it will hurt my whole family."

"How much time passed between Brandon seeing your picture in the shop and spying on you in the street?"

"About a week."

"When did you tell Melody the truth?"

"It was the next day, Saturday before last. I called her on the rooming house phone. We met in a café downtown. She wanted to know everything. I told her what I knew about him, trying to help her understand. You can only live with a lie for so long."

"It must have been a shock. How did Melody respond?"

"She was flabbergasted when she found out he was worse than Dad. I was surprised at how mature she was about it. She said she understood perfectly why I hadn't gone to the police."

"Did that surprise you?"

"Not right away. I told her I'd found some comfort after I joined the United Church. Our minister doesn't preach the God Almighty version we were brought up with, which I think of now as the Church of Satan. They talked more about the Devil than God. Dad wouldn't recognize Jesus Christ if he saw him on a throne in Paradise. I've tried hard to forgive Brandon. Our minister says forgiveness helps clear your mind. Melody comes to church with us, although not every week. It's so nice having her beside me."

"Morgan," I said, craning my head forward to look at her around Lauren, "I could see Melody was having a difficult, upsetting term, but I didn't understand why. Something happened to her in January, and I believe it had to do with her boyfriend, Aaron Campbell."

"He raped her. Did you know that? I couldn't believe it. Poor Melody. That's why she understands my predicament, all those years ago and now. I was the only one she could talk to about it. Hers wasn't the same as mine. She went to him willingly, not really knowing what she wanted. Once he got started, there was no stopping him, no matter what she said or tried to do. After he got what he wanted, he just threw her out. I'd never seen her so miserable. I suffered along with her. For the first time I knew how my poor mother felt when it had been me."

"Now that Melody knows the truth, have you two gotten closer?" I said.

"Oh yes. When we were in church last, a little over a week ago, she held my hand the whole time. Just before she left, she gave me a long, tight squeeze and said she loved me. We both cried. I think she was feeling as sorry for me as she was for herself. Neither of us wanted to let go."

"Did Melody intend to get in touch with her actual father?" Lauren said.

"She liked that Philip Lockhart wasn't her father, and the idea she had a real one worked its way inside. She couldn't stop the questions from eating at her. She wanted to meet him, to see him and decide for herself. I said I didn't know where he lived. I hoped she'd stay away from him, but I don't think she intended to."

"What's Brandon's last name and where *does* he live?" Lauren asked, with some urgency in her voice. Her patience had become a thin veneer under the pressure of a belt sander.

"Gould. Brandon Gould. He lives over in Crediton."

Lauren was ready to jump at this new scent, but I put a hand on her shoulder.

"One more question, please," I said. "It appears that Melody has a new, serious boyfriend, someone who might be connected to her disappearance. The relationship began sometime after her rape and before spring break at the college. Did she tell you who he is?"

"Not who. In her eyes I've become her mother, not a sister for sharing confidences. But yes, she does have a boyfriend. He seems serious about her. I wanted to know all the details, but she wasn't very forthcoming. She said how special and strong he makes her feel. Her boyfriend wants her to stay clear of her biological father. He's so protective. I think he might be a little older, though. 'Not a young prick like that bastard Campbell' is the way she put it. I'd never heard her swear."

My mind began an internal workout.

"I should get back to my family," Morgan said, rising from the bench. The evening mist was belly-slithering across the grass and creeping through our soles. "When you find anything that might bring back my daughter, please tell me. Deep down, I know Melody is still alive. We'll see each other again."

"We'll make sure you know whatever we find," Lauren promised. "You've been a great help. I think we're making some real progress."

Even though Lauren had turned on the car heater full blast, Morgan was shaking when we dropped her back at her brick-façade house. The kids she was desperate to protect from the damaging effects of her truth met her at the door.

"I'm going to take this information back to Sergeant Young," Lauren said, steering her cruiser in the other direction, toward the college. "I feel so sorry for Morgan. I dread finding Melody's body and what that will do to her mother. I'll let you out at your car. I want to explain my new lead to Sergeant Young in person."

You mean without me being there. It was her career and the simple file she had inherited from Dobson was growing into a filing cabinet.

Philip Lockhart couldn't derail the investigation now that Lauren had a suspect who wasn't him. A suspect for what, though? Did Melody find her father and was staying with him without telling anyone, not even her birth mother? Was she getting to know him, imagining the past she might have had? Maybe they're so out of touch with the world, they don't know the police are looking for her. Approaching that scenario would be a delicate matter. We couldn't just barge in like the Emergency Response Team, assuming it's a kidnapping or worse.

"I'll search Brandon Gould on the Police Information System," Lauren said, interrupting my wandering mind. "The next step is to go to Gould's. I'll give you a call when I'm leaving the detachment and come pick you up."

I agreed eagerly, even though I heard a church bell tolling sombrely in my head. I'm a born pessimist. I didn't believe anything positive was happening to Melody.

15: Gould's neighbourhood

I sat behind the wheel of my black coupe, thinking about Morgan's tale and trying to convince myself she wasn't about to face more suffering. The memory of her Irish stew lingered in my olfactory nerves.

I've never encountered a circumstance that could kill my appetite, but I didn't want to cook. The college faculty can barely sustain one classy restaurant. When one collapses, a replacement soon opens in the same space.

The Samurai Sushi and Ramen had committed *harakiri* last fall, less than a year after it opened. If you can't make it during the tourist season, it's over. The newly-opened Curry Planet was suitable for a nice, romantic dinner, but I was alone.

Take-out was tonight's solution. Town Council's anti-junk food rule doesn't apply to locally owned joints. I drove past the greasy spoon with the window sign that read Full Coarse Meals. Truth in advertising. Chinese take-out would do.

I ordered some spicy fried green beans with mushrooms and garlic from the closer-to-real page on the menu, although I knew the sugar and MSG would overwhelm any other flavour. Every dish came with chicken fried rice and a few veggies.

The chicken was AWOL. If anything, it had been wafted over the rice like incense from a High Anglican censer. My appetite slackened halfway through. A Guinness from my fridge helped the food's journey south.

I've wasted too much time waiting for Lauren to arrive or for the phone to begin bouncing cartoon-like in its cradle. I put down the hard-boiled mystery I'd started, unable to concentrate on the narrative. Like a character in a book, I felt like a single, plot-driven arc was overwhelming me.

A car honked twice outside, jerking me from the reverie I'd fallen into. Lauren was in a fully equipped model with lights on top. She had added a telescoping truncheon and a flashlight to her heavy weapons belt.

"Brandon Gould lit up the CPIC information system. He had a couple of charges of assault and sexual assault in Alberta in the early '80s. One resulted in a conviction and a provincial sentence. In 1985 he was sentenced to six years for aggravated sexual assault. The Parole Board turned him down after two years. He was released on mandatory in 1989. The following year, he was convicted again, this time for common assault, and only received probation. Must have lucked out with the judge. That's his last conviction in the system."

"It was almost a decade ago, but his record is consistent with what Morgan told us," I said.

"Totally. He had no criminal record from his time in Nova Scotia."

"That's only because Morgan didn't make a police complaint."

"It probably wouldn't have made a difference," Lauren said. "Those charges are hard to prove."

"Do you know where we can find him?"

"A Brandon Gould lives on Queensport Road. He's probably staying with his parents. That's where we're headed."

"Just the two of us?"

"Corporal Smith assigned Andy Graham as back-up. He'll wait en route and follow us to Gould's address."

It's not usually that simple in the county to arrange police backup on short notice. But if a member calls a 10-33 for immediate help, every other one in a 100-mile radius converges on the scene.

"Andy's a good choice, but he's working Highway Patrol."

"The Force rotates members through a variety of roles. It fosters careers and increases morale. Andy's done just about everything there is to do."

"What else do you know about Gould?"

"He's my number one suspect. Ident phoned to say they'd brought out that thumbprint from Melody's flat. They said it's reasonably consistent with Gould's."

"Reasonably might not be enough in court. Do you have a search warrant?" Lauren's probable cause seemed as porous as beach gravel.

"I have enough for one, maybe even tonight, depending on how cooperative the JP is, but I don't want to wait."

I understood her optimism about the warrant. The local cops have a close working relationship with county judges and prosecutors.

Lauren took Highway 361A towards the North Mountain. Andy was waiting for Lauren outside the Baptist Church and pulled out after her.

The Gould house was hard to spot. Most properties displayed their white-on-blue, fluorescent civic numbers on the roadside mailboxes or on posts by driveways. Gould's address was unmarked, a toothless gap between his socially conscious neighbours a hundred meters away in either direction.

The one-and-a-half storey house had been painted and maintained by the sun, rain, and sudden changes in temperature. A flickering electronic light escaped from the partly curtained living room window. Wood smoke swirled above a metal chimney. Someone was home.

The only vehicle in the driveway was a red F-150 truck. Lauren parked her cruiser directly behind it. Andy followed her in.

A large Rottweiler snarled and barked outside the car. It backed away a few paces when Lauren stepped out of the cruiser and withdrew her long flashlight from her belt.

A curtain in the front door of the house shifted briefly. The front porch light came on and a man we presumed was Brandon Gould the younger opened the front door. He called in the dog, stepped outside and stood under the light, scowling at us like potential home invaders, which we were.

Lauren holstered her flashlight and began to climb the stairs. I was close on her heels. Andy lagged behind in the yard.

I had a long look at Lauren's chief suspect under the glare of the porch light. I would have recognized him even without the plaid shirt, the thin beard, the husky build, the glowering eyes. Andy was staring at him, too. Gould returned my gaze without a flicker of recognition, although only yesterday he'd given me the evil eye.

I glanced quickly at his truck. The red and white Alberta plate didn't need to be surrounded by sparkling lights to confirm his identity. I remembered Plaid Shirt flying down Trunk 11A in a frantic rush. Was it merely a coincidence or was that time and place linked to Melody's disappearance?

Lauren stopped a couple of steps short of the top step, which led directly to the door. "Mr. Gould, we want to talk with you about Melody Lockhart."

Gould grunted his compliance and pulled open the screen door. He grasped the dog by its spiny collar and hauled him inside.

The door opened to the small living room. A few coats and caps hung on hooks screwed into the wall behind the door, with slippers and shoes strewn randomly on the floor. Nothing in this space suggested a hint of a young woman inside.

Gould took the Rottweiler into the kitchen. Lauren watched him from the door. I could hear him opening drawers, rummaging through them, and slamming them shut, as though Gould was performing his own search.

An older woman sat in an armchair in the corner of the living room watching the cops trooping in. Gould's mother, we figured. I sat on a wooden chair near her.

Gould had said his mother was so unwell, she needed permanent, residential care. To me, she looked elderly, but not frail. There were no oxygen tanks or bottles of pills beside her chair. Her hair was straggly and grey. She wore a flowered apron, although supper was over. You never know when the men of the house will want a beer or a snack.

Looking closely at her features, I noticed some resemblance to her son, mostly in their dark eyes and skin. She wasn't well suntanned but appeared naturally that shade of melanin.

Skin tone is an unreliable index for classifying people, although we do it all the time. I was curious whether Gould had been perceived as a 'visible minority.' If he had not, his long rap sheet, printed starkly in black and white, might have been considerably shorter.

Mrs. Gould scowled at Lauren, who was still standing in the doorway. She rose from her chair, proving she was still spry, switched off the situation comedy she had been watching, and closed the curtains. She sat back down, turned to me and said, "What the hell do you want here?"

I repeated the purpose of our intrusion, and identified Melody by her full name, not as "your granddaughter."

"Those Lockharts were always holier than us," Mrs. Gould said. "I'm glad Brandy got away from them when he did."

He didn't leave soon enough.

Gould stopped rampaging around the kitchen. I could hear him complaining to Lauren, but not what he was saying.

"You must be glad to have him home," I said.

"His dad got sick last fall, but that's not why he come home," Mrs. Gould said. Her son had told Andy the same thing, although the timing seemed different.

She lifted her head a little and leaned forward. "His wife run off on him. He don't care much for his dad anyways, 'cause he used to call him 'Heinz 57.' But he hates his own first name, too. 'Call me Antonio,' he says, like he's Italian." She pronounced it with a hard 'I.'

Gould came back to the living room, shutting the door in the Rottweiler's face. He had a half-empty bottle of Keiths in one hand and an opener in the other. He sat on a chair near the entranceway, stretched out his legs, and put the opener on a side table next to an identical one that was lying there waiting to be used. Lauren remained standing near him.

"What have you been jabbering on about?" he said to his mother.

"Nothing concernin' you. Of course, you spent most of your time on the mountain, hunting."

She turned to us. "Now he's talkin' about selling the place, both of them, and putting me in an old folks' warehouse. Nothin' wrong with me. I can look after meself."

"Ma," Gould said sharply, "that's between you and me."

"You and me and your damn lawyer."

"You know you're having a hard time, Ma," Gould said, making an obvious effort to control his temper. "I'm only home for a little longer. You can't live here alone and I've got to get back out west to visit my kids."

"I never seen 'em. And you never call 'em."

"Jesus, woman, these people aren't here to talk about that stuff."

He gave her a menacing look that should have made her chair quiver, then switched his attention back to Lauren, the uniform in his space. "What do you want to hear about this Lockhart girl?"

"Thank you, Mr. Gould," Lauren said. "Melody's mother told her that you'd come back to the Valley. Did you contact her? Is she here now? It's only natural Melody would want to hear your side of the story."

"Me too," Gould's mother said, bitterly.

"My side of the story?" Gould said with a raspy edge in his voice. "Since when does anyone want to hear that, least of all you cops?"

"We're here to listen," Lauren said, half-truthfully. *Perhaps a quarter.*

"Well, that's crap. Listen to this. Melody Lockhart's not here. She's never been here."

"Did you meet with her somewhere else, Mr. Gould?" Lauren said.

"She called here, on the weekend," his mother said. "You told me you didn't want to talk to her, so I just hung up. Maybe I should'a let her have her say."

"I don't want to talk to her, see her, nothing. I told you, that 'I'm your daughter' crap is just that—bullshit."

"So, you never met her somewhere downtown, at the college, in her apartment," Lauren said.

"Right. I never laid eyes on her."

Andy opened the front door, stepped in, and stayed in the entranceway, looking passively at Gould.

"Did you try to contact Morgan Conrad, Melody's mother?" Lauren said.

"No way. I want to stay away from that bitch. In fact, I don't think I can help you with any more of your nosy questions," Gould said abruptly. He began to pace in the small room. "I don't know what you people want from me. Sure, I got in some scraps years ago. Everybody does. Alberta's tough country. You've gotta look out for number one, but I was still screwed over every time. Everything was my fault. No one listened to me, not even those piece of shit lawyers they gave me. Plead guilty, they said. They'll give you a break. Yeah, right. You know where I ended up, and it sticks like crazy glue. You try getting a decent job with a criminal record."

Andy looked at him impassively. Lauren shifted her weight from foot to foot.

Gould stared angrily at the blank TV as if it represented the world that mistreated him. He wasn't finished. "I got a kids to look after out west, and that's where I'm headin', soon as I settle things here. But you cops are never going to leave me alone. Some woman complains, some kid gets lost, and the next thing I know, my house is surrounded by cops with their guns out. I can't count the number of line-ups you people have put me in. Now you're trying to pin another one on me. The hell with you."

Gould opened the kitchen door and called, "Spike!" When the dog appeared, he seized its collar. "I'll keep the dog in so you can leave in one piece."

Lauren walked to the door past Andy, who stood his ground. "Thanks for your help, Mr. Gould, Mrs. Gould," she said dryly.

I had barely a moment to speak to Mrs. Gould as I eased through the living room towards Spike. "You've got a nice spread here, Mrs. Gould. It should fetch you enough to make your next place comfortable. And it sounds like you own a second property."

"Yup, right on Pitch Lake. It's beautiful there. I love the sunset all down the water."

"That's enough gossip," Gould growled. "These people aren't those old crones you call friends."

I made my way towards Andy and the door. Gould looked as though he were considering letting Spike sample my thigh.

On our way back to the cruisers, Andy was the first to vent. "Assholes like him believe they're victims. It pisses me off."

"Me too," Lauren said. "No point arguing with him now. We'll have our say soon. What took you so long to come in?"

"I looked around outside the house and in an outbuilding. Then I shone my flashlight into the basement windows. It's just a big space with an oil furnace, way too damp to store much. I didn't see anything suspicious."

"I didn't ask for permission to look around inside," Lauren said.

"He'd have refused," Andy replied. "I would have brought up that fingerprint, though."

"Not yet," Lauren said. "We'll drop the evidence on him when the timing's right."

"Something else may be important. I stopped Gould yesterday morning just past Pitch Lake on Trunk 11A. He was flooring it."

"Do you think it's connected with Melody's disappearance?" Lauren said.

"I wouldn't be surprised. They have that property up there."

"I didn't get to ask Mrs. Gould its location," I said. "Gould's father was also called Brandon. Did you get CPIC hits on him, too?"

"No," she replied thoughtfully. "But one of the members whose been here a while might know him. Computer data doesn't go back very far."

"We'll be in the detachment soon," Andy said. "We can ask around."

Corporal Smith was watch commander that evening. Lauren filled him in on the early evening's work. He didn't know the Goulds. She phoned a couple of other members and had no better luck.

"There are a lot of properties along that lake," Lauren said. "I'm not waiting for morning to check the deed registry. We'll have to go door to door. Melody could be up there right now."

"Excuse me, Constable Martin."

We looked around to see Mavis Delaney, one of the civilian clerks. Most members called them girls. Mavis had worked at the detachment since 1971, when it was an outpost of the Bridgetown detachment. Access to her vital institutional knowledge would evaporate when she retired.

"What's up, Mavis?" Lauren said.

"About the Goulds: years ago, Brandon Gould was the biggest bootlegger on the South Mountain. We might find some old case files that show his address."

We followed Mavis to the back of the building. A dozen army-surplus filing cabinets that looked like scarred survivors of a bombing lined one wall.

"The cabinets are arranged by year," she said. "We should start with the one on the left."

We began thumbing our way through the residues of the criminal past. Mavis and Lauren pulled out some promising files, but the only address they found was "Pitch Lake Road, North Branch."

"As if the Gould's place was the only homestead on the lake," Andy said, disappointed.

"We can ignore the South Branch," Lauren said. "That narrows the search down by half. We have the rest of the night."

"The house is probably near the east end," I said. "Mrs. Gould could see the sunset reflecting down the lake."

"We can start by asking the neighbours at that end where the Gould property is," Lauren said. "They might remember the Goulds even if Ian is wrong about the location."

"Okay," Andy said. "That's our best shot. I'm up for another search, but I have a bad feeling about this one."

16: Warrantless search

Pockets of long-term poverty peppered the Valley floor, not just on the small Reserve or in the even smaller Black community. On the South Mountain, signs of affluence were scarce, although every year developers implanted more upscale houses like porcelain teeth. The migrants were usually come-from-aways, looking for acreage or privacy on a lake.

Most other folks lived in small, ancestral farmhouses or in higgledy-piggledy shacks with grotesque additions protruding like tumours in random directions. Car bodies bordering many of the driveways awaited a resurrection that would never come. Last season's flowers had shrunk to a tangle of dead, wind-blown weeds, testament to the daily struggle of life above the Valley. Making a living in too many Sterling County homes is a creative process of networking and barter, always precarious and generally unreportable in any revenue ledger. You'd need an army to enforce the tax laws.

Pitch blackness surrounded us, dispersed briefly by the front beams. Lauren slaked her speed, turned off the overhead lights, and took two right turns to the North Branch. We were searching for an older couple who knew their neighbours.

A generation ago, most mountain people lived on what they could scratch from the thin soil. They used any resources they found on their property, including hollow logs to carry well water to the kitchen sink. Like their garden gnomes, they and their houses were dwarfed by those of their better-fed and healthier offspring.

The lake properties consisted mostly of cottages battened down for the winter. A few gravel driveways disappeared through the trees, leading to nowhere we could see.

Lauren turned into the driveway of the first house we found with lit windows. We saw a renovated house with a steel roof, a bright red barn beside it, and a blue Subaru. It smacked of young professionals gentrifying the neighbourhood. Andy and Lauren reversed back to the North

Branch.

We liked the look of another farmhouse not much farther along. It appeared to have begun its existence as a small homestead that had become swollen with children and toil. An old Dodge Ram sat in the driveway, hoping we weren't auto undertakers.

Lauren alighted from the cruiser and walked to the front door. Andy joined me beside her car. The man answering Lauren's knock appeared to be the right vintage and stature. Lauren apologized for the lateness of the visit and asked if he knew where the old Gould property was.

"You're too late," he chuckled. "He died just a few months ago. And he stopped sellin' booze a long time before that. I guess that's not news to you. His old place is right on the lake. Just keep going past the Johnsons on the other side of the road and look for a clearing. You'll be able to see the lake. The old house is down near the water. It's still in decent shape. You can't miss it."

"How far along the road?" Lauren asked.

"Just a couple of minutes, depending on the shape the road's in. It can be dug up some bad this time of year. Better watch your muffler."

Lauren didn't give the cruiser's undercarriage another thought, nor one for her passengers. As we jostled our way west, the headlights bounced eerily off the ice puddles on the road and the remnants of snow mulching the bushes beside it. Most of it had melted in the warm weather.

After five minutes, Lauren wondered if she had, indeed, missed the geezer's directions. Country time is like a country mile.

A little further along the North Branch the clearing was obvious. The small, one-storey house on what we assumed was the Gould property was oriented so the front faced the lake.

Not venturing down the driveway, Lauren aimed her overhead spotlight on the house from the road. Whatever Gould's intentions, we didn't need a 'for sale' sign to lure us onto the property. Judging from the ruts, the access road had been used by a substantial set of tires more than once since the recent thaw.

We walked to the back of the house. From the outside, it looked like it had been abandoned to the gnawing of mice.

Lauren pointed her flashlight at one of the three rear windows and said, "Interesting. Look at this." The glass was shattered. A few shards clung to the edges. The window had not been covered. It was too high off the ground to look inside.

We followed the beam of the flashlight around to the front. We'd missed today's sunset over the lake by a couple of hours. The steps to the low veranda had been recently repaired. Three windows faced the lake. A large single-pane window to the left of the door enjoyed the best view. Drapes inside tried vainly to obscure our peeping into the private living room.

It looked live-in-possible, furnished with an old sofa, a couple of stuffed chairs, assorted tables, and knickknacks, all cottage-style, like a home for rejects from the main residence, postponing their eventual trip to the dump.

The stone fireplace in the centre of the far-left wall was soot black from the down draft. Some chopped wood and kindling leaned listlessly in a wooden box next to the concrete hearth. A faded, felt tapestry of a large buck covered much of the right wall. Three doors were aligned along the back. Bunk beds were visible in the middle room.

Lauren moved to the second front window and aimed her flashlight inside. I saw a small kitchen, too cramped for eat-in, with a sink and a rustic hand pump directly beneath the window.

Checking inside the third and final window, Lauren said, "This one has been used recently." Two heads joined hers for a view.

The room appeared to be about ten by ten. There was a mattress with a partially-open sleeping bag stretched on top. A couple of empty beer bottles lay passed out on the floor beside it. A red hunting jacket hung on a hook attached to the back of the door leading to the kitchen. A pair of large, high-sided hiking boots lay on the floor.

What focused everyone's attention, however, was a laptop computer, one corner exposed, lying in the open end of the sleeping bag. The computer's dull, metallic lid was closed to keep its secrets safe.

"Right in plain sight," I said. "Gould didn't make much effort to conceal it. All it would take was to zip the sleeping bag."

Even though the computer made no sound, Andy was the first to hear it invite us in for a closer look. "That gives us grounds for a search."

"I'm going in regardless," Lauren said.

Andy had no difficulty jimmying the lock on the front door.

Lauren went in alone and shone her flashlight around each room of the possible crime scene. "Melody isn't here," she said. She didn't sound disappointed or relieved. Something in between.

"We have to get Ident out ASAP," Andy said. "The site is as secure as it's going to get."

Lauren led the way back to her cruiser, turned it on for warmth, and asked Dispatch to alert forensics in New Minas. Andy sat in front. The heat reluctantly penetrated the plexiglass screen to my rear seat.

"Ident will take a while getting here," Lauren said. "In the meantime, we should write our notes about the interview at the Gould's, as best as we can recall, what led us to this address, what we've observed. You too, Ian." She deployed an extra notepad for me.

We avoided most corroborating chatter. Too much similarity would cast doubt on the narratives, making them appear contrived. I was still scribbling after Lauren and Andy had finished. Writing detailed notes was one of my specialties

"The key thing is Gould saying he didn't contact Melody. That's a lie we can unravel," she said.

"I hope it's not like peeling onions," I said. "There's nothing at the centre of them except more onion."

Corporal Smith showed up first, parked on the road, and walked over to Lauren's cruiser, avoiding the rutted driveway. We stepped out of the heat, and Lauren told him what we'd found. He went into the house for his own quick inspection.

It took Ident another thirty minutes to arrive from New Minas. Both Sergeant Akerley and Corporal Kemble had been roused from their TVs to make the pilgrimage. If I'd caught a whiff from their home liquor cabinets, I'd have filed it in my did-not-observe drawer. The detachment weekend begins Friday afternoon in the member's lounge. I suspect they pry into the exhibit locker for confiscated alcohol.

Akerley donned his evidence-preserving coveralls and pulled on blue plastic gloves and galoshes. Kemble mixed some dental stone with water to make a plaster cast of the tire tracks in the driveway, keeping clear of the well-defined edges.

"I'm interested in the victim's laptop," Lauren said.

Akerley went to work inside while we huddled near Smith's cruiser. The early spring dew made it too damp for a leaning post.

After about twenty minutes, Akerley carried out an IBM-sized evidence bag and brought it over. "You wanted to see this," he said. "It's college property. Melody Lockhart's name is on the nameplate. There's something worse. We found a pool of dried blood on the floor near the sofa."

"Shit!" Lauren said and rubbed both hands over her face.

"I've scraped some samples to send to the lab and covered it for preservation."

"Any idea how long the blood's been there?" she said.

"It's not fresh. We'll be able to tell more from the lab analysis. There's also a hatchet with blood on its blunt end. We also found a distinct footprint in the dried blood that appears, on first inspection, to match one of the boots we found in the bedroom. We'll know when we have a closer look at the accidental markings. You'll have to put your suspect in that boot."

"Is the computer working?"

"We'll dust it for prints. You're not going to get much out of its guts. The hard drive is gone. Without that, it's just a piece of high-tech garbage."

"Gould must have removed it," I said. "Finding it intact is important."

"What about the sofa and sleeping bag?" Lauren asked.

"With a quick pass, using the brightest white light we brought, we found lots of black hair in the sleeping bag and a couple of blonde ones with dark roots. There were more of both on the sofa. We found the same blonde strands on the end of the hatchet. They're probably the victim's. If there's any semen, the UV light will bring that out."

"The computer and hair tell us that Melody had been in the cabin, probably not long ago," Lauren said. "That really worries me."

"And the shattered window?" Smith asked.

"Looks like it was taken out by the bullet we found embedded in the bedroom door frame. Probably a .303 fired from the outside. Judging from the glass and the condition of the room, it wasn't long ago."

"One more thing for now," Akerley said. "We found dried marijuana scattered over the floor in one of the back bedrooms, like it had been hung there to dry." He turned curtly and went to rejoin Kemble in the crime scene.

"We've done all we can here," Smith said. "We've got enough to bring Gould in for questioning. Before we do, we should see where we think this file is." He turned to Lauren. "What do you make of what we have so far?"

"Melody and Gould met up Thursday night, the last time anyone's seen her. I think Gould brought her up here after that. Melody either agreed or was coerced. We found evidence of the way it ended."

"Why did she take her laptop here?" I said.

"That's got nothing to do with what happened to her," Smith said. "The next question is, what did Gould do with her body?"

"There's the woods and the lake," Andy said, pointing at both with a wide sweep of his arm.

"We'll have to get in ground search in the morning," Smith said. "It's a hell of a rough area. And we'll need the dive team to search the lake."

"Gould probably knows the trails a lot better than the search volunteers will. He grew up here." I said.

"Let's see what we can get out of Gould tonight. We have reasonable grounds for an arrest," Smith said.

"Shouldn't we confirm the ownership of the lake property first?"

"We go to Gould's now. We'll do the checking tomorrow."

Lauren followed Smith to the Queensport Road on the north side of Halstead. Andy trailed her. Three cars created the illusion of more members.

Sterling County farm fields had just been released from their winter suspension. We didn't need sunlight to know we were travelling through farmland. The malodorous by-product of the pig industry had been lavishly spread as fertilizer. Many locals called it the smell of money.

The mini cavalcade drove marginally over the speed limit, with lights flashing as the moon emerged from behind the clouds. We sped left through the ninety-degree curve at Tedburn and continued west, following the base of the mountain.

The police radio focused everyone's attention. Dispatch reported a gun complaint in Crediton. That was Gould's village.

Smith picked up immediately and demanded specifics.

"A Mrs. Gould phoned 911 with the complaint. Someone had called her son to say the cops were on their way. He pointed a loaded rifle at her and demanded that she tell them he'd left a couple of hours ago. Otherwise, she was to keep her mouth shut or he'd make her sorry she didn't. Then he tore out of the driveway in his truck. He'd been drinking, but not a lot."

"Did he turn left or right on the main road?" Smith said.

"She didn't say."

"Phone her back and find out. And get us some back-up ASAP." A gun complaint was like a magnet for cops, but rural distances affected response time.

A long minute passed waiting for Dispatch to reply. We were fixated on each on-coming vehicle, anticipating a speeding red truck.

"Mrs. Gould said he went out of the driveway, straight across the highway, and down a gravel road that ends at a cemetery."

Andy picked up his mic. "That cemetery road splits into a bunch of sidetracks. They go through the woods and end in farmers' fields."

Lauren glanced at me. "He's hiding until the coast is clear."

We followed Smith and Andy into a church parking lot. Andy unlatched his trunk and drew out a short, single-barrelled shot gun.

About Face

We huddled near the cruisers. Smith looked towards the main road. "Back-up's about twenty minutes away," he said.

"We shouldn't wait," Andy said. "He can get back on the highway through some of the fields."

Smith didn't hesitate. "Andy, you take the first trail. I'll take the next one. Lauren, you block the exit, We might flush him this way. Follow us in when back-up arrives."

Lauren drove behind Smith and Andy until they peeled off down different tracks, their headlights disappearing among the bushes. She stopped before the gravel road narrowed at the first fork, doused her lights, opened her window a couple of inches, then switched off the ignition. "I want to be able to hear," she said. She hadn't removed the keys.

We sat in utter silence, straining to recognize the shape of danger among the moon-cast shadows. Lauren's cruiser was awash in the pale light. She squeezed her eyes in total concentration.

Time slunk by imperceptibly.

I remained still, but my mind was in turmoil. Gould was angry and desperate. He was nearby and toting a loaded gun. He knew what was in store for him. He was armed and skulking around, probably on foot. He hated cops. Lauren's silhouette made an easy target. So did mine. There was so much I needed to say to her.

"Bloody hell," I groaned.

Flickers from headlights squeezed through the bushes, too scattered to make an impression.

I startled suddenly. The stillness had been broken by the slam of a car door. It's hard to gauge distance at night, but it sounded close.

My scalp prickled. If I had hairs along my spine, they'd be rigid. Every nerve in my body jangled.

I realized abruptly that I was staring out the bottom of the windshield, just above the dashboard. I'd settled in my seat, shrinking from the dread enveloping us.

I urged my body to slide slowly back up. Subtly, I hoped. Lauren stared fixedly ahead, but she had a tight grip on the steering wheel. I could still hear nothing but the swaying trees and the few cars whining along the highway.

Suddenly, headlights slashed through the darkness about ten meters ahead. I hadn't heard a thing.

The floodlight exposed Gould's motionless truck at the beginning of one of the sidetracks. He was sitting behind the wheel.

Lauren put her window down all the way, drew her sidearm, opened her door, and crouched behind it.

"Stay inside and put your head back down," she told me. Her warning throbbed with tension.

"Be careful," I said. "Rifle bullets go through a car door."

The scene unfolded in slow motion. Smith took position behind the door of his car. Gould stepped gingerly out of his truck, holding his rifle loosely and pointing it slightly downward. Lauren aimed directly at his centre mass.

"If this goes sideways," she said, "reverse the hell out of here to the highway and call 911."

Smith ordered Gould to lay his rifle down, slowly and carefully. Gould stood like a statue.

A car approached through the woods, braked, fishtailed, and came to a halt. Andy leapt out with his shotgun and took up position on the sheltered side of his cruiser. He aimed at the same target.

Smith forcefully repeated his command and warned Gould he'd be shot if he didn't comply.

No one moved. If Gould twitched a muscle in any way that could be construed as a threat, Andy would be the first to fire. Sirens sounded in the distance.

Cars squealed off the highway and approached quickly along the rough, gravel road. Back-up had arrived: two cars and two more members.

Gould stood there, either calculating the worsening odds or wondering whether he had anything to lose. He didn't have much time to decide.

Cautiously and deliberately, he took one hand off his rifle, slowly lay it at his feet, and resignedly raised both hands. He didn't say a word. I'd expected more spit and bile.

The gun had barely touched the ground when Andy reached him.

"Put your hands behind your back," he growled. He grabbed Gould's arms and pushed him, face-first, onto the ground, snapping handcuffs expertly on his wrists. Gould winced as the metal crushed his loose flesh.

When Andy hoisted his suspect to his feet, he objected to the treatment only with passivity and attitude.

I got out of the cruiser to join the members as they gathered around and visibly relaxed. Exposed to the icy fingers of the night air, my clammy skin was rattled by cold shivers despite my leather jacket.

Smith glanced briefly at me and made a show of brushing some of the dirt off Gould's clothes. "I'm arresting you in connection with the disappearance of Melody Lockhart," he intoned.

He frisked Gould and emptied his pockets. Lauren sealed their contents in a plastic bag. Then Smith nudged Gould towards his cruiser, chanting, "You need not say anything. You have nothing to hope from any promise or anything to fear from any threat. Anything you do or say may be used as evidence. Do you understand?"

"Hmmpf," Gould replied.

"You have the right to retain and instruct counsel without delay. You can call any lawyer you like. You have the right to legal advice without charge from the Legal Aid programme. Do you understand?"

"What the hell good has Legal Aid ever done me?"

"If you wish to call a lawyer, you can do it at the detachment."

"They're nothing but crap, and this is bullshit."

The police caution sounded less textbook than Gould's stereotyped response.

Smith bundled Gould into the back seat of his cruiser. As soon as Smith slammed the door, Gould slumped against it. He couldn't inadvertently trigger the inside handle. It had been permanently removed for his inconvenience and that of his ilk.

Smith turned to Andy. "You and Lauren go across to his house and check on the complainant. And look around. You, too," he said to Dobson, who'd been the first back-up to arrive. "And don't be long. I want to interrogate this asshole before it gets too late. I'll hold him in the lock-up in the meantime."

Transferring a suspect from the car to the jail cell was often the toughest step in the arrest process.

"I'll call a tow company and have Gould's truck impounded and secured," Andy said.

While Smith led the way back to the highway and turned right towards Halstead, three cruisers pulled into Gould's driveway for a second time that night. The flickering, blue light was still radiating around the edges of the drapes. Mrs. Gould was still awake unless the TV was watching itself.

Andy took the steps two at a time, stood just right of the door, and pounding on it. "Mrs. Gould, this is the police. Open up."

Lauren stood just beyond the doorframe on the opposite side. Dobson and I waited at the bottom of the steps. Cops never know what to expect when they drop in with barely an announcement.

Mrs. Gould pushed the door ajar and stepped back, her scowl as deep as the Rottweiler's growl.

"Restrain her dog," Andy said to Dobson. Then we thumped our way in.

"We have your son in custody," Lauren said. "He won't trouble you again tonight."

"I weren't afraid of him. He's all jabber and a do-nothing. But he told me you cops would come back tonight."

"Is that why he took off?" Andy said.

"He figured you'd pin this Lockhart thing on him. Goddamn cops. Can't you leave the poor man alone? Nothin' better to do 'cept harass innocent people."

Lauren guided Mrs. Gould to her recliner in the living room. "Sit down, Mrs. Gould. Do you have some place you can stay the night? You can't remain here."

She looked at Dobson. "Arrange for a volunteer to come from Victims' Services, then take her to a safe house."

"This is my house. I'm stayin' put."

Lauren sized her up for a few seconds and said, "Okay. I'll get Ident here when they finish at the cottage." Then, to Dobson, "You secure the site until they arrive. Tell them I want to know whether they find anything of Melody's, including her fingerprints. And that hard drive."

"They'll love doing another house tonight," Andy said.

Lauren began a cursory search of the living room.

"You have a warrant for that?" Mrs. Gould said.

"Don't need one."

Andy headed up the stairs. That left the kitchen for Dobson. He drew his telescoping truncheon to help with letting the dog out the back door.

The searchers came away empty-handed. No one had expected to find Melody in the house, bloody or dead.

Back to the detachment, we convened in Smith's office. "Gould's in the lock-up, snoozing," he said. "Andy, you can stay and observe the interrogation through the one-way-mirror if you want. I imagine that's what you plan to do, Wallace."

"For sure."

"I think I'll call it a night," Andy said.

Lauren turned to him. "Thanks for having my back." Andy nodded acknowledgement and headed for the back exit.

"We can't let Gould sleep much longer," Smith said. "I'll pull him out of it in a few minutes."

That gave enough time for a few necessities, including pouring out the mucous coffee and making a fresh batch, courtesy of Lauren.

She added the statements we had written at the lake to her file and set it on Smith's desk. It included the information she had gleaned from CPIC and a photocopy of Gould's prints on permanent file.

"I'd like to postpone his lawyering up as long as possible," Smith said. "It's late. He'll be susceptible to suggestions and mistakes." He turned to Lauren. "I'll take the lead. We'll let him spin out his story, then confront him with the evidence. Jump in when it's helpful. At some point, I'll step out and you can work on his sense of morality."

"If he has one," Lauren said.

Smith found a well-defined enlargement of a fingerprint from an unrelated case and put it in Lauren's file. "I expect to get the partial print from Ident this evening, and whatever else they've come up with," he said.

He gathered a stack of papers from the recycling bin, built a small portfolio of additional "evidence" and stuffed it into two empty file folders. He placed them at the bottom of the stack under Lauren's folder. The false fingerprint aside, this ruse was useless. Gould would know all that counted was what they took out of the files and what they had to say about it.

Smith collected the real and fake files and led the way towards the lock-up. Gould's free accommodation was about three by eight, with a narrow cot underneath a wafer-thin mattress. A seatless toilet stood in a back corner.

He roused Gould unceremoniously and reattached the handcuffs, then latched his arm tightly around his bicep. He eased him out of the holding cell, then slammed the door shut, its metallic exclamation punctuating the confinement.

The interview room was a short walk from the cell. I slipped into the darkened observation room beside it, invisible behind the one-way mirror.

The interview room was about eight by eight and designed for claustrophobia. A table with three aluminum chairs stood in the middle. The beige walls were intentionally plain to focus the suspect's undivided attention on the interrogators. It wouldn't prevent him from staring at a screw working its way to freedom through the cracking drywall compound.

Lauren had interviewed many suspects. Smith innumerable ones. I'd sat in on several, where my role had been to detect contradictions or information the suspects shouldn't have known.

In these situations, interrogators presumed guilt. Denials and claims of innocence were falsehoods to contradict and dismiss. The objective was to manoeuvre the reluctant suspect towards a voluntary confession of the official truth. None of us was optimistic Gould would follow anyone down that hole tonight.

If you're assumed to be guilty, either way you play it is consistent with that supposition. An innocent person doesn't need a lawyer. Demanding one makes you look guilty. On the other hand, who could trust the system or the truth to set them free? Certainly not someone like Gould, or anyone with his indefinite colouration.

In my mind, no one is ever innocent, but that doesn't mean they're guilty of what they're accused of doing at a given moment.

Gould sat back in his chair and rubbed some blood into his hands. Judging from his attitude, he anticipated an easy session. He hadn't asked to call a lawyer, leaving the option on hold in case he needed it.

Smith and Lauren sat down on the opposite side of the table, so everyone was in profile to the mirror. Their suspect was in energy conservation mode. He would need it.

17: Detachment sauna

Smith placed the stack of files on the table. A microphone sat on the right, next to a yellow, porcelain coffee mug with dark, brown stains around its rim. Smith turned on the mic. He could switch it off to keep something out of the record or if the police wanted to utilize extra-legal tactics.

Looking around the room, I didn't see a thick phone book that could deliver a solid, skull-numbing blow without leaving telltale marks.

Smith announced the date and time for the record, named the people present, and said the suspect was being interviewed in connection with the disappearance of Judith Melody Lockhart. Then he read the police warning once again, this time from a card to be sure of precision. Gould continued to waive his right to call a lawyer. For the moment.

I wondered what impression Gould would try to give. His gaze was focused on Smith, the member in the room with two stripes on his shoulders. Gould had been belligerent when he'd stood on his own terrain. Now, he sat casually, his eyes calm rather than defiant. He was as professional as any of us. He'd played this role before, successfully sometimes, and was prepared for another performance. He looked as keen to know what the police thought they had on him as they were to spring their mind traps.

Smith produced a package of Export A from his coat pocket and offered a cigarette to Gould, who wasn't about to turn down the gifts of a smoke and a brief delay. Smith flicked his lighter and slid the stained coffee cup towards Gould, breaking its cover. It was half-filled with cigarette butts. Smoking wasn't a courtesy extended to every suspect, but it reduced the tension following an arrest and eased the way into the suspect's version of events.

"We'd like to establish when you came back to Sterling County, why you came back, and what you've been doing since you returned."

"I came back last fall when my father had a heart attack. We thought he was gonna die quick. He hung on until January. Then I stayed home to look after things. I've listed the property and found a home for my ma. She can't cope on her own. I'm going back to Alberta when I'm done."

"Did you come home prior to this visit?"

"No. I don't like leavin' work or my family. This business here is takin' too long."

"Have you found a way to make an income here?"

"No. I've just been busy tryin' to repair the house. Since my father got sick, no one's been lookin' after it."

"How are you supporting yourself?"

"I got some savings. Things are cheap here if you know how and where to get 'em."

"Your family has some property on Pitch Lake. Do you spend time there?"

"Yeah." Gould didn't appear concerned about the revelation. "I did some huntin' in the woods last fall and stayed in the cabin to get out early in the mornin'. And I fished for trout."

"Have you been back to the lake this spring?"

"No. But if this real estate thing takes much longer, I'll soon be fishin' again."

I wondered when Smith would add some choice cuts of bait to his multi-hooked, fishing line.

"So, you've lost your father, and your mother is fragile and unwell. You'll have to get power of attorney to look after her and her affairs."

"Yeah, I have that power."

"What were you doing on that back road this evening?"

"I had enough of my Ma's whining. It's quiet back there, a good place for a smoke and a beer."

"Last Monday, coming down the mountain on Route 11A, you were given a speeding ticket. Can you tell us why you were on that road?"

"I was checking out an old folks home in Bridgewater. Them places aren't easy to get into unless you have a lot of money. Social Services has an opening there. It looked pretty decent to me. Ma hates the idea of it, but it's for her own good. It's called the Sunrise Manor." *More realistically, the Sunset Manor.*

Gould shifted in his uncomfortable chair. I inferred the adjustment was a non-verbal cue to a falsehood, although I was squirming around in mine, and my lies were simply the ones I fool myself with.

"Can you please tell us what connection you have with Melody Lockhart?"

"I was married to one of her sisters, about twenty years ago. I didn't like her family and they didn't like me. I had an affair with her other sister. It didn't last long. They accused me of making her pregnant. They named the baby Melody. I never believed I was her father. But you have my DNA on file, so you can check that out. The Lockharts treated me like some kind of devil. That's why I left for Alberta and stayed there until last fall."

"Were you interested in this daughter you were supposed to have?"

"I didn't give her a second thought, even after I got back. I didn't even know it was a her."

"When you came back home, were you surprised to find that Morgan Lockhart—the name you knew Melody's mother by—was living in Halstead?"

Gould hesitated before answering. "What do you mean?"

For the first time, Smith consulted the top file on the table.

"Kate Lawrence owns a craft shop on Bank Street where Morgan Lockhart—Conrad now—sells her pottery. Lawrence identified you as the man who came into her shop and asked questions about Morgan." Smith looked at the file again. "She gave you Morgan's last name and phone number."

"Yeah. I saw her picture in the front window, and it made me wonder what she was up to. She'd been pretty hot for me back in the day. I made up some excuse to get the information."

"Did you call her or try to visit her?"

"No. She's married."

"Morgan saw you in a Ford 150 with Alberta plates parked across the street near her house."

Gould sighed. "Yeah, I drove by. I wanted a look at her, after all these years."

"Do you know Melody Lockhart?"

"I knew there was another sister, that's all. Nobody ever blamed me for being her father. Not until she called me."

"When did she do that?"

"Last Tuesday."

"What did she want?"

"She said Morgan was her mother and I was the father. And that she wanted to see me. I told her straight out that I wasn't her father." Gould shifted again.

"What did she say?"

"That she believed her mother."

127

"Was that the only time she called?"

"No, she called again last Wednesday. That's when my Ma told her to go to hell."

"Are those the only times you had any contact with Melody Lockhart?"

"Yeah."

Smith returned to look in the file. I assumed he would bring up that partial print from Melody's apartment, prying threads loose from the yarn Gould was spinning.

After doubling back to reconfirm that Gould had never seen Melody, Smith said, "Last Thursday, Melody had a visitor in her room. A man. Do you know anything about that?"

"No, I don't." Gould stopped fidgeting.

"He and Melody had a beer and talked for awhile. They didn't want anybody to overhear."

"He sat in a chair by her desk and drank a Keiths," Lauren said.

Gould said nothing.

Smith placed his elbows on the table and leaned forward. "What we don't understand are the fingerprints we found in Melody's room. On one of the beer bottles and a couple of other places."

He drew out the enlarged fingerprint prop he had plucked from some other bugger's case and lay it on the desk. Then he took out the official sheet with Gould's fingerprints and full name typed boldly on the tab and lay it with a slight flourish on top of the first.

No reaction.

"The prints we found in Melody's apartment match yours. Can you explain how your fingerprints were found in Melody's room?"

Gould blinked a few times and readjusted his position. It looked as though he was trying to concoct a plausible lie. He drew a deep breath and glanced at the door, as if Legal Aid was on the other side waiting for a grand entrance.

"I'm sure there's some simple explanation," Lauren interjected. "Morgan told Melody you were her real father. She tried to contact you twice. It makes sense you would want to see this Melody for yourself. See whether she looks like you? Whether she may actually be your daughter?"

After thinking it over, Gould said, "Okay. I'll tell you what I know. I wanted to leave Melody out of this. I met her twice. She called me that first time and said she wanted to meet me after supper at the Main Street Café. Somewhere safe and public. I said it was too public. People could eavesdrop. She suggested the college library. I met her in the lobby. She led me to some place where she liked to sit. Almost nobody was around."

"How did the two of you get along?" Smith said.

"Melody was pretty hostile at first. She believed what her mother told her."

"Did you deny you were her biological father?"

"I said it was possible. But I wanted to tell her the truth about me and her sister."

"How did she react to the truth?"

"She sat there all quiet and nodded a coupla times. Then I told her how hard I was brung up. Every day my drunken old man told me I never done nothin' right. He was always pissed off at me. I got scars to prove it. What kid like me wouldn't get into hot water? But I didn't do what Melody's lyin' sister said I done. That was all consensual, like." Gould had used a word he'd heard more than once in court.

"Did Melody come around after you told her about your past?"

"Yeah, after a while, and I started to feel better about her. Like maybe she was really my daughter. It helped that we both hated her dad, the one that raised her. We had some laughs about him. It was like talking to Morgan all those years ago. I wanted to say something nice, you know, to compliment Melody, so I said how pretty she is. That she looks a lot like her mother when I knew her."

Both Lauren and Smith shifted in their chairs but said nothing.

"After that, Melody told me what was going on in her life. She's doing good in college. Got lots of friends. Likes somebody, she said, but wouldn't tell me nothin' about him except he was older. I told her she's got a half sister and brother out in Alberta she didn't know about. I said she could take a flight out when I get back home and school's out, you know, when she could scrape together a little money."

"Did she like the idea?" Smith said.

"Why wouldn't she? She bet I can hardly wait to get home."

"What did you say?"

"Sure I can't wait. What would anybody say?"

Gould's impression was giving off more than he realized, making me wonder what Melody had actually thought of him.

Smith followed with the obvious question: "You met Melody twice. Was the second time in her apartment last Thursday night?"

"Yeah. That was my idea. It was about that boyfriend she kept to herself. When I thought it over afterwards, I didn't like that he's older than she is. I called her and said I needed to talk. She didn't say yes right away, but she was proud of her room and said she'd show it to me. The beer you found was hers."

"Did she identify this other man in any way?" Lauren said.

"She hardly said a damn thing and didn't like that I was asking questions. She got pretty mad and we both said some things. She's got my temper, that's for sure. In the end, I said to hell with her and her boyfriend. They deserve each other. I felt sorry afterwards about wrecking what we'd built together. But it's best not to drag this father-daughter thing out any longer."

"What did you do after you left Melody's room?" Smith said.

"I went home."

"Did you contact her again at any time or meet her?"

"Nope."

During the pause that followed, Smith glanced at Lauren without giving anything away. Gould seemed unburdened, like he had stepped out of a church confessional. He sat back, relaxing from the effort of his speech and asked the time. It was quarter to one.

A knock on the door interrupted the interrogation. Dobson brought in some papers, probably faxed over from New Minas Ident.

Smith glanced at them and said, "Constable Martin, I want a chance to discuss these with you." To Gould he said, "We won't be long."

As she and Smith stood, Lauren said, "Would you like another cigarette?"

Gould nodded. He was staring at the papers in Smith's hand. What else would he have to explain away?

Smith proffered a second cigarette and lit it, giving Lauren a sideways glance.

I stepped out to join them in the hallway, where Smith summarized the findings from Ident. "They found Melody's fingerprints at the crime scene, including on the two beer bottles. The blond hair on the sofa and the strands in the sleeping bag are consistent with the ones from her hairbrush. The blood at the scene is the victim's type. So is the blood trace from the hatchet. The boot with blood on it had a small nail poking through the sole, near the big toe. Ident wants to inspect Gould's foot. The tire tracks showed incidental marks that match the wear on Gould's truck."

"And the hard drive?" Lauren said.

"No sign of it indoors, in the crawl space, or anywhere near the house."

"We've got a strong case for Melody being assaulted and probably killed at Pitch Lake," she said.

"Exactly," Smith said. "I'll unfold the evidence, but we need enough to make the homicide charge stick. He's not the confessing type."

I went back to my viewing post. Gould's version had to be plausible, I thought. The better to take us in. You don't tell the cops more than you have to.

When Smith and Lauren marched back in, Gould had finished his cigarette and was staring at the door.

"We have some more questions," Smith said.

"Hopefully, they won't take much longer," Lauren said as they sat and Smith turned the mic back on.

"When was the last time you were up at your property on Pitch Lake?" Smith said.

"Early last December, for hunting."

"Do you let anyone borrow your truck?"

"No one drives it but me," Gould said slowly. I could see where Smith's questions were heading. It must be dawning on his suspect.

"We found fresh tire tracks in the driveway of your lake property. They're from your truck. We found other things in the house. Is there anything you want to tell us?"

Gould leaned back on his hard aluminum chair. "Yeah," he said reluctantly. "But first I want that damn machine turned off." He pointed at the mic. "I don't want things I say to come back and bite me."

"I'm glad you've being cooperative," Smith said. He glanced at Lauren. Self-satisfaction gleamed in his eyes. "I'll cut the recording, but I have to read your rights again. Nothing is ever off the record in a case like this. Anything you say can be brought into court." Police credibility was unassailable in the county.

Smith switched off the mic after rehashing the legal formalities. "What do you have to say?"

"I drove up last weekend, to check on the property. It's for sale. I went into the house. Somebody had been usin' it to dry marijuana. It was all over the back bedroom."

"Is that it?"

"No. The window was smashed."

Smith gave a long, exasperated sigh. The interrogation was going nowhere. He pushed his chin towards Gould. "We're interested in Melody Lockhart, not some damn weed. Did you take her up there?"

"No way."

"We have evidence she was in the house, and not many days ago."

"What evidence?"

"We found two empty bottles of Keiths with her fingerprints on them."

Gould just stared at him.

"We also found Melody's laptop on the mattress in the front bedroom. Some of the hair in the sleeping bag was hers. From as recently as last Monday."

"No way. She couldn't have found the house on her own."

"That's what we think, too," Smith said.

Gould looked around the room. He could see the questions pinpointed him. "Christ! I had nothing to do with her disappearing."

"That's not what we're saying," Lauren said. "We're looking for information. Who else has access to the lake house? We have to look at every possibility."

"Every possibility means me."

"We found blood on the floor that matches Melody's," Smith said. "Stop beating the bulrushes. Did you drive her up there Thursday night after the two of you had an argument? Did she go willingly?"

"Jesus, you cops are all the same. You're only a person of interest. Help us out. All we want is some information. You must think I'm some stupid."

"Look," Smith said, his tone more threatening. "We want you to tell us what happened to Melody and where she is. We know something serious happened between you two."

"We think it was just an accident," Lauren said. "Things can go sideways so fast when there's an argument. The best thing for you is to come clean. It won't go down so badly if you help us out."

Smith stretched in his chair. "I'll get us all coffee and give you some time to think about your own best interests here."

"Just throw your shitty coffee down the drain," Gould said. He looked at Lauren. "I see what you've been doing. You sound so nice but you're a lyin' bitch, worse than any of them. I want a fucking lawyer, and I want him now. And I want a lie-detector test."

He sat back, staring once more at the door, expecting his counsel to appear instantaneously, like a genie he had summoned. I wondered what his three wishes would be.

Smith answered his demand. "I'll arrange for a telephone." He handcuffed Gould and propelled him back to the holding cell.

We reconvened in Smith's interrogation central. "I'd hoped we'd get further tonight," he said. "We have lots we can use, especially with his lies. When I played out the evidence, he knew he was caught. That's when he lawyered up."

"We'll take him over to the county lockup and I'll lay an information tomorrow," Lauren said. The file was supposed to be hers. "A member should go back to the lake and talk to the neighbours about what they saw or heard around the Gould property."

"Also about that shot that broke the window," Smith said.

"Someone may remember hearing a rifle Monday morning," I said.

"I'll call ground search and alert the dive team. We'll need to search the lake," Smith said. "I want to get moving on this right away."

"According to Gould's version," I said, "he and Melody talked about a boyfriend. I think we shouldn't lose sight of that possibility, however remote it looks now. I'd like a chance to ask Gould more about what Melody had to say about him." *Otherwise, Gould's lawyer will tell him to clamp shut like a Venus flytrap and I'll get nothing out of him. I still might not.*

"I think there's been too much about what he said she said. It's the facts that count," Young said.

Or what count as facts.

"Maybe we can let Ian have a shot at that angle before you bring Gould out for his telephone call," Lauren said. "He might say something else we can use."

Gould stood and put his hands behind his back as soon as the key went into the lock of his cell. "Before we take you to a telephone," Smith said, "Dr. Wallace has a question he'd like to ask. You don't have to answer it, but it may help you and Melody both."

Gould straightened his arms and glowered at me. "You again," he said. "I don't know who you are, but right now, you're the Man. Get this over with so they let me make my damn phone call."

"It's about Melody's boyfriend. She was keeping him a big secret. Did she say anything else about him? Anything that could help to find her?"

A long sigh. "I don't know why I should care, but I did say some nasty things to her. But she said some pretty mean things back. I remember her saying he was way smarter than me. She called me ignorant and stupid. She said she could tell from the shape of my forehead. What crap do you teach them?"

I'd lectured about phrenology to discredit the false belief that people's physical appearance mirrors their intellect and morality. I hadn't expected anyone to believe it.

"Remembering that makes me want to walk out on her all over again," Gould said. "Look, this is going way too long. I want my lawyer."

"Thanks, Brandon," I said.

"Turn around and put your hands behind your back," Smith said.

He and Lauren led him out to the main office where they gave him the use of a telephone and a phone book. He went straight to Legal Aid in the Yellows.

Sterling County had a duty counsel who could be called in an emergency. All Gould heard was an answering machine's voice message. He left some details about the accusation and his name. "When can I meet her?" he asked Smith,

"Tell her you'll be in the county lockup overnight and be arraigned in the morning," Smith said. "She'll meet you then."

Gould finished his message to Legal Aid. "I'll get somebody who knows nothin' about nothin' with a long list of other poor people being screwed over," he said, summing his situation, which must have felt normal for him.

Smith shut him back in the cell. He wasn't ready to deposit him in the county jail.

"Maybe we should have pressed the evidence on Gould earlier," Lauren said, when her suspect was back under lock. "I hope Melody's still alive. Gould is the only one who can tell us where."

"Alive and missing a lot of blood," Smith said.

Having a prime suspect focuses the investigation to a narrow point, like a magnifying glass some kid uses to make ants spontaneously ignite. Gould was the solitary insect under the police lens.

"Wallace, your boyfriend angle is a red herring," Smith said. "With what we've got against Gould, that kind of speculation in a lawyer's hands could block a conviction."

He closed the file and placed it on his desk, ready to call it a night. Lauren offered to drive me to Livingstone Street.

"How sure are you Gould is guilty?" I asked quietly when we were alone.

It was two in the morning. We were both emotionally wrought, but I didn't expect her flash of anger. "I'm surer than ever he absolutely is. You heard him lie to us and backtrack on his story. Only guilty people do that. What about the evidence?"

"Gould had a clean sheet for the past ten years."

"He learned to be careful."

"It didn't stop him from being harassed. That may say something about his appearance."

"You're making excuses for him," Lauren said.

"I'm trying to understand things."

"That's not important. My job is to hold him accountable for what he did."

I shook my head. "Unless someone else did it. That second boyfriend is the other missing person in our case."

"Our case? You and I are reaching an impasse on this file."

"I'm not ready to wipe my hands of it because you think it's solved."

"You're just an armchair rationalist, not an investigator. I need tangible evidence. Melody's blood in Gould's house will be the clincher."

"Not if there's another explanation. I might be a rationalist, but I listen to people and see things, and build a synthesis from it all."

"You see what you want to see. I don't need these complications."

I wondered what else she might not need. *Maybe me.* "Thanks for the offer of a drive, but I think I'll walk. It'll give me time to clear my head."

"Whatever," Lauren said, like a dismissal.

My heart felt heavy as I headed into the night air. The solitary walk reflected my withdrawal from the official side of the case. I was some distance from constructing my own version.

Either my nostrils hadn't completely expelled the odour of pig fertilizer, or something was decidedly off. I clung to the idea that Melody had had only one heartthrob after her Aaron Campbell-induced suicide episode, despite the lack of clear evidence.

I needed Mary's help. Like her finely tuned sense of smell, her instinct for people and their stories was much sharper than mine.

Other than the Halstead Police Force, Tim's coffee shop is the only 24/7 operation in town. I pictured a lonely raisin and bran muffin sitting on the shelf, feeling abandoned and unwanted, like an ex-husband waiting for someone's affectionate attention.

Tony Thomson

18: Debates

Wednesday, 31 March

Halstead is about as busy this early in the morning as a beehive after all the bees have left. I walked listlessly down Main Street with my hands deep in my pockets to shelter them from the frosty air.

All the motor vehicles in town had been given the night off. Stoplights were forbidden in Halstead to simulate rusticity, so there were no red-amber-green sentinels to keep me company. The lonely stroll wasn't post-apocalyptic, merely the normal, late-night absence of visible life other than foraging raccoons.

As I walked under a streetlamp, my truncated, formless shadow appeared darkly at my feet. It gradually grew longer and took human shape. Just as it became almost palpable, my spectral companion slowly began to dissipate as I neared the next light down the street, and it finally disappeared without a whimper. When I looked over my shoulder, I saw it reemerging behind me.

Tim Horton's was the exception to the rule barring fast-food chains within town boundaries. A so-called first-family descendant owned the franchise. He got the business license through what everybody assumed was a political favour. The owner never showed his mug in the place. I followed my elusive search for truth inside the café, hoping for the final raisin bran.

I recognized the server behind the counter as a post-delinquent. She had run afoul of the law when she was fifteen and couldn't be identified publicly, the legal anonymity designed to prevent negative social labelling. Within her first week of community service, everyone in town knew her as "that young offender."

She was working alone even though it had been obvious for years that solitary, past-midnight employees were an in-danger species. I hoped she wouldn't become the victim of something sufficiently gruesome to induce protective legislation.

Someone had beaten me to the last muffin. After deliberating longer than for anything else over the last 24 hours, I asked for a black coffee, decaf considering the time of night, and a maple-glazed doughnut. The artificial topping bore only a vague resemblance to the genuine product. When it first dripped from the spigot, plunged like a mass murderer's knife into the vein of a still-leafless tree, maple syrup was little more than water—except to the tree.

One other loner was taking advantage of the only pre-dawn, indoor space in town you didn't have to break into. A man was slumped in his booth with his head turned toward the window. He wore a hoodie that hung down over his eyes against the glare of the light and had turtled deep into his jacket. All I could see was a clean-shaven cheek and a wisp of blondish sideburn. Probably had a fight with his girlfriend.

I left him in peace, carried my snack to a corner table near the window, and rehashed the Gould interview.

Smith and Lauren were creatively piecing together their exact narrative about Melody's disappearance. Cops are accused of tunnel vision when they fixate on one suspect and sometimes suppress evidence or manufacture it to strengthen their narrative.

Gould sounded like the author of his own misfortune. He'd shifted his bad faith onto everyone else, starting with his bootlegger father. By carelessly juggling fact and fiction during the interrogation, he had confirmed the cops' worst suppositions.

They would leave out of their notes my hypothesis about a second boyfriend. Nothing would impede the tidal bore bearing towards conviction.

The defence is entitled to full disclosure of all police evidence pertaining to the case, including the notes. The cops' most prudent strategy is to keep reasonable doubts out of the record. But if I reveal my theory to Gould's lawyer, I risk my credibility with the police and my relationship with Lauren, assuming I still have either.

The evening newspaper was on a table near mine. The lead article, with the byline S. Starr, claimed, "Missing Girl Second in Six Months." I grabbed it.

The article began with a brief biography of Melody Lockhart, much of which I knew to be wrong. Slim considered the police scenario of Melody running away with her boyfriend highly unlikely.

The second part began by asking whether a connection existed between the Lockhart case and that of Bridget Dennis. She had been reported missing in Annapolis Royal last October. Both were college students, Bridget at the Centre for Geographic Sciences in Lawrencetown. They were of similar age and build, with blond-coloured hair. They rented apartments in their respective towns and were generally solitary. Neither was known as a party-goer or to have a boyfriend. Bridget seemed the more independent because she occasionally hitchhiked along the Number One. The Annapolis Royal Police Force—all three of them—hadn't gotten far in their investigation before it froze more quickly than apple blossoms in a hard, spring frost.

Slim concluded his piece by speculating that the two missing students may have been victims of the same dangerous stranger, who might now be stalking a third.

I hadn't heard about the Bridget Dennis case in any RCMP briefing I'd seen. That was going to change now that Slim had exhumed the case. Smith would quickly rebury it if they couldn't make it fit Gould.

The possible connection between two missing students was intriguing. I imagined multiple murder expert Cathy Clarke's violin changing its simple, lover's-quarrel-turned-violent refrain to Slim Starr's tune.

I stepped back onto Main Street. It was too early for the first signs of humanity's new day dawning. Walking with my head angled downward, I didn't have the energy to reconstruct meaning from all I'd heard. I needed a sieve that could catch the relevant details identifying an alternative suspect.

Would the result be any better than the current vision at the end of the police tunnel? Corporal Smith had not paid much attention to Gould's information about Melody's current boyfriend. They had accused me of seeing only what I wanted to see. Nothing guaranteed my pieced-together story leading to the name of another suspect would be more reliable.

My thought experiment was complicated by the problem of remembering exactly what I'd seen and heard. It's not as if I could just read it again like a novel and pick out the parts that seemed to belong together.

I needed someone to talk with who knew the case but wasn't involved in it. Slim Starr was my best choice, except that he'd make it public. So, I began a shadow debate with him, detailing my thoughts about a second boyfriend.

I imagined Slim's rejoinder. *'It's your duty to inform the defence about another suspect. Just let her know you don't have two clues about who it might be. In fact, you imagined he may exist based on some cryptic notes the victim wrote, which you think are vaguely suggestive. But who knows? Why wouldn't a defence lawyer be ecstatic to hear that?'*

Slim was right. Three people had said that Melody had a new boyfriend, but I didn't have a clue who he was. And I had a nagging feeling that, somewhere in the interrogation, I'd missed something important.

Maybe that fragment would surface in the middle of the night, like my better ideas. I'd force myself out of bed to write it down before it disappeared along with my dreams. Usually, I couldn't decipher what I'd scribbled in the dark.

My head was growing as weary as my thoughts. Yesterday morning's jog along Pitch River felt like last month. Maybe I should have conserved my strength.

I raised my eyes from my ever-reversing shadow often enough to make my way past the darkened Bridgeside to Livingstone Street and my flat. I barely remembered falling into the sack.

An hour and a half past jogging-time, the radio alarm dutifully announced reveille from the kitchen counter. I rolled over, hoping the mellifluous, radio-quality vocal cords of the CBC host would serve as a sleeping tonic. CBC elocution training erases any vestiges of a regional accent as thoroughly as the rest of their training stifles the capacity for critical thinking.

What brought me out from under the covers, however, was a soundbite from Corporal Smith that announced a suspect in the Melody Lockhart case would be arraigned at ten o'clock. He made no mention of the Bridget Dennis case, but coupled with Slim Starr's article, the pitchfork brigade was bound to be at the courthouse for the morning session.

No media campaign had lit a torch under the RCMP to solve the case *tout suite* in the interests of justice and story deadlines. Too often, the demand for haste can produce quick but false results. This case had started without the immediate, gory sensation of a mutilated body lying in the shallow grave our mass murder expert had predicted.

I glanced at my night table. I hadn't scrawled any brilliant note to myself in my semi-consciousness.

Despite the four hours of sleep I'd managed, I felt surprisingly alert after morning ablutions, a couple of cups of Just Us coffee, a grapefruit sliced meticulously to extract the pulp from the sinews, and a bowl of sugarless oatmeal with chopped almonds and blueberries plucked from the depths of the freezer. With luck, some of that sustenance would fuel the adrenaline I'd need today.

Two classes needed cancelling, and not in person. I dialed the department secretary. Darlene Morse comes into work early and leaves late, trying to finish her work when needy students aren't queuing at her door. Department heads complain she's inefficient. Ambitious profs want her to do more of their work. Students say she's the best thing about the department.

I let her know I'd be absent for the day without offering an excuse, which she didn't request. She agreed to write a cancellation note on the blackboards and pass the information to the head when he wandered in later in the morning.

"You sound terrible," Darlene added. "Make sure to stay at home and lie down."

"Excellent advice," I said. Not that I planned to take it.

Gould's arraignment was next, to be followed by the casting of curses by the righteous few. Being dragged in front of a judge with a charge over your head is sufficient evidence of guilt for the kangaroo court of public opinion—opossum court in Canada, since it's our only native marsupial.

My last visit to the county courthouse was fewer than twenty-four hours ago. Today's destination was the main floor courtroom.

The room was almost full and not by last night's arrestees. Gould was somewhere in the lockup at the rear of the courthouse or in the small exercise yard with its razor wire fence, built in the vain hope of separating the bad from the outside world.

Gould's case was a hand-written afterthought on the court docket posted beside the courtroom door. Today's slate was light. Mondays were the busiest, when the court processed the weekend's sad assortment of the Valley's underclass. Crime kept police, criminal lawyers, and the complex correctional apparatus employed. And criminologists.

The principal courtroom was no library. Two sheriffs' deputies guarding the door had no interest in subduing the chatter. They were intent only on keeping the crowd from bringing sharp farm tools and torches into court.

Lauren was sitting at the front near the prosecutor's table. I stood in the SRO section to the left of the door and scanned the room, looking for a Montreal Expos ball cap with brown hair spilling out around its rim.

Slim Starr, notebook in hand, leaned on the back wall on the other side of the entrance. He was looking around, as though he were judging the mood of the mob he had helped assemble. I lumbered across the floor to stand next to him.

"The police have arrested Brandon Gould, thinking he's connected to the Lockhart case," I confided quietly to Slim's left earlobe. "He's a long-time offender with convictions for sexual assault."

Slim makes his living gathering facts from likely and unusual sources. I'd offered him a sip of information, the better to drink from what I hoped was his much larger fount.

"That's nothing new," Slim said, matter-of-factly. "You said they think he's connected. Do you think he isn't?"

"He's connected, all right. I'm keeping my options open."

"The RCMP brought him into the lockup well after midnight. He was making a stink about being accused of something he didn't do." Slim was letting me know he'd questioned one of the turnkeys.

"That's what they all say."

"Yeah, and sometimes they mean it."

"If there's more to the story than we have so far, you're the one to find it," I said. "You've been digging into the Lockhart case and also Bridget Dennis's. Do you have anything else to show they're related?"

"Nice of you to read my column. Are the local cops looking into both cases?" He had ignored my question or had no answer for it.

"I bet they are now," I said. "You gave everyone something to think about, including this potential mob in the courthouse." I pictured Slim's Expos cap turning into the cone-shaped hat of a sorcerer's apprentice.

"Even the hint of multiple murders creates an uproar in this sleepy burg," Slim said. "More than serial arsonists, although they're more common."

"Was that structural fire on the mountain arson?"

"No one knows. They're thinking an electrical malfunction. The fire was intense, fuelled by gasoline stored inside. It was lucky it didn't spread to the house or woods."

"Was there anything valuable inside, enough to make it a worthwhile insurance fraud?"

"The owner is a Dr. Davenport, from the College. When I interview him tomorrow at his spread on the lake, I'll mention you suspect him of fraud," Slim said.

"No worries there. What caused the fire?"

"There wasn't enough left to determine a cause. Some people like to see pretty yellow and blue flames and hear things that don't belong to them go bang in the night."

"He'll still get the insurance money," I said.

"He didn't bother with insurance. Too much nuisance for a nothing shack, is the way he put it."

"That's not how I remember it." June, now his ex, had invited Mary and me for a barbie one summer five years ago. Barry had shown me around while our wives went for a walk near the shore. He had begun the tour at his shed. "It was a fully equipped carpenter's shop. He had table saws, a band saw, handsaws, hatchets and other tools. It looked valuable to me."

"Some folks hate the whole idea of insurance. You have a good memory."

"He practically pushed me through the shed door and brought me face-to-face with a newly severed deer head with a full rack of antlers. Its blood was puddling under my feet and spreading beneath a large roll of greenhouse sheeting. He enjoyed a good laugh over my reaction."

"He's a practical jokester. I'll have to watch out."

"I can't imagine him doing any kind of manual labour. He said his wife doesn't let him slaughter animals in the house."

The courtroom chatter subsided abruptly when the Provincial Court Justice entered, dressed in his traditional, Westminster garb minus the white wig and the square, black cap. The junior Crown Attorney was decked out in a black silk gown with partially open sleeves, which trailed in the back below her dark gray skirt. A white two-pronged cravat hung down from her neck.

Everyone stood as requested. The men doffed their hats, following custom, not necessarily expressing respect for the system the judge represented.

A Breathalyzer refusal case, the first item on the docket, dragged on interminably, adding to the voluminous case law on drinking and driving. When people with money to spare are snared in roadside checks, they can afford expensive lawyers. The rest of us aren't so lucky.

When the judge pronounced the impaired driver guilty, he left the courtroom, arguing with his hired help. Gould's arraignment was next.

A couple of burly, waist-bulging deputies, ex-town cops supplementing their tin-watch pensions, led him in through the back door. His lawyer hovered behind like a small, black shadow detached from its body.

Gould would have been high fashion only in a lumber camp. His appearance fit the role for which he'd been advertised.

The incessant whispering resumed, intending disrespect although not for the judge.

Since everyone else had come to gawk at the spectacle, including me, the announced intent of Gould's session was superfluous. Gould was charged with second-degree murder. The prosecution wanted him held in custody pending his trial.

Gould's duty lawyer asked that he be released on his own recognizance. "I met with Mr. Gould for the first time this morning. I have preliminary information about the evidence the Crown has, but what little I know sounds entirely circumstantial. We are a long way from full disclosure in this case."

"Mr. Gould is a resident of Alberta, Your Honour, and a risk to flee the jurisdiction," the Crown said. "He made an attempt to escape when the police came to arrest him last night. We ask that he be remanded in custody."

"Mr. Gould has been living in Sterling County for seven months, looking after his aged mother, your Honour," Gould's lawyer said. "He's not a danger to the public and he's not a risk to abscond."

The back and forth continued for a few minutes until the judge cut it short. "A murder charge is serious," he said. "I order that Mr. Gould be held in custody, pending a hearing to determine whether a pre-trial remand is warranted."

The consultation between the justice and the clerk to set the date for the show cause hearing took longer than Gould's initial appearance. Two Sheriffs Deputies led him through the back door to await transport to the Correctional Centre.

The courtroom herd decamped out the front door, feeling justified in their indignation. They headed to the parking lot behind the lockup, intending to shower the Sheriff's van with spit and curses. Slim followed them along with the Global TV cameraman, who had been waiting outside. At least I knew which channel to record.

I stayed inside by the door, waiting to see where Lauren was going. She had a brief conversation with the Crown Attorney and spied me on her way out.

"I'm happy with the decision," she said, walking briskly to her cruiser, with me a half-step behind. "He'll be held in custody for now and the hearing will be a slam dunk."

"Gould is used to being caged," I said. "You'll have another go at him soon with more damning evidence, although not without his lawyer. It shouldn't take long to check the DNA from the blood and match it with Melody's hair fibres."

"Right. Once we have the case sewn up, Gould's lawyer will be a big help. When she sees everything we have against him, she'll tell him confession is his best option."

"Convincing him might not be so easy," I said. "Trying to make the marijuana in his back bedroom his big revelation makes no sense."

"He was leading us on. I think he changed his mind about what to say even as he was telling us about it."

"I don't understand why Gould didn't hightail it up to the lake after we left his mother's place, to mop up the evidence."

"Being caught cleaning up a crime scene is more damning than pretending to know nothing about it."

My energy to argue had expired. This was an important case for Lauren. As the lead investigator, she had solved it quickly, or so it seemed. Annual performance assessments build or break careers.

Maybe she felt her hat becoming tight, because she turned to me before getting into her cruiser and said, "You know, identifying Gould as the suspect and the location of the crime scene were key to this case, and you helped with that. I still have some loose ends. We can't get together tonight to celebrate, but we will soon."

"No worries," I said, relieved we might have a future.

Lauren drove off in search of I didn't know what. She thought Melody's file was a wrap.

I still had persistent questions of my own. To me, a missing body is a lot more than a loose end.

The Sheriff's van carrying Gould to his new digs pulled out of the courthouse parking lot. The onlookers began to disperse, among them Slim Starr. He waved to me. I waited for him to draw abreast.

"Davenport's a colleague of yours," Slim said. "What can you tell me about him?"

"That dig about me suspecting him of fraud won't be an embarrassment. He's a much bigger fish in the College than me. His résumé is longer than your reporter's nose. I'll know more when I read your interview."

"You don't have to talk with Davenport long to realize he has an interesting story, at least a local interest piece for the *Herald*. You know, a down and out young man finds success."

"I look forward to it," I said. "He comes across in the college as standoffish."

"Yeah. He wasn't happy to see me at first, and neither was that big dog of his. He barked loud enough to disturb the neighbours across the lake. So did his dog. But after we spoke for a while, I could see a switch flip and he agreed to be interviewed. Everybody really wants their story told. You just have to know how to approach them. Anyhow, I need to file this courthouse story."

He hurried away. They wouldn't hold the presses for this one.

I had immediate needs of my own, starting with the latest search results from Pitch Lake.

Members regularly convened at lunchtime in the dining room of the Knight's Hotel, a clone of a budget US chain. I'd joined them occasionally to hear detachment gossip. The hotel was off the beaten track, so the cops could avoid being surrounded by prying town eyes. Sergeant Young had ordered them to limit the size of the gathering. When too many cops met for coffee breaks, county taxpayers complained about the wasted time and money.

Today's chat would rehash the Gould case. It was an opportunity not to miss.

Tony Thomson

19: Steaks and knives

More RCMP cars than usual occupied the choice spaces near the lobby entrance. I wondered how many tourists their presence turned away, thinking something bad must be happening other than what comes out of the kitchen.

Several tables had been jammed together at the back of the dining room with Corporal Smith strategically at the centre, hanging with the regular members. I took one of the two vacant seats next to him.

Other noon-hour patrons in the dining room kept a respectable, earshot distance away.

The collective guffawing around the table wasn't case-related. It was trash talk that had spilled over from last night's recreational hockey game. The inequitable dishing out of insults and put-downs was part of macho sports culture. If you didn't have the bravado to give out the trash, you needed the thick skin to endure having it dumped on you.

A server came around to take our orders. The second order of business was how you liked your steak. I opted for coffee.

When the hockey laughter subsided, Smith switched the conversation to his own agenda. "It was a long night," he said.

Everyone knew what was coming.

"Did it ever go well. That asshole mouthed off high and mighty at his mother's house. Once we got him in the interview room, he put on this 'I've got nothing to hide' act, so I let him spin out his yarn and caught him in a lie. You could hear his transmission grind as he jammed her in reverse. When I hit him with the fingerprint evidence, his jaw hit the floor. You saw it all, Ian. That's how it went down, isn't it."

It wasn't a question.

"Sure was," I said. "He changed course two or three times. You and Lauren got a lot out of him he wasn't expecting to give."

"Yeah, he still thought he could outsmart me. I strung him out a long time before he finally lawyered up. And I'll hit him with lots more next time I bring him in."

No doubt, although it was Lauren who had kept Gould talking when it looked like he was about to quit.

"No confession, though," Andy Graham pointed out.

"Not yet. If he wants a break on his sentence, his lawyer will tell him to pretend remorse and own up to what he did."

"What's happening with ground search?" Andy said, gesturing towards the South Mountain, framed by the window behind him.

"You know what the terrain is like," Smith replied. "Thick brambles, uneven ground, bogs, boulders scattered all over the place, uprooted trees. It's a tough slog at the best of times. The search team is using some hounds. Nothing so far. My money is on the lake."

"Pitch Lake's pretty big and deep, and really dark," Andy pointed out. "They don't call it Pitch for nothing. It's from the peat and the iron leaching out of the rock. It won't be easy to find a body anywhere in that water until it gasses back to the surface."

"The dive team's going to begin tomorrow. They'll start offshore from the cabin unless ground search finds something today. Either way, it's going to be a matter of time."

"Can you dig a grave at the bottom of a lake, you know, with an air tank and all," Paul Dobson said. "And put a body in it and cover it over? If you could, I bet we'd never find it."

"You got somebody in mind, Dobson?" Andy said.

"Well, now that you mention it…. But, seriously, can it even be done?"

"There are a lot of simpler means of disposal," Andy said, as though he had seen them all. "Besides, the lake looks calm on the surface, but it's fed by a lot of gullies, running high this time of year, and underground streams. There's a lot of moving water underneath, and erosion. Nothing buried would stay that way."

"They better find the victim's body," Dobson said. "Can't get a conviction without one,"

"Bullshit," Andy exclaimed. "It's not that simple to get a 'stay out of jail forever' card. All you need for a conviction is solid investigation and conclusive forensics."

"On top of a confession," Dobson said.

"That's just lazy policing. GIS counts too much on squeezing a confession and leaving no visible marks. Remember the Shakeston murder, a few years ago?" Andy said. "We think he buried the body. Nobody's found it yet, but he was convicted of first-degree murder."

"Yeah, because of a ton of circumstantial evidence and convincing

DNA," Smith pointed out.

"Like I said."

"What about that Bridget Dennis girl that went missing over in Annapolis last year?" Dobson asked the Corporal, probably imagining a graveyard under the lake.

"We're looking into that file today," Smith said. "Gould was back from Alberta by then, and the two cases look a lot alike."

The cops in Annapolis Royal will love the Mounties muscling in. Town cops resent their interference. But once a case becomes a homicide, small departments lose jurisdiction.

Smart members know it's better to cooperate with local police instead of taking over their case. I wasn't including Dobson in that company.

"Have we ever had a serial murderer in the Valley?" someone asked from down the table. "We can't be immune to that virus." I looked to see whether Cathy Clarke had joined the table and was throwing her voice.

"None I'm aware of. There are a lot of unsolved homicides of females. We're lucky we solved the Lockhart case so quickly," Smith said, allowing a smile to transform his usual demeanour, his teeth stained with coffee and self-satisfaction.

"I was the first member on that file," Paul Dobson said proudly, now that the case had become important. "Something suspicious happened last Monday on the mountain. I talked to some of the suspect's neighbours this morning. One of them heard five or six rifle shots coming from Gould's property. The next thing, he sees this truck tearing up the road hightailing it out of there."

"That had to be Gould," Andy said. "He was still running away when I spotted him. He didn't see me driving toward him or turning around. I figured he was impaired. He came up with a story I didn't believe. From what the Corporal says, he's still making stuff up."

"Yeah, no wonder," Dobson said, retaking the initiative. "He was the one being shot at. Ident pulled a .303 bullet out of the back of his truck."

"I guess you didn't notice the bullet hole," Corporal Smith said to Andy.

"Hell, no. That truck was filthy and beat up. I could hardly tell where the license plate was from."

"Who'd be shooting at him?" I said.

"According to New Minas Drugs," Dobson said, "he was selling marijuana that he'd stored in the lake house. They figure he harvested it from somebody else's grow-op in the woods. Looks like the guy he ripped off found out who took it."

"He did a piss-poor job if he was trying to kill him. But it sure scared the hell out of him," Andy said. "Did the neighbour stay away from the property or go check it out? He didn't bother to call 911."

"He said he thought the guy driving the truck did the shooting," Dobson said. "He didn't hear any other vehicles. He waited a bit and took a closer look down at the shore. All he could see was a man in a canoe heading west across the lake. Fishing, he thought."

"Did you ask any of the other neighbours about the shots?" Corporal Smith said.

"Not yet." Dobson looked around the table, his body language implying an NCO shouldn't come out and spoil the members' lunch. The brief silence around the table suggested it was a common sentiment.

The arrival of slabs from a recently dissected cow, dripping something red that only appeared to be blood, with mushrooms and onions on top, broke the uncomfortable moment. About half the crew finished their coffees and disembarked. My info cruise being over, I followed them down the gangplank.

Not that I wasn't hungry. My stomach led the way downtown.

The Main Street Café was the first and busiest coffee shop in town, independently owned by a local developer. He'd taken over a convenience store near the college, gutted it, built a kitchen addition on the back, and outfitted two floors for the latte and lunch crowd. A couple of tables and chairs congested the sidewalk to the right of the front door, at the diagonal corner of the building.

Johnnie Walker sat at one of them. More than once he'd insisted a paying customer relinquish the table for his use as his right in perpetuity.

Johnny kicked a chair a few inches out on the sidewalk, opening a space for me to squeeze in. If I didn't accept his silent invitation, he could blame my blindness rather than his ambiguous signal.

I joined him. "Hey, Johnnie. What's up?"

"Everybody's talking about the Lockharts. They don't deserve this kind of heartache. Georgina's one of the nice ones, despite her nasty husband. Or maybe because of him."

"Opposites attract."

"Nah. Opposites repel. They don't know it until they're married."

"Do you know Melody well?"

"Since she was a kid. Always smiled at me when she tagged along when the mom stopped to say hello. Last year, she came into the café once in a while and still turned on that shy smile. It made me happy. She never sat with me, just found a table by herself to read or write. You can't tell how kids will turn out, though."

"How so?"

"I saw her last fall holding hands with some guy."

"Do you know who he is?"

"Nope. I only saw them from behind."

"Well, that relationship didn't last very long," I said.

"You're telling me. She graduated from boys to men."

That certainly piqued my interest. "Do you know who's she's with?"

"Nope. They showed that guy they arrested on TV coming out of the courthouse. I've seen him hanging around town, dealing drugs. But I might have seen Melody with him."

"What do you mean, you might have seen them?"

"I didn't really see him. One night last week, I was walking on Main Street and I saw Melody crossing the bridge to SoHa. I stopped to watch her. She went around a street corner. Then, I heard a truck take off. It didn't come back to this side of the river."

"You recognized a truck by its sound?"

"Well, it was kind of a loud rumble. I've seen that guy they arrested driving a truck."

"Observant as always, Johnnie."

"Got nothin' else to do."

"Have you told the cops about this?"

"No one's asked me."

"Try Crime Stoppers. They won't ask any questions. I'm going to get lunch. Can I get you something?"

"Sure. Another black coffee."

I stepped into the café. Two baristas, as they called themselves, worked at the L-shaped counter along the front. The display case tempted me with a variety of sandwiches, salads, and wraps.

The Thai red lentil soup served with two scones won the competition. Customers crowded the tables by the side windows. I carried my tray absent-mindedly into the back, oak-panelled room, thinking sorrowfully about Melody.

Suddenly, I saw her leaning over a table and holding a man's hands.

20: Xavier and Janelle

The mirage lasted for a double-take second, then disappeared as instantaneously as it had come. A woman I didn't know was sharing a table with Xavier Benoit.

He saw me and invited me to sit. "You look haunted," he said. "Like you've seen something otherworldly."

"Yeah. The last couple of days have been unreal."

"And that's a bad thing? This is Janelle Thibault," he said, touching her arm.

"Hey."

She looked to be in her early thirties, an ex-student or a come-back, mature one. The two were at ease together.

For several minutes, they continued their conversation in French while I tucked into the soup, a touch salty, and the buttery scones. A café mocha and a slice of chocolate mousse cake awaited their turns.

Janelle pouted when Xavier interrupted her in English to initiate a conversation with me, the unintroduced. "Do you believe Melody Lockhart is dead?"

"That's a difficult question."

"I'm not asking what you think. I want to know how you feel."

"I want her to be alive."

"Don't be obtuse. What does your gut tell you?"

"Xavier, the last thing it told me was, I'm hungry."

"Est-il un idiot?" Janelle asked Xavier without otherwise acknowledging my existence, as if the third chair at the table had remained vacant.

"Astute, Janelle," Xavier said, beaming. "Ian here is thinking simplistically."

"I just didn't want to say aloud what I think is probably true," I said.

"You've answered my question. My next is, who killed her?"

"The police think it's Brandon Gould. He's Melody's biological father."

"They always get it wrong."

"You don't read enough detective novels, Xavier. They never get it wrong."

"I've read one and that's enough. Once I finished it, I promptly forgot everything I'd just read."

"Touché," Janelle applauded.

Xavier shot me an appraising look. "You say 'the police think.' Whom do you suspect?"

"The 'whom' is my problem. When I walked in, I thought I saw Melody sitting right here, at your table." I pointed blindly through Janelle at her chair.

"Bravo! your unconscious mind isn't entirely gone," he said. "I am its suspect. You were looking at Janelle and seeing the victim. She does have something of the late Melody's facial construction."

"Quoi! Ce n'est pas vrai! Melody n'avait rien avec mon flair," Janelle complained. I found her adoption of the past tense more annoying than Xavier's. Among other annoyances.

"Absolutely true, Janelle. Ian's just looking at you superficially. Now, Ian, what led you to your brilliant but obviously flawed conclusion about me?"

"Seeing the two of you together," I replied, begrudgingly.

"Ah. You mean our juxtaposition. What was it about me that made you imagine the man you truly suspect but don't realize it yet?"

"Geez, Xavier. My mind doesn't work that fast."

"Quel penseur!" Janelle threw in from the bleachers.

"Your thinking mind is not the issue. It's just leading you in circles. You need that sudden flash of unconscious insight, which your conscious mind takes literally and interprets as a mistake. What pattern did you detect in that momentary impression of, we'll call them Xavier and Melody, 'appearing together in the café'?"

"Shouldn't that be Xavier and Janelle?" she asked, speaking English with no trace of an accent. I wondered whether a native French speaker would detect an English twang in her *français*.

"Yes, of course! I am the key to Ian's vision, not the false Melody, and not actually me. You need to paint a pentimento over my image. Look at your palette. What colours do you mix first? What do you know about the mysterious Monsieur X?"

It occurred to me that I'd forgotten Johnnie Walker's invitation and his black coffee. I felt entrapped by one of Xavier's dramatic improvisations and let out a long, uncomfortable sigh.

"You win. What colours? Thinking hair, maybe a base of medium brown, speckled with white, especially around the temples."

"So, not as old as me but no youngster."

"Maybe a goatee, or a light beard, even more salt and pepper. And glasses."

"An egghead. Plenty of them around town," Xavier said.

"A brown corduroy jacket, worn sleeves and elbow patches."

"Goes without saying."

"Secretive and private," I said.

"That's more promising."

"Seductive, knows how to worm his way into a woman's affections."

"Now you're just back to me again."

"Qui parle ainsi?" Janelle said, snickering.

"Ha!" Xavier laughed appreciatively.

"Manipulative and self-seeking?" My impression canvas was reaching its limits.

"That's good. Now stand back and have a look at the new me that's not me. Who do I resemble? Who comes to mind?"

"Nobody. Everybody."

"Give me the first name that pops in your head."

"Xavier."

"Oh, Ian. You disappoint me. I felt you were getting close. You're just thinking too hard. Let the pigments dry a bit and let your mind work behind the scenes on the overall impression. You'll come to your answer when you least expect to."

"When it's too late, you mean."

"It's already too late for Melody, which is what's truly important. You said so yourself."

"Not exactly," I said, rising from Xavier's table. "I'll let you know the next time sugar plum fairies dance in my head."

"T'es un terrible danseur," Janelle complained to Xavier, taking the improvisation in a new direction.

I bought a large, black dark roast on the way out. Johnny wasn't there. I left it on his table.

I felt more overwhelmed than tired. I followed my feelings back to the college until I stopped at twin metallic doors. Exercise was exactly what my body knew I needed.

Basketball carried me to an alternate universe. Whenever I entered the gym doors, every other thought disappeared from my mind.

Last week's basketball clothes were standing in the locker, tolerable for one more use if no one was within ten feet.

I was in luck. A few stragglers had erected a volleyball net at the near end of the gym to practice killing the ball. I walked past them to the empty end of the gym, under the main basketball hoop. Today's noon-hour basketball game was over.

The game always started slowly and politely until a flagrant foul occurred or someone was grievously aggressive. Then it became seriously competitive and winning was all that mattered. That style suited me fine. The only regular player who was more competitive than me was a pastor in his real life. How you play ball wasn't an accurate index of how you presented yourself in other realities.

With the main backboard and two practice hoops attached to the walls on either side, a triangle of targets beckoned to me. Being quick off the mark and fast, which aren't the same thing, were my only weapons. I'd neglected to add height and bulk in university.

I divided my time equally among all three hoops, driving for lay ups and reverses or pulling up for jump shots and low-percentage hooks. I'd left my dunking days in high school, along with most of my bad memories.

By the time the scheduled workout crowd arrived, dressed in fashionably designed aerobics tights, my heart rate had maxed and my pores were holding my shirt in a close embrace. I headed back to the locker room, Body Movin' to the beat of the Beastie Boys.

Once I was off the hardwood floor, Melody's disappearance flooded back into my mind. I hoped all the jumping and running had rearranged the bits and pieces of her story into a plausible chronicle. I had a few suspicions about people I'd talked to but didn't have a lot to go on. It seemed logical to sort out where I was before moving further.

My main visual was that apparition of Melody holding hands with a man who'd turned out to be Xavier. Was he a likely suspect?

Cathy Clarke had suggested a dominant man in a position of authority. Xavier thrived on women's admiration and rumoured affairs. But I'd heard hardly any gossip about him acting inappropriately with his students. 'Hardly' because everyone has someone who dislikes them and wants to undermine them.

It doesn't take much. A negative word or two from someone you trust substitutes for independent judgment. Just because Xavier had acted the concerned innocent didn't mean he was.

Xavier was more dramatically romantic than John Percy Byron, even though he was considerably younger. In many ways, however, the romantics prof also fit the pattern I'd fashioned for Xavier. I'd wondered about his keen perception of Melody's mood and attire. And all the talk of love and romance made him popular among students, particularly impressionable women.

Was it reasonable to suspect him? He worked with his partner in the same department. Like the whispering wall in the Temple of Heaven, the faintest sigh of what Byron did at the college had echoes at home.

It struck me that I'd tried the suspect shoe on Xavier's foot and Byron's, a second faculty member. But I hadn't realigned my information sieve. I'd fallen naturally into an academic approach and used facts to potentially disconfirm two of my colleagues as suspects.

A few other possibilities flew across my internal monitor: Robert, the tenure-committee hack with the wandering eye. Davenport the suave. The womanizing guidance counsellor in Psychology. Maybe Clarke herself, the murder expert. *Theory or practice?* I wondered.

For any of them, my sieve was practically empty of facts, disconfirming or otherwise. I reminded myself that it's been just three days.

I wandered slowly through the A&A Building until my mind's gears ground to an abrupt halt. I was an academic, used to demolishing other people's theories. I usually took it for granted that the fundamental error began with a flawed assumption, on which the whole argument was built. My initial supposition was the likelihood of a connection between Melody's presumed boyfriend and the person responsible for her disappearance. Was assuming that a relationship had turned sour the best tack?

My suspect pool was dangerously shallow. Maybe the best I could hope for was some *deus ex machina*, a last-minute psychopath emerging from beyond the College professoriate and thrusting into the headlights.

Maybe the link was with Slim Starr' second disappearing student. Both women may have had fatal encounters with that dangerous stranger found so often in pulp fiction and occasionally in real life. In the Maritimes, even highway cops patrolling alone at night have met them with tragic results.

If Melody's boyfriend was bright, as Gould had suggested, he didn't have to be a faculty member. Young Campbell played the intellectual. Would a few years older count as a significant difference in Melody's eyes? Campbell wasn't the only student candidate for *Jeopardy* on campus, although no one we'd talked with had connected her with any other classmate.

In my thinking, Melody's disappearance most likely originated in intimate relationship troubles. I wondered momentarily whether my judgment was blighted by my own troubles. My old relationship was vexing and my fledgling one stalled on the ground.

Thinking about Lauren brought Barry Davenport to mind. I was irritated by the personal attack on my character he'd launched in Lauren's presence. I knew more about Davenport than anyone else I'd talked to so far.

I took the stairs to the second floor. Davenport was considerably older than Melody, although his looks narrowed the age gap. Over the nearly five years since June left, he had had temporary liaisons with many women. For a mere college teacher, he appeared to be well off. He'd gone for an extended spring break last February. Melody might have joined him. Perhaps his money had funded the adventure.

Second thoughts—perhaps third or fourth ones—troubled me as I headed down the corridor to my office. I couldn't understand how someone like Melody could see Davenport as attractive. He was abrasive rather than charming. Unlike the fawning Byron, Davenport came across as disrespecting students. Disdain for people in general might be more accurate.

But no rumour mill suggested a liaison with any woman at the college. He had influenced Aaron Campbell's thinking and, perhaps through him, Melody's. He was reclusive, though, living alone on the mountain far from everything. It went with being an elitist, although I didn't understand his antipathy to Britishers. Being right-wing had nothing to do with intelligence.

Assuming the existence of a Davenport and Melody relationship, demanding absolute discretion would be a reasonable precaution for any faculty member. I doubted they'd meet in her room in town.

Johnny Walker believed she met Gould last week. From his story, Gould may have driven her to the lake. But it could have been Davenport. From what I'd seen, his house on the mountain was a more romantic destination than Gould's run-down shack.

I looked down to the end of the hallway and saw Davenport's closed door. *I should do something*, I thought, *not just think*. Talking to him would be a good start. Of the faculty members I'd considered, he resonated the loudest.

I wasn't sure that talking counted as *doing* anything. *When in doubt, equivocate.* I had more other hands for deliberation than any Indian god.

I looked into the departmental office and saw Darlene at her desk. She was surprised to see me come in.

"I thought you weren't well today," she said.

"I'm not, after being up most of the night working on the Melody Lockhart case."

"It shows. It's so sad, poor girl. I feel for her parents. They've charged some guy from Alberta. Does that mean they found her body?"

"No. That will take some time. And I don't want to lose hope she'll be found alive." *It was becoming more difficult to still have hope.*

"I don't remember hearing about the other girl over in Annapolis, and that was just last year," Darlene said. "Was the Alberta guy involved in that case, too?"

"The police haven't charged him because their investigation isn't complete. They weren't doing him a favour."

"Speaking of favours, I cancelled classes for you this morning, like you asked."

"Yeah, I should have said thanks."

"At least you always give me some notice, which is more than I get out of Barry. He's missed his classes for a week. Usually when he goes off to a conference, he lets me know beforehand. Not this time. I gave him a call at home to see how he was. He didn't answer. In fact, I called three times."

"Just to see how he was?" I asked incredulously.

"Well, not exactly. I saw him briefly in the hallway yesterday, so he's around. But it's odd he's not teaching. Students have complained to me about it. They hate it when he misses classes."

"They hate other things about him, too, like his student put-downs."

"He's always saying inappropriate things," Darlene said.

"Yeah, but offhandedly so he can disavow them. Lately, he's more direct about his beliefs, like he's beyond caring."

"I've noticed that, too."

"I wish I'd known how racist he was before I voted to hire him."

I walked slowly down the hall to my office, my perplexed eyes on the carpet. The term *slope head* surfaced out of the blue in my mind. That's how Davenport had described his supposedly dim-witted students. According to Gould, if I remembered precisely, Melody had said the shape of his forehead was a sign of his stupidity.

The similarity was jarring. Perhaps it was Davenport who had taught Melody by example to judge character from people's physical appearance. Had she been around him that much?

I followed the hallway to my office, put the key in the lock, fiddled with it until it reluctantly agreed to work, and then stopped without turning it. Davenport's unusual class avoidance coincided with Melody's absence. Curiosity overwhelmed my sense of inertia and propriety.

Pocketing my keys, I retraced my steps to the departmental office.

"Hey, Darlene. Sorry to bother you, again. I need a favour. Yeah, another one. When I left home, I forgot to bring my office keys. Can you lend me your master? I'll need it again to lock the door later."

"Just as long as you don't expect me to wait for you before I go home," Darlene said, reaching into her drawer for the open-sesame key that unbolts all the doors in the department.

I went back down the corridor and listened quietly at Davenport's door, feeling furtive and guilty.

21: Break and enter

No sound came from inside Davenport's office, not the groan of a chair, the shuffling of papers, a whirring fan, a single metallic keystroke. I turned the master key as silently as I could. Only the final click of the retracting bolt broke the silence.

I took the key to the office, remembered to say thanks, and returned to the scene of my unauthorized B&E. I opened the door wide enough to poke my head in. Davenport wasn't inside.

I closed the door behind me, switched on the light, and looked around. I was searching for something tangible to link Davenport and Melody.

Not much appeared to be different at first glance. Davenport's portable typewriter wasn't on his desk, as I had expected.

The left-hand wall was one long bookshelf. I was immediately struck by another absence. The only personal objects Davenport displayed in his office were framed photographs showcasing different locales and his random partners. The series of pictures now had a visible gap, like two missing teeth. I couldn't recall which ones were gone.

More surprisingly, Davenport's coveted, leather briefcase lounged nonchalantly beside his desk. He never went anywhere without it, like some invisible chain tied it permanently to his wrist. 'It's got all the drafts and notes for my new book,' he'd explained, if anyone asked. 'I need to have it near me.'

I lifted his sacred totem and placed it on the desk. It felt about as weighty as it should.

The first things I saw inside were reprints of the article he had proudly distributed to department members. I pulled a file folder out next. Inside were three hand-written pages, on which Davenport had written a summary of the main arguments and evidence from the article. They looked like talking points for conference presentations.

The bulk of the material in the case consisted of computer print outs. I hoisted them out, placed them on top of the outline, and thumbed through them. What I had thought about them was belied by what I had exposed to the light on Davenport's desk. They were merely random papers, nothing that couldn't simply be tossed back in the recycling bins from which Davenport had repurposed them. They resembled the draft of a new book as much as the false evidence folders Smith had assembled to fool Gould.

I was stunned. Davenport's briefcase was an elaborate prop. But why had he left it in his office for any nosy colleague to snoop into? I'd heard of writer's block, mythologized in academia and fiction. He had seemed out of sorts lately and more prickly than usual. That made sense.

But his long résumé reflected no previous affliction. I wondered how he had time for anything besides publishing. Had his succession of accomplishments been impeded by a mid-career crisis, marring his stellar reputation? I had seen no signs.

Checking elsewhere in the office, I found no indication linking Davenport with Melody. His filing cabinet was practically empty. The desk drawers contained random stationery supplies and unused paper. I didn't find the missing photos.

Disappointed, I replaced the papers in the briefcase, fastened it, and left it where I'd discovered it. Was the fake manuscript a one-off writer's block or did it represent some deeper layer of dishonesty?

I could learn no more in his office. I opened the door softly, checked the coasts, closed it stealthily behind me, and returned to Darlene's office for the master key.

"You didn't stay very long," she said.

"I had a couple of things to pick up. You know I do a lot of work at home."

"Ah ha," Darlene said neutrally. She kept track of professors' comings and goings, assembling resentments and anecdotes. I was glad she didn't have supervisory responsibilities.

I completed the clandestine lock-up and, once more, dutifully surrendered the key.

In my office, I drew Davenport's application and academic CV from the hiring committee folder in my filing cabinet. These documents contained almost all I believed about his past. Did they contain additional nuggets of disinformation?

The college library was in a wing perpendicular to the A&A building. At an empty table near the circulation desk, I examined Davenport's résumé skeptically. His cover letter date was April 27, 1994. It didn't appear suspicious. He had arranged for two letters of recommendation from Australia, written on University of Adelaide letterhead. Neither was from his PhD supervisor. In his cover letter, Davenport had explained that the supervisor had recently died.

Both referees had testified *ad nauseum* about Davenport's brilliance and unique perspective and had predicted the stellar career that was his for the asking. They would be pleased to hire him themselves should they have a suitable opening.

Yet he ended up in Halstead.

Both letters were larded with generic superlatives but short on details. They mentioned Davenport's proposed dissertation research on rituals but not any of the articles he had bragged about publishing as a student. And they didn't comment on the completion of his PhD or the quality of his defence.

His application included a photocopy of a letter from the VP Academic in Adelaide certifying the completion of his doctorate. The coloured letterhead and ink signature on the original had made it appear genuine.

The detailed CV of his scholarship listed the titles of the articles he'd published, the journals in which they appeared, and the specific issue numbers and dates. It was time to hit the references section of the library.

Davenport's application file included three reprints of his articles, two from *Anthropology Forum* and one from the *International Journal of Ritual Studies.* The college library subscribed to neither. The reprints were bound in glossy journal covers and appeared to be above-board.

Anthropology Abstracts summarized articles published in the field. I found only the one publication Davenport had copies of in his briefcase. Perhaps his articles hadn't been abstracted because of the limited number of scholars in his sub-specialty.

Ulrich's Periodicals Directory answered that question. In many cases, his purported articles cited non-existent journals, or ones with only a slight variation in name from an actual one. When the journal was genuine, the issue numbers did not exist. For instance, no volume five existed for publications appearing quarterly.

I couldn't tell whether any of the CV entries were authentic, but there were so many that were false that the academic dishonesty was astounding. My opinion of Davenport was taking an about face.

Nothing about him now seemed real. I wondered whether his identity was counterfeit along with that faint lilt he described as Australian.

What was equally disturbing was the depth of our gullibility. We had accepted his CV *prima facie*, for reasons of convenience and because he came across as extraordinarily superior to other applicants.

If Xavier were to ask again whose name came immediately to my tongue, it would be Barry Davenport's. But I couldn't connect his scholarly pretensions with Melody's disappearance.

Beyond that, who was Davenport? Why had he buried himself in Nova Scotia, and how had he managed the pretense so successfully?

I wanted to confront Davenport with my findings and witness his egoistic self wither away, if that were possible. Before that, though, I had to share my findings.

Back on the second floor, I called the detachment and asked for Lauren. The clerk said she had left before noon but wouldn't say where she went. Next, I tried to reach Corporal Smith. He was out, too.

As a final resort, I asked for Sergeant Young, the detachment commander. He picked up his phone but didn't sound pleased to hear from me. "Wallace, you've become a nuisance."

"You'll change your mind after you hear that I've a strong suspicion about who Melody's boyfriend is. He's Barry Davenport, a colleague of mine."

The first response was a loud squeak from Young's office chair, badly in need of greasing. "You better have a lot more than a suspicion. What's the evidence that implicates this colleague in the disappearance?"

It was my turn to hesitate. "I've put together a lot of pieces of Melody's backstory, and Davenport fits neatly into them."

"That's nice. We've got a ton of physical evidence, and none of it implicates anyone other than Gould."

"Davenport could have planted it."

The groans from Young's chair grew louder. "Leave that investigation to us," he said.

"There's more. I have concrete evidence Davenport's academic credentials are forged. He may be living under a false identity. That's fraud."

"That's for us to decide. But even if you're right about his qualifications, that's a long way from implicating him in a murder. Bring in your evidence and we'll see what we shall see."

"Okay," I said slowly. "I'll do the paperwork. But I still think he's connected to Melody Lockhart."

Young had taken my revelations cavalierly. My credibility in the detachment had become as fragile as a Chinese paper cut. I haven't been able to convince anyone, not even Lauren, that there was another boyfriend.

If Melody were still alive, I'd find her at Davenport's. He had arranged his exposé interview with Slim Starr for tomorrow. I was afraid he wouldn't stick around for it. He might be gone already. I had to go now and hope I wasn't too late.

I left a message on Lauren's home answering machine about Davenport's fraud and my larger suspicions. I said I was hoping to see him this evening and asked her to meet me at his house.

It was almost half past five. I retraced my route up Trunk 11A, remembering Monday's patrol along Pitch Lake with Andy. I wished I were riding shotgun with Lauren.

Tony Thomson

22: Gerald and Darryl

When Pitch Lake Road came in sight, I made a right turn and followed the same route I had patrolled at the beginning of the week. The sun was just sinking beneath the horizon.

Facing Davenport felt compulsory. I'd have to concoct an excuse for dropping in uninvited. I wasn't sure whether to hit him first with the fraud or with Melody's disappearance. I still had gnawing doubts about the second narrative. I'd have to wing it and present my suspicions as fact. Young was right about lacking something concrete to connect her with Davenport.

Signs of habitation thinned as the wilderness crowded the rough roadbed. I navigated carefully through the spring potholes, hoping to keep my muffler attached.

A wooden mailbox shaped like a train locomotive emerged from the gloom on the right. I hit the brakes, steered out of a fishtail, and reversed back to the driveway.

G. Balsom was hand-painted on the mailbox. Gerald had built my applewood desk and was Davenport's irregular Mr. Fix-It. If anyone knew something about his comings and goings, and with whom, it would be Gerald. His panel van was parked by his work shed.

He answered my impatient knock before my knuckles had time to complain.

"Have you eaten yet?" he said. "Mildred's got a boiled dinner on the stove and there's beer in the fridge."

"Sounds good, but I'm heading to Barry Davenport's, and we'll both eat and drink too much."

"Come and join us anyway."

Gerald sat down at the kitchen table in front of his nearly-finished plate. His long-time wife, Mildred, smiled at me from her seat as I took the chair opposite Darryl, their unattached, twenty-something son and Gerald's workmate.

"I have another job I'd like you to do," I said to Gerald. "I want to pair the desk you built with a big, applewood bookcase that I can take when I move out of the rental."

"Bookcases aren't hard. I'll let Darryl finish it. It'll cost you less."

"It'll be worth more than you charge me. I haven't seen the work you did at Davenport's, but he's real proud of it. It sounds like an expensive reno."

"That was a hell of a job. His house is a hundred-fifty years old if it's a day. It looks great on the outside. Any time you pry something loose and see what it's hidin', you find nothin' but a rat's maze."

"Well, I won't go looking. I'm heading there for some bachelor company. He's gone without a girlfriend since June left."

"That's what you think. When I go back for another job, I never find the same woman."

"And sometimes you see a lot more," Daryl said. "Last Sunday—"

"Leave your dishes on the table when you're done," his mother interrupted. "I'm going for a smoke and to watch my show."

"Darryl, you've got me curious," I said, when Mildred was out of the room. "What did you see that drove your mom out of the kitchen?"

He was dying to spill. "I was comin' back from checkin' my snare line. I got three beauties and Barry'll buy some rabbits if they're still alive when you find 'em. He's got that big guard dog that raises hell when anybody comes close. But I got a way with dogs and been there plenty of times. So, it greets me, all tame like, and doesn't make a peep. I walk up on the deck. That's when I seen her."

"Seen who?"

"I don't know. This blonde girl's lying in the sunroom on one of them long chairs with nothing on. I mean totally. It made my week!"

"Pretty cool, Darryl. What did she do?"

"Not a thing! She looked out of it."

"Then what?" I said.

"Barry paid a lot for the rabbits. So I go back out and she's still lying there."

"She hadn't moved?"

"Nope. Like she didn't care."

"Barry didn't mind?"

"He told me to keep quiet about it. But I heard him yellin' when I was goin' down the driveway. He was pissed at his dog."

"I'll be sure to honk my horn when I pull into his driveway."

"No need," Gerald said. "That dog'll let everybody on both sides of the lake know." I wondered how many times his father had shared vicariously in the vision of Darryl's encounter.

"Call me with the dimensions for that bookcase," Gerald said, seeing me out.

"Thanks for everything. Keep that beer cold for next time."

I turned around in the Balsoms' driveway and continued toward the western end of the road. I felt sure that had been Melody at Davenport's. She might still be there.

I passed the "Private Property! No hunting!" sign near Davenport's driveway and switched off my headlights. I parked short of his driveway and walked through the screen of spruce trees, into the open field leading to his house.

A tangled heap of metal appeared in silhouette near the lake where his shed had been. The blue moon hadn't risen in the partly-cloudy sky.

I listened carefully for the watchdog's first snarl. The only sounds were my sneakers crunching on the gravel. Light filtered through the blinds at the back of Davenport's lake-facing house. His Land Rover was parked next to the house. My career in breaking and entering wouldn't continue tonight.

Still no barking.

I turned the corner and approached the cedar deck in front of the house. The forest crowded it on the right. Between stands of bare hackmatack, I saw the opening that led to a two-rut trail leading into the bush. The rough track turned to the right a few metres in, following the curve of the lake. It was the only route to the north side of Pitch Lake.

I found the dog lying under the cedar deck. I could only see its hindquarters: no marks showed.

I climbed the two stairs to the deck, shivering in the twilight and at the evil omen underneath it. The collection of gas cans lined in front of the sunroom window could fuel a car race.

I trod cautiously on the cedar planks. But before I could knock on the door, it suddenly opened, jamming my elbow hard into my gut.

I looked squarely into the business end of a rifle.

23: Shadow of doubt

The .303 looked like a bazooka. Davenport lowered the rifle and rested it in the crook of his arm, like he was on a hunting expedition and hadn't found worthwhile game.

"I might have known it would be you," he said. "Where's your car? You didn't walk all the way down this lonely road."

His tone was neutral rather than false friendly. He must have checked out the back window, thinking the cops were onto him. Considering the message I'd left for Lauren, that might not be wrong.

He stepped aside and beckoned with his rifle for me to enter. I focused on the immediacy of the moment.

Davenport followed me in. I remembered the open concept space from the time Mary and I had visited. A backpack and bulging army-style duffel bag lay in the nook by the dining table. If he were planning to leave tonight, he had packed lightly.

A map or chart lay on the dining room table with what appeared to be an airline ticket. I looked over at the small nook off the kitchen where his expensive-looking ham radio was housed.

He prodded me in the back with his rifle, directing me towards the stone-faced fireplace on the rear wall. A blaze sizzled between the narrow mantle and the wide, concrete hearth.

Following instructions, I sat on one of the two stuffed chairs angled towards the fire. Davenport leaned his rifle against the wall on the left of the fireplace and sat in the other.

"I doubt you'd accept a drink," he said. "And I need to think clearly."

His accent seemed thicker, more authentic. Tilting his head slightly to the right, he stole a glance at the mantle clock, then relaxed in his chair. Both of us stared into the blazing fire.

"It's not a social visit," I said.

"Neither was my greeting. I'm curious what you think you're doing."

"I know you're taking a permanent leave of absence to avoid being fired. And you're lying about your part in Melody Lockhart's disappearance."

"What you think or believe isn't important."

"It's what we think."

"We, meaning the police."

"I let them know where I was going and why."

"You looked like you had a monkey up your sleeve. But you're the one who's lying. You've come here all on your lonesome," Barry said smugly. "The police are no worry of mine."

A log slipped from the burning stack, flinging embers into the metal screen.

"No one's gets immunity for murder."

"You're making some monumental leaps of faith, if I can use that incorrect phrase. But you're right about my evening's plans." He shrugged. "I have to admit, you surprise me."

"Would it surprise you that I know your so-called manuscript and CV are as fake as that Rolex you flash around?"

"You have such a minuscule imagination. That wasn't my real career. It's not hard for someone like me to stand out when I'm surrounded by pea heads. Any time academics sneeze, they put it on their resumé. My credentials were impeccable."

"Your manufactured ones. I doubt you arranged the fraud by yourself."

"That snout is getting you into trouble," he said, with a hint of annoyance.

"I also know your identity is bogus."

Davenport stood from his chair more quickly than I expected and, for the first time, looked me hard in the eyes. He grasped the iron poker lying on the hearth. Opening the screen, he gave the fire a few nasty strokes, then placed a couple of logs carelessly on top. He checked the clock before resuming his seat, still looking comfortable.

"Which one?" he said.

"One what? Identities? Victims? Escape plans? You won't get away. I told Sergeant Young everything I know about you."

"Hummn." He said, mockingly. "So what?"

"Meaning you don't plan to be around to worry about it?"

"Something like that. Once a loose end wiggles free, things unravel quickly. The faster you jump, the cleaner the break."

"There's nothing clean about this one. What did you do to Melody?"

"You're such a *dummkopf*. The idiocy isn't what you believe to be true with all capitals. It's thinking you, of all people, can waltz in here, apply a truth poultice, and I'll say what you want to hear. That cliché only happens in the trashy books you read."

"What do you have to lose?" I said.

"Interesting question. Now I'm thinking what I might have to gain. You're going to do me a big favour."

"Not if I can help it."

"You can't."

I let that sink in for a few seconds, thinking of the gas cans on the deck. "You'll do the same favour for me you did for your shed."

"That fire turned into the loose thread I mentioned."

"No wonder. It was your arson."

"That nosy hack reporter wanted it to be arson. He showed up, poking his Cyrano around. He was hard to get rid of."

"Starr wanted your personal story. You'll have to wire it to him. The book version could make his career. When he comes for the interview, he'll find nothing but ashes."

"Don't be too sure of that. Maybe they'll find my remains."

The image of a buck's head and antlers flashed before me.

"You mean a substitute's—mine. That'll buy some time, but burnt corpses can be identified."

"What makes you think there'll be any teeth? That would be careless."

Better to keep him talking. "You set fire to the shed to destroy the murder evidence."

"Melody again. You're like a broken record. The cops have the guilty bastard."

"I told the cops Gould wasn't her lover. You were. They're looking for you."

"Interesting. The cops think their suspect was also her lover."

"Melody became a liability when she figured out who you were. That's why you killed her. Not in anger, deliberately. It was probably Sunday night. A witness saw her here with you that day. What did you do, keep her drugged? Strangle her? Throw her body in that big freezer you have in the back room? Drag her down to your butchering shed?"

"I've got to hand it to you, Ian. You have more imagination than your tiny head suggests. But you're off track. The baboon you want is in custody, as I've said."

"I don't buy this pointing the finger at somebody else."

"You don't want to hear the truth."

"I hear you and assume the opposite of what you say," I said.

Davenport looked at the mantle clock again. This time he shifted forward in his seat. I wondered what time his flight was leaving.

"Face this truth. You're dying to hear me talk about the Lockhart girl. You envy the way women are turned on by me. I have what you only wish you had."

"I've got lines I won't cross."

"You can't cross, you mean. You even envy that bloody toady Campbell."

"What about Melody have I been missing?"

"Melody wasn't just easy pickings, she was fun, for a while. She came to me all broken-hearted after that Brit had her. It didn't take long for her to become a creature of my making and, I admit, hers. Soon, she was bringing exciting ideas to me."

"What soured it for you?"

"Simply, that hick father of hers, her real one."

"How does he fit in?"

Davenport glanced at the clock, crossed one knee over the other, and looked at me appraisingly.

"Melody found out he existed from her real mother. She became obsessed with meeting him. I couldn't talk her out of it."

"Doesn't that make sense after she learned her past was a lie?"

Davenport hesitated again and adjusted his pose. "Last weekend, she told me what happened. She went to meet him. After his absurd pity story, Melody told him about us and said she wanted to make it public. We were in love, weren't we?"

"So? It wouldn't be the first time a mucky affair like yours surfaces."

"He had a conniption fit and left. She called me and I drove her up here for the weekend. I'd never heard so much anger from her. Such spirit. I took her back to her room Sunday night. I haven't seen her since."

I looked at the flames reflecting off Davenport face, astonished to feel the first flicker of doubt since I'd left the valley floor. He gave me a crooked smile and added wood to the fire, lightening the gloom.

"Melody's clever," he said. "And I discovered why. You know it, too."

"Because she thinks the way you do?"

"Don't be a donkey's ass. It's racial."

"What?" I said, puzzled.

"I spied on her in the library when she met that Kaffir father of hers."

Davenport glanced briefly at me knowing what his expletive had revealed. Only a South African would use that variant of the N-word.

Then he continued as if nothing had changed. "His black hair and dark skin gives it away. Melody is mixed race. She's got the instincts of the coloured and the intellect of the Caucasian. It's a dangerous combination."

"There's got to be more behind killing her than your Afrikaner racial prejudice. She spent time here with you. What did she learn about your past? Your identity? Maybe your politics? She became a threat."

"My politics! You make it sound so bloody constitutional. What a country this is. It's war in South Africa. When that sell-out Botha surrendered to the Blacks, he hamstrung the Civil Defence. We had to take things into our own hands. Assassinating Hani should have been the beginning."

"Hani?"

"The communist. That terrorist ex-con should have been next."

"Mandela."

"Not everyone gets their just desserts."

"Obviously. But Mandela's working on reconciliation. He wants truth, not revenge."

"There'll be no reconciliation for white families, massacred or driven out of their own country. Civilization is being destroyed in South Africa. Five years of Black rule and we're becoming a third-world country. You wait till that happens here. Guilt-ridden Kaffir-lovers like you will feel so guilty, you'll sell out your birthright. Then the tail will make the elephant tremble."

"You could go home."

"Not a chance. There's a price on my head. They put me in Nova Scotia because no one's ever heard of it. I've visited some of my other haunts. They're starting to feel safe again."

"*They* put you here?"

"It's a helluva lot bigger than you can imagine."

"Now I'm an inconvenience, like Melody was."

"Ach, man! You've got it."

Davenport glanced at me and narrowed his eyes. I looked to his left at the rifle leaning against the wall near the fireplace. Davenport was becoming increasingly agitated. He rose and stabbed the fire with the poker, then lay it on the mantle. A thin wisp of smoke trailed from the red-hot end, like it was wafting a prayer to heaven. I didn't like my chances.

Davenport remained standing. "Church is out."

Tony Thomson

24: Pick and roll

Davenport looked straight at me with dull, dead-man's eyes. He flexed his fingers and began moving behind me.

With all the blood I could summon, I pushed off from my chair. My shoulder rammed him like I was butting into a heavy pick, and I pushed my fist hard into his solar plexus. It felt like I'd hit an offensive tackle.

He reached back for the rifle while I rolled towards the fireplace. I snatched up the poker with both hands and swung hard for his temple as he was bringing the .303 around.

He jerked away. The blow landed on his right carotid. He fell to his knees, his hands on the floor, his right hand still clutching his rifle.

I swung down the poker violently and crushed his fingers between my weapon and his. I heard a crack and a grunt.

He grabbed the poker forcefully with his left fist and tugged it. My grasp loosened. He rose slowly, fumbling with his other hand to align the rifle.

Davenport pulled hard on the poker. I let go suddenly. When he stumbled backwards, I made a fast break towards the door, bolted through, and pivoted left.

A bullet hit the frame beside my head, sending splinters flying. I heard the rapid bolt action. His second shot went harmlessly toward the blue moon that had risen above the lake.

The railing needed only a simple vault to clear. I sprinted toward the opening of the ATV trail, close to the deck.

Another shot ripped into the bordering hackmatack as I made it through the first curve and into the straight stretch.

My run was more stumble than speed. The ruts were icy, the wet muck dry and frozen. Cold air was settling. Darkness loomed far ahead where the trail veered to the right, following the lake. Davenport was doubly advantaged. He was armed and knew the terrain.

"There's no fukken place to run," he yelled.

I looked back but couldn't see him.

He'd have a clear line of sight before I reached the second curve. And a steadier grip on the trigger.

Dense brush lined the trail. It thinned irregularly beyond the fringe. When I spotted a small opening, I rushed through the brambles towards the darker, tangled forest. Davenport still wasn't visible. I planned to cut through to the logging road and find my car.

A little illumination penetrated the canopy. I could avoid the large, shadowy trunks but not the tree roots that spread along the surface of the shallow soil. They took turns catching my foot. Hardwood trunks, snapped off at their weakest points, hindered my progress. Rocks larger than basketballs littered the ground.

I fell more than once. My knees and hands took the most damage. Every branch and root I cracked sounded like another gunshot.

Checking back, I made out a light bobbing along the trail. Davenport had found his deer-jacking flashlight.

I froze momentarily when it cut through the branches in my direction. It was mostly pointed ahead and down.

Would he expect me to run like a startled deer? Or freeze like a startled rabbit? Either way, I'd be betrayed by sound.

I stopped and peered around, squinting my eyes. A vertical snarl of roots and soil showed where a few large spruce trees lay on the ground. The largest of them appeared to offer the most protection.

Looking beyond it, I made out the horizontal remains of another spruce. It was suspended slightly above the forest floor, supported by its fallen mates. It would do.

Crawling past its lower branches, I reached the dense foliage at its crown. I wormed my way in until I was surrounded by the tangle and burrowed as deeply as I could into the moss and lichen. My taste for black and dark blue clothing offered a semblance of camouflage.

I took several deep breaths. My pulse rate slowed. I wished it were pitch dark.

The flashlight beam revealed that Davenport was near where I had gone into the bush.

"Good thing you have big boots, Wallace. I thought you'd try for your car."

I heard Davenport push through the snow and brush into the forest. His light glowed around in a wide arc. He stood still, listening for the scurrying creature he was hunting.

"Holed up like a frightened rabbit. You can't have gotten far."

Flashes of light showed he was moving away from my refuge, more silently than I thought possible. Judging from the waning light penetrating my hiding place, clouds were scudding across the full moon.

The woods were otherwise soundless. Where was the mournful cry of a coyote or the warning call of a loon?

The thunk of a car's trunk slamming shut carried across the lake until it found me in the woods.

Davenport's painstaking search was getting closer. I buried my neck in my coat. My hands clawed into the ground, seeking a rock worthy of David.

Twigs snapped. His flashlight beam flitted about.

"This looks promising," Davenport said. He was nearby. I hoped he'd found the large, fallen spruce.

Time passed slowly, achingly.

"You're not going anywhere without my help," he said into the darkness. His light flashed angrily here and there.

"Goddammit, you're wasting too much of my time."

His boots closed in on my temporary sanctuary. Light began scanning from its uprooted bottom. I turned my face slowly away, toward invisibility.

The light slid along the tree trunk. My muscles tensed. My eyes closed. I held my breath. Hopeless last-second heroics flashed through my mind.

Wedged in, I had no way to spring into anything. Not even when the double ratchet of the rifle readied another bullet. My haven would become my tomb.

Time felt interminable. You can feel death before the bullet hits, like a prisoner on the gallows with a rope around his neck waiting to hear the trap door open.

Davenport fired his cannon. Knowing it was coming didn't prevent my startle reaction.

The bullet smashed into the tree trunk inches below my tucked-in feet.

"I don't have time to finish this!" Davenport shouted, almost as loud as the shot. "Remember what I told you!"

He stalked noisily towards the trail, his boots crunching the frozen mud.

I waited for silence, then crawled out from my refuge, shivering violently. My cuts and bruises throbbed, like the pain of being reborn.

I struggled to free myself from the tree branches and tried to regain my bearings. Knowing the direction of the trail, I moved cautiously in the opposite way, towards the logging road, antenna finely tuned to limit bodily damage. Finding that road meant going back towards Davenport.

The rumble of an explosion from the direction of the house shook the forest. Flames rose rapidly, propelled by Davenport's accelerants.

Beneath the roar of the conflagration, I heard a two-stroke engine cough to life. Headlights illuminated the trail. Davenport was leaving the scene. His route would take him to the other side of the lake. He must have stashed a car on the North Branch Road.

The growling of the engine advanced a short distance into the forest, then sat idling. The woods in that direction burst into flames. I couldn't go back the way I had come. His four-wheeler growled around the second curve, then slowly faded as it headed north.

Behind me, a gas tank erupted, followed by a second—my soon-to-be blackened Accord.

The flames jumped to the treetops. I reached the logging road and found it was strictly no exit. The fire had spread to either side.

I pushed through more bush on a circuitous route. Navigation through the dense, new growth was a nightmare. The branches clawed at me like arthritic fingers and slashed my face. Smoke wafted above the trees, obscuring the moonlight.

The first wail sounded faintly in the distance from the Pitch Lake Volunteer Fire Department. I was going in the wrong direction. I veered toward the call of the siren.

The woods grew increasingly dense as I pushed my way east, the terrain soggy and difficult. I stumbled upon a spring stream trickling north to the lake, and used it as an uncomfortable pathway. The new-growth alders on either side met above the stream bed, enclosing it with a foreboding canopy. *Shouldn't this be over now, with the underdog emerging triumphant?*

The wail of a nearby fire truck suddenly cut off. I stumbled onto the South Branch Road, near Davenport's *No Hunting* sign.

The fire tanker sprayed my car with foam and aimed streams of water toward the woods around it, which were spewing heavy smoke and steam. The tanker had only a limited supply of water. The nearest fire hydrant was down in Halstead. Every engine from the county would be converging on the forest fire, and pumpers would soon be queuing along the lake to refill their tanks.

The flames won the first skirmish. The tanker quickly went into reverse, heading for a refill. It was going to be a long night for the crew, even if reinforcements were on the way.

Tony Thomson

The firetruck stopped abruptly near the spot where I stood transfixed and totally bushed on the edge of the road. A firefighter jumped from the rear. He looked at me as if I were the culprit behind the chaos.

25: Round one

The volunteer firefighter took a blanket from a side compartment of the truck and placed it over my shoulders, then led me along the road away from the fire to where I could sit on a stump. The truck resumed backing down the road in search of a clearing close enough to the lake for reverse pumping.

"You look like hell," he said.

"That good?"

"What's your name?"

"Wallace. Ian."

"It that your house?"

"It belongs to Barry Davenport, but he doesn't exist."

"Is anybody still inside?"

"Nah. He took off. Try the airport. Or look for a submarine off the coast."

"Okay," he said, drawing out the word. "An ambulance is on its way, and the police." He emphasized 'police.'

"I should have waited for Lauren. He was lying to me. Nothing else makes sense."

"You're telling me."

Judging from the number of sirens in the distance, the fire had started alarms all over the county. I pictured them all trying to get into the narrow road at the same time.

One siren belonged to an RCMP cruiser. I hoped it was Lauren's.

Another fire truck arrived. Two teams carried heavy pumps down to the lake and were soon spraying the woods near the shore. Saving the house was a hopeless cause. Or my car.

An ambulance and police cruiser parked down the road in a space wide enough to allow vehicles to pass. Two paramedics jumped out and came over to me, accompanied by an RCMP constable. He was a greenhorn I didn't recognize, likely new to Halstead. He looked at the scene with wide eyes.

The firefighter who had helped me followed the medics as they half carried me to the ambulance. The constable stood with him outside the ambulance door.

The paramedics began a triage, first examining the cuts on my head. After the evening I'd brought upon myself, it needed examining.

The cop watched me carefully as he spoke with the firefighter. "Who's he?"

"His name is Ian Wallace. He came out of the woods, near that burning car down the road. I think he may have started the fire. He says nobody's still inside, but I wouldn't take his word for it. He's not making much sense."

"Been drinking?" the cop said. He sounded excited.

"No sign of alcohol."

The paramedics completed their assessment and lay me on the stretcher. "You'll need some stitches on your right hand and both knees. Maybe on your lip. You've got some wood splinters in your left cheek. Nothing looks broken, mostly just nasty scratches and cuts. And no burns."

"Don't give him anything for pain," the cop said. "I need to talk to him."

I looked at his name tag: Reginald Swinimer.

"He's exhausted and in shock," the female paramedic said. "We're taking him to emergency. If you're arresting him, you'll have to come along."

The cop frowned and peered closely at me. "I'm doing both," he said.

He ratcheted one handcuff to my right wrist and closed the cuff around a bar of the stretcher. He didn't ask if I understood I was under arrest. He stood next to the stretcher, keeping me under close surveillance, as if I were about to propel the gurney out the back and roll away.

The ambulance made a tight turn and reversed direction towards the highway.

I wanted to close my eyes and sleep, but I had to start making sense.

"The fire was started by Barry Davenport," I said to the cop. "It's his house. He's a suspect in the murder of Melody Lockhart and he's probably heading to the Halifax International Airport. Call the airport detachment. Have them detain him for questioning. Barry Davenport."

"I'll do that."

He called dispatch. "Swinamer, en route to the Halstead Hospital with a suspect, under suspicion of causing the fire at Pitch Lake. 10-5 the information to Corporal King, Halstead detachment. No bodies yet discovered." He'd emphasized 'yet.'

"It's all a misunderstanding. If anybody's body is supposed to be found in the fire, it's mine."

"Sure it is," Swinamer said. He braced himself and started writing in his police notebook, marking the beginning of a fresh page and probably hoping the same for his budding career. His tongue protruded slightly between his teeth like a contented cat's. He'd bite it half off if someone slugged him with an uppercut. I didn't have the strength or the inclination. In my line of work, aggression was usually verbal.

"OK, Bud," he said. "Let's start with your name."

"Didn't you learn anything at Depot?" I said, vexation winning out over exhaustion. "That firefighter who fingered me gave you my name. Ian Wallace."

He narrowed his eyes but didn't respond other than by laboriously writing in his notebook while the ambulance bumped along the gravel road.

"Am I under arrest?"

"I don't hand out bracelets to everyone."

"Did they suspend the rule about giving a police warning over-night?"

"I did that. You forgot."

He was growing on me. "Look Reg, we're wasting time here. I have to talk to Sergeant Young or one of the corporals. It's urgent."

"Just relax. You'll get your day in court."

"You're new here. I'm a criminologist at the Halstead College. Constable Martin and I have been working on the Lockhart disappearance. That's why I'm here."

"She nailed that file down pretty quick," he said, somewhat reluctantly.

"Maybe you'll get lucky with this case. There are major loose ends and you're right in the middle of them. The guy who started the fire is the key to it, and it wasn't me. He's slipping away as we speak. You've got a great career ahead of you, Reg, but not if you let this one slide through your fingers."

I'd aimed for his tender, self-interest belt. He looked like he wasn't sure whether it landed above or below.

"For the record, I don't believe you. But I need to be sure."

Swinamer called dispatch and said he had a 10-14 information he wanted passed along to Corporal King, the Number Two in the detachment. He slept with the procedural Manual.

"I've got an Ian Wallace here in connection with the 10-95," Swinimer radioed. "He claims to have information about the Lockhart file."

King picked up. "Wallace. What information."

"It sounds complicated." I admired Reg's quick thinking.

"It would be. Where are you?"

"We're 10-17 to the hospital. Wallace needs medical treatment. Our 26 is about 15 minutes."

"How serious is it?"

"Just superficial."

"Okay," King said, not sounding relieved. "I'll meet you at Emerge. After they finish with him, it'll be my turn."

King signed off. I had something to look forward to.

"10-4," Swinamer said. Fortunately, the rookie had run out of 10-codes.

Once we made the turn onto Trunk 11-A, the ambulance siren began to howl. I lay uncomfortably on the flat bed wondering why Lauren hadn't come.

The paramedics wheeled me into Emerge, followed by my conspicuous police escort. Reg left the cuffs attached to my wrist and the stretcher, waiting for King to arrive. He had dithered about taking them off, probably trying to remember what the Big Book had said about cases precisely like mine.

After the nurse examined me, it was the doctor's turn. When she finished, she said, "The lip's still bleeding. The cuts on the knee are deep, but they don't bleed much. You'll need stitches on some of the cuts."

She took out a kit for some quick suturing and some surgical-quality alcohol. It looked good enough to drink until she began to swab my cuts. I wanted to numb my aches, both moral and physical, not aggravate them.

The doctor gave me some pain meds and a prescription. With Reg in tow, the nurse wheeled me out of Emerge. I appreciated the ride until I realized our destination was a room occupied by Corporal King.

"Ian Wallace," he said. "What have you been up to tonight?"

"Nice to see you, too. Right now I can only give you the *Reader's Digest* version." And so I did.

King didn't show any visible reaction. "I hate *Reader's Digest*, except for the jokes," he said. "I hope this isn't one of them."

King reluctantly gave the Airport detachment a one-sentence version giving them Davenport's name as a person of interest and requesting that he be informed if he shows up for a flight. He looked at me as if he were deciding what to do next.

"You look like shit, Wallace," King said.

Was shit an improvement over hell?

"Somebody's put you through the wringer. I'll drive you home. Your meds will wear off in the morning. I'll swing by at eight and bring you in. Sergeant Young will want to hear all of your tall tale. Whatever was going on, it looks like you were in way over your head."

Young Swinimer had suspected me of arson. I hoped Young would know better, although he'd play it by the book. Round two of my ordeal would start tomorrow.

My lonely bed had never felt so good. Not counting catnaps during the TV news, I hadn't fallen asleep this quickly for a long time.

I wasn't sure how much time had passed or how long the phone had been ringing when I recognized it had something to do with me. Long enough to break through my pain-killer haze. It might be important.

"Hey," I said into the phone.

I heard Lauren's worried voice. "Thank God you're finally home."

"Hi. Such a nice voice to hear."

"I just found out what happened. What the hell did you think you were doing? Why didn't you wait for me? Are you all right?"

"Sure, if you don't count the absurdity of survival."

"I'm coming right over. You sound really groggy. You must have been sleeping."

"You didn't come," I said.

"I went to Annapolis County to check into the Dennis case. When I got back to the detachment, King and I were alone. I heard about the big fire on the South Mountain, but had no idea it had anything to do with us. King kept me in the dark about what was going on. Concentrate, Ian."

"I am concentration," I said, fuzzily aware that that didn't sound right.

"Get up and get a drink of water."

"Okay. I think it will hurt," I complained.

The cold water on my face helped me open my eyes. I hoped the vodka in my glass would soon help them close again.

"That took a while. I wondered if you'd passed out."

"Not nyet."

"Listen. I want to say I've felt so bad about letting you walk home alone. I was pretty worked up and I'm sorry about what I said."

"No worries."

"Something important came up last night in the detachment I need to tell you about."

"Oh?"

"You're trailing off, Ian. I should let you sleep. We can talk tomorrow.

I'll come by early in the morning."

"My meds are kicking in." I forgot to mention some were self-prescribed.

We said a few more things before she hung up. I think they sounded nice.

26: At last

Thursday, 1 April

I expected King to come in an hour and had a lot to do, beginning with getting out of bed. The clock radio described the effects of NATO bombing in Yugoslavia. I felt too close a connection with civilians caught in the carnage, and switched to the local station.

That show's host worried about the likelihood of more arson after two suspicious fires in a week. If it had been an open-mouth show, I'd have phoned in to say the real culprit had pulled an Elvis and fled the province.

The mirror told me I'd gone a first round with a lean and hungry Muhammad Ali. But my appetite had reawakened.

Cereal with cold milk would have been simple, but a Montreal bagel with cream cheese and lox won out. *A good sign.* And lots of strong coffee.

A car stopped outside my house when I was carrying breakfast into the living room. I heard steps on the veranda. It was barely ten past seven. I checked to make sure I'd gotten dressed.

Somebody knocked on the door. Seeing Lauren was a surprise.

"Hey. How nice of you to come over."

"I told you last night I was coming over."

"Oh? That was awfully nice."

"You sound hung over. You invited me to spend the night."

"Why didn't you?"

"You were ready to pass out. Your snoring would have been annoying."

"I'll have to work on that."

"I was really worried about you. But you sounded your normal self last night, minus the pain-killers, of course."

"Can you stay for a while?"

"I'm sorry, not long. Young told me to coordinate the search, not that it needs supervision. I told dispatch I was on my way to Pitch Lake. Want to help us scour the woods? You're the expert."

"King's picking me up at eight. My needlepoint knees hurt like hell. Don't ask me to kneel."

"I planned to say you look worse than you sound. Now I'm not so sure."

Lauren's eyes began to devour my breakfast.

"I'll make one for you: a Lauren Bagel," I said.

"Not funny."

I tried to stifle my hobble while she followed me into the kitchen and sat at the table. "Did you find out anything useful in Annapolis Royal?"

"The town cops opened a file but didn't do much. Bridget Dennis is an aboriginal from Bear River. No one from the area would talk with them."

"Cops have a fragile relationship with any of those communities."

"A member from Bridgetown began investigating at the Lawrencetown college. He figures she's somewhere east of Shag Harbour with her boyfriend. That file was hit by a polar vortex."

"I've got news about Davenport," I said. "That's not his real identity, and I found out he and Melody were having an affair. I believe he killed her. I told Young all about him, but he wasn't impressed."

"That makes sense. Something puzzling happened after I got back to the detachment last night. Young was in his office with the door closed. He only does that when he's on a private phone call. Then, he opened it, saw me, and slammed it shut, like he does when he's pissed off at someone."

"His idea of effective communication."

"The phone call must have been from someone higher up. The next thing, he tells King to come in. They spend about ten minutes. Then Young summons me into his office—and that's not too strong a word. He orders me to lay off Davenport and make sure you do, too. 'Concentrate on Gould,' he said."

"When was that?"

"Not long before the alarm came in about the fire. Maybe Davenport's in Witness Protection? No one in the detachment would be told about it except Young."

"That sounds much too innocent for the man who tried to kill me."

Lauren looked at me with consternation, taking in the implications of what I'd just said. "Witness Protection would simply have assigned him a new identity and moved him along."

"I'd say he had a specialized military career, something like Black Ops...or White Ops, since he's South African. If he was a witness, it was to mayhem he created. Some treacherous things went down while Apartheid was collapsing, and he was deeply involved in them. I'd sure like to know what Melody found out about his past."

"And you went to see this man without me?"

"Going there was a 'now or never'. He was getting ready to pull out. I figured he and Melody had a fight and she ended up dead. Until I looked deep into his eyes. The intent I saw told me her death wasn't a simple case of manslaughter. It was a good thing I didn't wait for you."

"How can you say that?" Her tone was accusatory.

"Davenport was in a killing mood. He'd already killed his dog. Your presence would have been threatening. We'd have walked into a war zone. When I showed up alone, he saw me as a lightweight. And he had some time to kill, so to speak, before his flight."

"I can't get over thinking what might have happened to you. To us." I saw dew in her eyes.

She took a first bite of her triple-cooked dough. Some of the generous dollop of cream cheese squeezed off the edge.

"I'm sorry. I was being reckless."

We tucked into our morning fare. Cream cheese and fish have always sounded like an unlikely, even unappetizing combination. Except smoked salmon isn't just fish. My tongue pushed the ingredients around in my mouth, teasing my taste buds, until the distinct flavours gradually merged, combining into a unique savoury sensation.

We ate slowly and tentatively at first, then enthusiastically, sharing the experience with appreciative murmurs. Our eye talk had its own auditory range. We swallowed our last bites simultaneously.

"I wish we had strawberries and cream for dessert," I said thickly.

"And champagne," Lauren added to the imaginary feast, a less bubbly tone animating her speech. "I guess I better get to the lake."

We held hands on the way to the foyer, where we shared an intimate kiss. The stitches in my lip stung pleasantly and Lauren didn't seem to mind the stiff threads.

I was stirred by feelings too long dormant. Fear of disappointing her went fleetingly through my mind. Tongues in cheeks, our embrace flamed into passion.

An impediment intervened.

"Ow!" I groaned, as I encountered her work garb.

"Sorry."

Lauren leaned back, struggling to tear off her bullet-proof vest and escape from her heavy belt and holster. The weapons fell on the hardwood floor with a loud thud. Nothing fired prematurely. That augured well.

I reached behind her head and pulled off the tie holding her braid in place. I slowly unravelled the strands, releasing cascades of silky hair.

I grabbed her hand and led her through the bedroom door as she pulled at the buttons on her shirt and hurried out of her Styrke pants, the stripes crumpling on the floor. Tossing my t-shirt aside, I fumbled to undo her bra.

"Out of practice," I said.

I yanked my belt loose, dropped my pants, and flung down the belt where it wound around Lauren's brassiere. We imitated the pair by collapsing on the bed entwined.

I stroked her silken skin with my hands and body as we moved in time together.

Lauren took my head into her hands. I squeezed her tightly. My mind went to a dimension of its own, drifting into thoughtlessness, lost in touch.

With our final movement, the headboard thumped on the gyprock. We lay sweating on the bed.

"Oh my God!" Lauren exclaimed a moment later, suddenly bolting upright. "Corporal King."

"We've got fifteen minutes," I said, calmly.

Lauren disappeared into the bathroom, moaning, "I've got to clean up." I searched here and there, untangled and sorted the scattered apparel, and followed her in.

"Time for a shower." We both squeezed in for a quick one.

Lauren dressed dervishly. I calmly followed suit.

A kiss goodbye, the most gently amorous of all, and she was out the door, but not before she delivered a romantic parting line: "Next time, Ian, take off both socks."

Next time!

By the time Corporal King arrived, I'd dressed, having found a shirt that didn't advertise organized crime.

King didn't comment on my well-being and got straight to business. "We've got a serious case of arson, a missing person—the owner of the house—and you, a person of interest. Investigators are searching the rubble for a body. If they find one, you'll have a lot to answer for."

He walked behind me to the cruiser and opened the back door.

"Am I under arrest, again?"

"Not yet."

I limped into the detachment and was ushered into the same interrogation room where Gould had worked his audience so inexpertly. I thought about the psychology and time management of police interrogation. But mostly I replayed in my mind the best parts of the morning.

Young and King jack-booted in with coffee. Mine had sugar and cream. I drank it anyway. No one offered a cigarette. Neither of them went through the police warning routine or gave notice about video recording. After all, this was merely a friendly discussion in a cozy room.

Until it turned out not to be.

"Let me tell you what happened. Interrupt if you have to," I said. I'd gone over it so often in my head, it was hard to avoid providing too much detail.

Neither of them moved a muscle other than their arms and mouths and swallow reflexes, as though I was saying nothing of significance.

"Melody's recent experiences made her stronger," I said, "and she realized the potential power of her sex. She was still expecting her relationship with Davenport to evolve into something normal. He seemed like an exceptional catch." I paused. Young and King remained irritatingly deaf.

"You know a lot more about Davenport than I do, like who he really is," I said directly to Young, in a tone he couldn't avoid hearing.

"Let's say he's no longer a person of interest in this case," he said. "Please continue."

"Of course he isn't, in your mind. Davenport brought her back to Pitch Lake Thurs-day night and kept her there until he killed her. She knew too much about him. And because, in his eyes, she wasn't white."

"Do you know why he thought that?"

"Because he's a South African white supremacist?"

"Don't go bringing politics into this thing."

"Funny you should say that."

"Are these facts or are you just speculating?"

"I'm using reason to connect the facts."

"So you say. Getting back to your story, why did Davenport leave, if in fact he did?"

"He was exposed and too much of his past was coming home to roost."

"Like what?"

"Beyond the obvious, his wife disappeared four years ago."

"You're stretching this story worse than a sloppy old pair of underwear, but it pongs about the same," King said.

I ignored the interruption. "Melody was isolated at Davenport's house and under his control. She had no way to get out and, I believe, was drugged into passivity. I think Davenport killed Melody some time between Saturday afternoon, when a witness saw her alive and stupefied, and this past Monday night. The shed fire was his effort to destroy evidence."

"I can't wait for you to get into that, Wallace," King said. "I think I'm in an episode of the *Twilight Zone*. Why and how did this killing come about?"

"Underneath it all was Melody's need for independence. Coming to define Davenport as a worse patriarch than her father was the beginning of her liberation and, I'm afraid, the end of it. My guess? Her dismembered body is in the lake."

"You forgot to say, 'I imagine.' Do you know how many times you said 'think,' or 'believe,' or 'seemed'?" King demanded.

The word accountant.

Young stood and began pacing in the narrow room. "Jesus, Wallace, why should we believe you're a reliable witness? Because you've been granted some privileged position?" A little spit spurted out with the p's. "Your students trust you to tell them truths. They don't have a choice."

Young removed his jacket and placed it on the chair. He didn't sit back down. "No one else has to believe your version, least of all us."

He grabbed his empty coffee cup and left the room, leaving his jacket to resume the rant.

"Sergeant Young says you've got a serious case of tunnel vision about Davenport," King said. "You thought he was Lockhart's lover. What feelings did you have for her and about their affair?"

I was suddenly aware of King's angle on the case. I looked at him, realizing he interpreted my hesitation as falsehood.

"My feelings for Melody? Last Sunday, I hardly knew her. It's been a hell of a week and Melody's been in the centre of it, like a character in a novel who's never present but always in mind. I'm sad and angry that Davenport took her life away so brutally. To answer your real question, I didn't go to Pitch Lake intending to take out my supposed jealously on Davenport, and certainly not to kill him. We didn't even get into a heated argument. I saw him leave the scene very much alive."

"Our ongoing search for remains may come up with a different story," King said.

I couldn't suppress the moral outrage in my furious eyes. I was ready to quit and had a couple of lawyers on friendship retainers.

Young rejoined us carrying a single coffee for himself, put his jacket back on, and leaned forward in his chair, crowding King.

"Here's something we know as a fact," he said. "Last Monday, Barry

Davenport booked a first-class seat on a flight to London, scheduled to leave last night. He never showed."

"He had another way out."

Young sat back in his chair. "Look at the evidence we've got against Gould."

"That was planted and easy to find. Davenport wanted a fall guy. Gould was too obvious a candidate."

"The evidence wasn't hidden because Gould didn't have time," Young said. "Someone shot at him on Monday morning and chased him away."

"A neighbour saw a man heading away from the scene in a canoe towards Davenport's end of the lake."

Young threw up his hands in exasperation. "Can't you hear yourself, Wallace?" he said. "Everyone with property on the lake has a canoe. And three-aught-three hunting rifles are as common as pocketknives." He paused briefly. "Tell me this. Did Davenport voluntarily confess to you about killing Melody?"

I hesitated, trying to contrive some details I could live with. But I'd sound like Gould, re-winding my story to change its direction.

King added, "Even if you say he confessed, it'll just be hearsay with no one to confirm or rebut it."

Whatever I said now would come up under oath in court. My mulling was brief. I didn't have a choice. "He said I was an idiot to think I could waltz in and he'd confess, like they do in the movies. He expected me to believe his lie that Gould killed Melody."

"This is exactly what tunnel vision is," Young said, raising his voice in annoyance.

He stood and leaned over the desk. "If you'd brought these ideas to us in the first place, we'd have investigated. Maybe you wouldn't be sitting here, a rank amateur, in deep shit that you may never get out of."

"Right. And you would have dropped it faster than a Breathalyzer charge against a county judge. Davenport's capable of cold-blooded, deliberate murder. I survived an attempted one. And he had plans for my body."

"Maybe you'll get a chance to make that complaint formal," Young said. "We're done here, for now."

They walked out, locked me in, and left me to stew. I lay down on the floor, wishing I could miniaturize myself and escape under the door. I felt disbelieved, mentally battered, and threatened.

As my consciousness began to dwindle. visions of pleasure craft buffeted by a slate-grey sea seeped in until they gradually faded to black.

27: Departure

"Wallace," Young said, jarring me out of my restless slumber. He helped me up off the floor. "I've got some information for you."

"I've got some, too."

I sat on the felon's metal chair. Young closed the door and resumed his place at the table. King's chair remained vacant.

"The fire investigators didn't find any remains," he said.

"Did the search teams turn up anything?"

"Nothing so far."

I hadn't detected a shift in his attitude despite the lack of a body in the rubble. I wondered whether the suspicions he harboured about my role in the case had remained intact. "Any sign of Davenport?"

Young wiped his forehead with one hand and fumed mutely at the one-way mirror.

"Did a higher-up in intelligence sell you the protected witness yarn?" I said.

"Nobody tells me how to run my detachment. Davenport isn't a person of interest in the murder file."

It was my turn to indicate exasperation. "Are you cutting me loose?"

"One more thing. You said you had some information."

"Nothing important," I said.

"I'm not surprised."

He opened the interrogation room door and directed me through the detachment.

"Stay the hell away from this file, Wallace," he said, loud enough to be heard throughout the building.

Then, quietly, as a warning for my ears only: "And stop dragging Constable Martin down with you."

"Who's driving me home?"

"Swinamer!" Young shouted, as if the constable had become the principal target of his displeasure.

About Face

Mavis, our helpful office clerk, answered the summons. "He'll be back any minute."

Young ushered me into the foyer, muttering, "Wait here for your ride. It wouldn't look good for you to wander into traffic."

"At least the insurance companies have my back."

I had no intention of acquiescing to Young's hands-off demand. Davenport was still my target. The photos he'd removed from his office had become an eye worm for me. Not one of them had shown anything that could fly. But he'd displayed photos of a sailboat and, more tellingly, a powerful speedboat off Queensport. I had an idea how he may have gotten away. His clock-watching hadn't been about a flight he might miss. He'd been concerned about the tide tables at Queensport. Without a running tide, the boats were stranded on the mud.

I'd withheld that information from Young out of spite. He'd like to know it, but he might take his sweet time getting into gear and ignore me when he did. Lauren was up the opposite mountain at the search site. From what Young had said, it was better for her if I poked around on my own before bringing her into the picture.

If I was right about Davenport's escape, he would have pushed off late last night and be well on his way to the Bermuda triangle. I still planned to lay low when I got to Queensport. I was in no shape for an encore confrontation. Either way, I expected to have news to share with Lauren or to gloat over at Young.

When Swinamer arrived, he acquiesced to me sitting in the passenger seat of his cruiser.

"Thanks, Reg. I really need the ride."

"I'll say, but it was Young's idea."

"He's being pretty decent right now. He fed me some important info from the search site."

"No remains in the fire?"

"That, and more, but the arson is your file. I'm guessing you were in the thick of the investigation this morning."

"For sure. A woman on the North Branch Road reported her car stolen last night, a grey Chevy Cavalier. I found an abandoned four-wheeler just off the ATV track by her house."

"Did anyone notice the Cavalier on the road out?"

"No one saw it during the fire. And it's not at the airport."

"Or at any of the local airports between here and Halifax," I improvised.

"I didn't know that."

I asked Swinamer to drop me at the only car rental in town. I decided against suggesting he let Young know about our chat. Why make the junior constable's life more difficult?

He let me out at Budget Rent-a-Car. A man in an ill-fitting suit and off-kilter tie sat behind the front counter, beginning his career in casual serfdom. I rented a brown Malibu. It was closer to my deceased coupe than the compacts he'd suggested. I directed the Malibu towards Highway 361 and Queensport.

The road takes a left through the village of Tedburn, where I'd shared a home with Mary. Then it follows the footprint of the North Mountain until it veers north and ascends a V-shaped crevice to the top. It follows the rim for a few kilometres and then gradually drops towards Queensport's narrow, picturesque harbour. I pulled over on the shoulder to survey the scene I was getting into.

It was early afternoon. The tide was still coming in. The small fishing boats moored to the floating docks told a familiar tale of seasonal work supplemented by government pogey. None resembled the motorboat I remembered from Davenport's photo. I parked in the public lot near the government wharf next to a light grey Cavalier that might be the stolen car.

An offshore breeze lowered the wind chill to barely positive numbers. I tightened my jacket around my neck and scanned the wharf, looking for someone who was familiar with the comings and goings in the harbour.

A handful of men were working on their boats or hanging around. I walked towards a youngish-looking man whose nimble fingers were busily repairing the curved slats and rope webbing of an old, wooden lobster trap. It was so badly broken that a lobster could more easily get out than find its way in.

He saw me staring at his handiwork and said, "I can sell you this one if you wants it." Every summer out-of-province tourists bought scores of traps, tied them haphazardly to car roofs, and took them a long way from salt water.

"No thanks," I said. "I'm from here. That's skilled work you're doing."

"Makin' and fixin' traps gets passed down. Mostly now, we use them metal ones." He pointed to a pile of rectangular, box-shaped traps neatly stacked on the wharf. "Nobody wants them for souvenirs."

"What do they think they're going to catch in their city backyards?"

He laughed. "If it was that easy, I'd wanna do it."

"You can make a good living on the lobster boats."

"I learned everything I need right here on the dock. But the livin's not great. Fish companies take most of the money. Even unions don't help."

I paid him twenty dollars for the lobster trap. "I'll pick it up before I head out. Maybe you can help me. Can you point out someone who's lived here a long time and knows the harbour and the boats?"

"My grandfather. There's him," he said, pointing to an old fisherman standing at the end of the wharf. He was looking out to sea, with his hands deep in his pants pockets.

"Thanks, man. Good luck on the boats."

His grandfather turned and walked toward me with a wide, cautious stride, as if the wharf was about to begin pitching and rolling. A thick, white beard flowed over the turtleneck of his beige, cable knit sweater. Heavy boots, baggy jeans, and a bright orange toque completed his outfit. He looked like a movie extra.

He closed the gap between us more rapidly than I could, as I limped along on alternate legs. A friendly smile proved he still had some teeth.

"Look at you," he said. "Gone arse over kettle some hard."

"Oh yeah? You should see the other guy's knuckles."

"You both pie-eyed, or what?"

"No drinking, just a disagreement."

"Well, that's some stunned."

"In more ways than one."

He fell in step with me as we walked slowly along the wharf. "I came down looking to find the guy. It's time we talked it out. Barry Davenport's his name. He's got a big motorboat that he keeps moored in the harbour."

"I knows the boat. It's a beaut. Nothin' else like it around here. Buddy's none too friendly. What he done to you don't surprise me. He ain't around if you got payback in mind. That was some blue moon we had, eh? Too bad the clouds rolled in."

"Like a half-lit sun in the clear heavens. I guess you know this harbour pretty well."

"Born on the Cape but raised right here. Fished all my life. One of my boys got the license now. See them boats?" he said, indicating the small fleet in the harbour. "Every one of them got their own story. It looks like a nice, quiet village. Underneath there's bile and jealousy stretchin' way back. Nothin' to do for me now except remember it all, mend some traps, and breathe the salt air." He inhaled deeply, with satisfaction. *You get used to the smell of fish guts, oily rope, and diesel fuel.*

"You fish for lobsters?"

"In season. You lookin' to go out?"

"A mite too chilly today," I said, hunkering down in my coat.

"Yup, it's right fresh, I find."

"The speedboat's not moored. When did he take it out?"

"I saw it headin' out about ten last night. The tide was comin' in good by then. He ain't brought 'er back yet."

"Does he take it out often?"

"Nope. He put 'er back in the water just last Tuesday. When I got up near midnight to pee—got an old man's bladder—I looked out and seen he'd pushed off. I saw 'er docked when I got up for breakfast at six."

Davenport's late, deep-sea trip hit me in the gut. I could imagine only one purpose. The dive team was searching the wrong body of water. Melody had taken over my life. I pictured the culmination of her horror. She'd been swallowed beneath the Fundy tide.

"Any idea where he goes?" I said.

"Could go anywheres. That's his business, for sure."

"I'll take that boat charter when the weather's better."

"Try July," he chuckled. "You'll have to ask my son, Eugene Jr. That's he standin' in the dooryard." He pointed to the bright green, double gabled house we'd been walking toward. It was perched slightly up the hill, giving it a view over the harbour and the bay.

"That boat there's mine—his, now," he said, pointing to the family heirloom Cape Islander, anchored near the end of the harbour. It was named *Sweet Marie*, after the old man's sweetheart or his sweet tooth.

"You'll be hearing from me," I said.

I walked along the wharf and watched as the tide slowly and inexorably encroached on the pebble beach, covering more of the rocks with each wave. A heavy mist in the bay rendered the distant New Brunswick coastline invisible. Melody's body was somewhere in between, gone forever. I was as close to standing astride her grave as I could get.

A Cape Islander pushed briskly past the navigation buoy as it tolled in rhythm with the slapping swell, its irregular clang like hesitant mourning. Breakers pummelled the pilings and splashed the planking.

The biting windchill caught me by the throat. I pushed my chin down onto my neck and wrapped my arms around my chest to stave off the biting damp. No prayers surfaced from the depth of my melancholy.

Visions of Davenport's late-night trip into the bay pushed insistently into my mind. I pictured each irregular, weighted piece of flesh wrapped in clear plastic, bound tightly with meticulously knotted yellow and green fibreglass rope. I heard the splash as he plunged each of them into the water and watched them disappear through the surface, their entry instantly erased by the turbulent sea as if the person they enwrapped had never existed.

I imagined Judith Melody Lockhart, forlorn and desolate, disillusioned to her core by the cruel inhumanity of her fate. Drops of salt spray stung my face like tears shed over the absurdity of death.

The Fundy chill inside and out urged me to turn away from the perpetual grey eternity and return to life. Multi-hued houses spilled out of both sides of the steep gully. A long, thin waterfall tumbled into a tidal stream finishing its journey back to the big pond. The fishermen at their traps materialized in their distinctness. Each discrete reality restored my sense of continuity.

The lad repairing the traps watched me approach from the windward side. His handiwork was meant to be pulled back out of the water, filled with a precious living. Davenport's havoc had been dumped once and forever.

"Are you okay?" Eugene Jr. said, as people do when you obviously aren't.

"I will be. A young woman I care about went into the water offshore and won't ever be found."

"Oh." He removed his toque and looked sadly at me because there was nothing he could say or do.

He helped me carry my unwanted trap to Hertz's Malibu and tied the half-closed trunk.

The car climbed the slope back to the top of the mountain, then down the precipitous incline to the valley floor and the village of Tedburn. My mind meandered between Davenport and his ex-wife and what June might also have discovered about her dangerous husband.

June had developed a friendship of sorts with Mary. Mary had said June's quick departure fit the scenario of an abused woman trying not to be traced. A second, less benign possibility gnawed away at me.

I drove to the old homestead in Tedburn, hoping Mary was in a friendly mood. Her blue Taurus was parked in the driveway. The Dodge Ram belonging to her live-in boyfriend was not in sight.

Even after so many months, it felt odd to rap on the door.

"I'm surprised to see you," Mary said, answering my knock. "Donnie's on his way home from work."

She stood in the doorway, looking unsure what to do. "Did somebody throw you down the stairs?"

"Not recently."

"Why are you here?"

"A few years back, you received a postcard from June Davenport. If you kept it, would you mind if I had a look? I want to know exactly what she said."

"I don't remember how she put it, but her meaning's perfectly clear. I never heard from her again. The card's probably still in the desk. Why do you want to see it?"

"Davenport was having an affair with Melody Lockhart, the missing woman, and they were together last weekend. I think he killed her."

Mary nodded. "He was abusive to June, so it doesn't surprise me that it didn't stop with her."

"The card June sent might help me convince the police that Davenport should be a suspect."

"Wait inside and I'll get it."

She handed the door to me and I stepped in. I could see the antique dining room table and the captain's seat I had habitually occupied. It was Donnie's, now.

It took Mary about three minutes to find the card. "June sent it about six months after she left, so she was alive and well. Reading between the lines, you can tell why she went and didn't keep in touch."

The card was from Muscle Beach in Venice, California. It showed a trio of ripped young men fortifying the beach's reputation. It had been mailed from Santa Monica and postmarked October 3, 1994. It was written in green ink with a feminine-looking calligraphy and signed June, with a little smiley face instead of the u in her name. The brief note read:

> Dear Mary,
> I'm sorry to have left so suddenly without giving you any warning. Your friendship is important to me. After your visit and our sisterly talk on the lake shore, you know what drove me to run. I'm not in California anymore, despite the beach scenery!!! I need to find someplace safe and private to settle down. Probably won't be able to write for a while. Take care,
> *June*

"You can see she was fine," Mary said assertively. When I didn't reply, she added, "You're probably wondering whether she actually wrote it. June and I went down to the beach by ourselves. She's the only one who knew we'd talked about her awful relationship. You and Barry hung out and drank too many cocktails."

"That part about the scenic muscle boys doesn't sound like the June I remember."

"You wouldn't understand. It's exactly what rebound June would say."

I handed the card back. "Thanks, Mare."

I continued along the 361 towards Halstead. Mary's new flame didn't notice me when he drove by on his way home. Donnie wasn't snubbing me. I hardly existed in his world.

I couldn't ignore him.

Mary was right about my thinking, though. Davenport could easily have written that postcard and June might have been his first or even one more of his victims, in the full meaning of the term. Davenport and I knew that Mary and June had been deep into a sombre, personal talk. What else would they chew over other than their partner woes? Particularly June, I thought. That sisterly tidbit in the postcard meant nothing.

When I reached the Trunk One intersection in Halstead, instead of going to the college, I directed the rental car toward my refrigerator and TV, feeling confidently self-satisfied.

28: Ethics

I spent an impatient hour waiting for Lauren to get home and reading *Gone Fishin'*, a Walter Mosley I'd borrowed from the library. A good choice for character and setting. Lauren's shift ended at four. I reached her at a quarter past.

"Something's come up," I said.

"I hope you've been resting at home."

"Not exactly. I've been down to Queensport talking to some fishermen. Davenport kept a big motorboat in the harbour. It looks like he stashed the stolen Chev near the wharf and went out to sea before midnight. He hasn't come back."

"Did you tell the Sergeant?"

"Not yet."

"I'll call him. He'll alert the Coast Guard and send a member to check on the car."

"And I know why the search team hasn't found Melody's remains." I paused for effect. "They're looking in the wrong body of water."

"Go on."

"Davenport also took his boat into the bay late Tuesday night and came back before dawn. I'm certain that's when he disposed of Melody's body."

Lauren was silent for a moment. "Did anyone see him go on board, and did he carry anything with him?"

"The chap I talked to noticed the boat was gone, but that's all."

"Did you make a note of the witness's name?"

"Eugene, if that helps. He lives near the end of the harbour."

"Policing is about details."

"I like details. Let's go out this evening," I said, "and take our minds off the case. A group from the city is playing at the Knight's Inn. Some music and dancing would do us good. I'll pick you up about seven-thirty. We can grab donairs on the way."

"Okay. Let's do it."

Lauren was ready to go when she answered my knock. I was delighted to see her. This morning's emotions flushed back into my face. It had really happened. I held her hand while we walked towards the car. She opened the door for herself.

As we drove, I kept glancing at her beside me. It should have felt familiar and comfortable. Instead, she seemed dissatisfied.

"Let's try Antonio's. They claim to have a genuine east coast recipe."

Her nod reminded me of a 'whatever' shrug.

I parked in a loading zone near the small restaurant. It was a busy night at the take-out counter. We watched as the big cone of processed donair meat they claimed to be lamb slowly rotated between vertical broilers.

A server in an Antonio's apron cut thin slices of the browned meat and placed them on flatbread, adding chopped onion and tomato. He topped it with a sauce of sweetened, evaporated milk and vinegar, and rolled the wraps in tinfoil. We carried them and a couple of coffees to one of the few tables for eat-ins in a back corner.

We nibbled on our donairs and tried to prevent the sticky sauce from seeping out the bottom of the tinfoil and all over our hands.

"Something's bothering you," I said.

"Sergeant Young believes Davenport's academic fraud removes a distraction from the case against Gould. His false identity was about to be outed, so his disappearance isn't connected with the murder investigation."

"He fashions contrary facts to fit his existing theory."

"Are you any different?"

"I'm right about Davenport. That makes the difference"

"Speaking about ideas fitting facts," Lauren said, "I don't understand why Davenport didn't brag about what he was getting away with. In his eyes, you were about to die."

"It was an unusual Hawthorne effect—choosing to do what you know is unexpected."

I looked searchingly at Lauren, aware of our differing narratives.

"I can't see how I can bring your Davenport story to the prosecutor and not be laughed out the door," she said. "The Crown will proceed to trial only with a reasonable chance of success. I've built a winnable case against Gould, even without finding Melody's body."

"The Crown needs to know there's a plausible second suspect. She can decide to drop the case, regardless of what the police want."

"Everything you say about Davenport can be explained away."

"Sergeant Young will think what he wants. What matters is what we think and do about it."

"It's Young I'm concerned about," she said. "And how the other members are seeing you. They have an 'us versus them' mentality, and think you're joining 'them.'"

"Davenport tried to kill me. I take that personally. Aren't you having second thoughts about the file?" I understood ambiguity and ambivalence as well as anyone.

"I have my career to think about. Sergeant Young asked me whether I still honestly believed the charge I'd laid against Gould. If I didn't, he'd take me off the case."

"The trial will continue with or without you."

"I'm trying so hard to make decisions based on facts and evidence. If I quit the file purely on conjecture, Young will say I'm letting my emotions rule my judgment. I'll have to put in for a transfer and hope my reputation doesn't follow me."

"I don't want either to happen."

"Neither do I, but I have to choose pragmatically. The trial is a long way off. Who knows what we may find before then? Maybe Davenport, himself. If not, we'll see what happens."

"And if nothing changes?"

"I'll present my evidence. What did you do? What did you find? Simple, factual questions. They won't ask what I theorized. If you're right and Gould isn't guilty, the defence will find a reasonable doubt. You're the one who doesn't trust the system to deliver a fair verdict."

"Too often it doesn't."

We sat and sipped our coffees, which were beginning to need ice because they weren't quite cold enough. The lad from behind the counter collected the dripping tinfoil and napkins but didn't offer to refill the drinks.

"The question of ethics doesn't apply just to me," Lauren said softly.

"I'm not following. I'll be strictly factual on the stand. Since I won't be an expert witness, no one will ask my opinion, either."

"If you'd told Young during your interrogation that Davenport confessed to murder, you could have repeated it on the stand. Davenport confessed to the affair and to having a racist motive. It wouldn't be much of a stretch to believe he told you he killed her. Think of it as a narrative giving your whole truth. You want to prevent Gould from being railroaded."

"I can't believe you're saying I should have lied."

"I'm not saying you should have. But you bend the truth all the time. I want you to think about why you didn't this time."

"I had debated what to tell Young, but I didn't know what might happen. Davenport could have been arrested. If Young believed I wasn't being honest, that would be it for me."

"That's what I'm getting at. It would be *it* for your police research, sure. But your career would still be intact." Her empathetic tone only slightly softened her words.

"You're saying I chose to protect my career over Gould's best interests. I felt I didn't have a choice."

"It's bad faith to say that. Deciding what is right is never simple."

"Like truth," I said.

"The file will be resolved one way or the other, and your role in it will blow over. You were a big part of the early investigation. We make an effective team. There'll be other cases for us."

She looked in my eyes and took my hand. "Let's head out to the Knight's."

"Sure. And leave the shop talk in the car."

Cops liked drinking at the Knight's because of the dearth of prying eyes. The lounge was about half full of patrons when we arrived. They had cleared a space in front of a small stage on the wall opposite the bar for dancing. Two young men with long hair, tight jeans, and black leather vests were belting out *Four Strong Winds* through portable amplifiers that didn't improve the singing. A drummer with a shaved head and handlebar moustache completed the trio. A few couples danced self-consciously in front. The evening was young.

We sidled over to the bar. Lauren ordered a strawberry daiquiri. I wanted a Cuba libre but the bartender didn't recognize the name. I asked for a dark rum and coke with lime juice instead.

We carried them to a table located far enough from the band not to need earplugs but near enough to feel part of the action. Our drinks went down fast and easy. A server replenished them more than once.

The trio played an eclectic mix of country and western, blues, and pop —older favourites for everyone. Nothing recent, from the '90s. They gauged the mood of the crowd and tailored their choices. Before long, Lauren began to sing along to the country choruses. I got caught up by *Ain't No Sunshine*.

When the band played *Brown-eyed Girl*, I put my hand over hers and nodded at the dance floor. We elbowed our way in. Lauren surrendered to the rhythm and danced fluidly, becoming in my eyes the only person on the floor. My tender knees made me an awkward partner for anything quick, but the rum helped.

We shared a laugh over my inept twist, then stayed on the floor while the band went through a long, set-ending medley of popular dance numbers.

We stopped at the bar for new drinks to slake our thirst. Lauren suggested tequila because it contained electrolytes. We downed them. The evening was going splendidly.

"I need to freshen up," Lauren said, slurring her words just a little. I followed her towards the loos and returned to the table before she did. The crowd and the din had increased considerably. Lauren zigzagged unsteadily around the tables on the way back but seemed oblivious to her gait. Her bloodshot eyes begged for a Breathalyzer.

She sat, then leaned on the table, swished the swizzle stick in her daiquiri, and took a sip. She squinted at me with bleary eyes. "I wasn't going to say this, but all last night, I couldn't get out of my mind how close you came to losing your life. This afternoon, though, I felt angry you did that to yourself. I should have been the one going up there."

"Not the way I saw it," I said, dismayed.

"You're not giving me credit for my training and experience, like members who don't want me for a partner because they think I need protecting." She sloshed around uncomfortably in her seat.

"Geez, Lauren, I didn't mean to be sexist."

"You can't help it. Men don't get women except from a male point of view."

"I need help with that, and you're the only woman I want in my life."

"That's sweet, Ian, but it takes a lot of habit-breaking."

"I'm sorry I hurt you."

Lauren was silent for a moment. I knew this conversation would come up again. Not tonight, though.

The band settled in for its final set. Lauren leaned closer and said, "I'm sorry I'm ruining our good time."

"You can't. Everything's got to be up front between us."

"Totally. You need to take dance lessons."

"Starting now."

The prickly interlude slipped into our memory recesses as we picked up the beat. The dance floor overflowed as more couples joined in for the slow ones. We sat longer and drank less.

As closing time drew near, the band began a loud and lively version of

Hey Jude. People stopped dancing and crammed in close to the stage, swaying in unison and bellowing, over and over, *Na, na na, na na na na, na na na na, Hey Jude!*

I suggested we leave the melee and find a room. We giggled our way down the corridor with our arms wrapped around each other, not playing it cool.

A teen-aged couple with fluttering eyes and eager hands leaned against the wall further down. They looked in our direction as we found our room and put the key in the lock. They frowned disapprovingly at us as if romance had an expiry date.

Tony Thomson

29: Trials

Friday, 22 October, 2000

All that remained of Davenport in Nova Scotia were unproven theories and scars left by flailing branches. Of Melody, a bottomless sadness.

The jury in the Gould trial had reached a verdict, a year and a half after he'd been remanded on the charge of second-degree murder. I awoke early to make the cross-province trek to Bridgewater to hear the pronouncement. A judge in Halstead had changed the trial venue to the South Shore. He'd ruled that public opinion was unfavourable to the accused in Sterling County.

The trial judge had prohibited the media from reporting any details of the case to avoid contaminating jurors' opinions. I'd been barred from the courtroom pending my testimony, for the same reason. Despite the bans, information had cascaded down the courtroom steps all the way to Sterling County's informal cable network. Lauren had shared a few bits of the trial with me, strictly on the QT.

She and I had worked out a mutually satisfactory relationship status for the impending millennium. We implicitly agreed to remain monogamous, although we kept separate apartments and often slept alone. When she came over, she usually stayed the night. When I went to her place, I was gone well before breakfast. Her neighbours applied the sexual double standard to single women. That she was a Mountie heightened their vigilance. Liberal attitudes about sexuality had made slow inroads in small towns.

Our relationship felt furtive, even as the need-to-know group had swelled like a creek in hurricane season. Most people who matter had read the signs.

We understood either of us might leave the Valley when a career opportunity beckoned or Lauren got a transfer. We hoped a long-distance, separate-together life would have enough elasticity to remain intact. Or one of us could follow the other. The uncertainty bothered me more than it did Lauren. I felt settled in the Valley and wanted to hang on to my position.

Each day of the nearly two-week trial, she had driven Melody's adoptive parents, Georgina and Philip, to and from Bridgewater in her civvy car, which attracts less attention than a police cruiser. I saw her car parked outside the courtroom when I pulled up in my new coupe.

I passed through the foyer of the blatantly-functional courthouse and pictured the intricate woodwork of the heritage site it had replaced. Onlookers milled about near courtroom number one and waited for the spectacle. Many had made the trek from Sterling County.

I stepped inside, past the Sheriff's Deputy, and hovered near the back. Lauren sat near the front, quietly talking with Morgan and her husband, Paddy. Georgina and Philip sat further along the same row. Of that group, only Philip Lockhart scanned the room to find people he knew, pointing fingers as if he were a minor celebrity.

Lauren came over when she noticed me at the back. "I can't stay. I want to be with Morgan. The verdict is going to be hard on her, no matter how it goes."

"This case isn't going to tie things up for her, with Melody's body still missing."

"She wants to try reconciliation with Gould."

"That's her church talking."

"It's not a bad idea. We'll see how he responds."

"I'm glad the trial is almost over—for us, I mean. Can't wait for the weekend." We'd booked two nights at Digby Pines.

"Copy that," she said, smiling in anticipation. It doesn't take long to develop evocative relationship memes and memories.

"I feel nervous about the verdict," I admitted.

"Me too. I've never been a witness and thought a not-guilty verdict might have some claim to justice. You did that to me."

"I can't say the same, that a guilty verdict would be just."

"I know. For Morgan, a guilty verdict might be worse."

"Why so?"

"She desperately wants to believe her daughter is still alive. Guilt presumes Melody can never come home." She glanced back to the front. "I see Morgan searching for me. I want to go back."

"Dinner tonight? We can celebrate the end of this affair."

"And the persistence of ours. Make a reservation for seven-thirty. Your choice."

I watched Lauren walk back to the front. I much preferred her in civvies.

I waited petulantly for the hearing to start, scanning the courtroom. Slim Starr hadn't arrived. I wanted to hear his take on the trial. I'd given him a so-called exclusive interview last April, laying out what I knew about the con artist formerly known as Barry Davenport. He had made it obvious in his exposé that I had little actual evidence for anything except his academic fraud and the arson. Once those facts were established, I hoped my half-truths and assumptions would gain momentum like a brakeless train on a downgrade.

Slim had used his resources to delve into South Africa's far right organizations. In his article, he had speculated about Davenport's probable connections with South African intelligence and the Afrikaner Resistance. Slim's digging had unearthed credible stories of a network of white supremacists in Western intelligence establishments. Among other clandestine doings, they helped white terrorists from former European colonies find sanctuaries. Insiders called it the under-cover railway.

Slim was pleased with his article, which newspapers across the country had reprinted. He hoped for something similar for the new one he'd post today.

As if my thinking about him had conjured him up, Slim squeezed into the courthouse, notebook in hand, and stood near the door. The judge hadn't yet made an appearance.

I moved beside him and leaned on the back wall, dodging the light switch. "How many versions of this story have you written?"

"Only three, with a little room to add unexpected details for each possible verdict."

"After that publication ban, you'll get first page treatment."

"That spot's mine, and I'll make the deadline if this circus ever gets going. Are you still sticking with not guilty?"

I had bet Slim a fifty-cent piece that Gould would be acquitted. Slim had suggested making it a silver dollar. That was too rich for my gambling-averse blood, so we stuck with the half amount.

"I hope to double my coin," I said, "but I'm not expecting it to go Gould's way. Did you bring yours?" It wasn't the kind of currency anyone normally carried.

"You'll find out when we know the decision," Slim said. "And to be precise, we're talking about today's verdict, not some possible appeal, right?"

"I guess we'll have to see about that, too," I said, even though he knew

I didn't mean it. "What does your first version predict?"

"It won't be first degree murder, no matter what you think. I didn't bother to write that account."

"Juries are strange animals," I said. "I've seen some dicey verdicts come down, and I think Gould will be nailed to a bigger cross than the one Philip Lockhart is wearing. I take it not guilty is your third and least likely write-up?"

"Definitely. My first story is guilty of second-degree murder. But it's hard to prove intent to kill in a case with no confession and no body."

"So, they'll probably come back with manslaughter."

"That's my third version. Only Gould knows how the homicide happened, if he did it, which you don't believe."

"Davenport hasn't come forward to say anything different. You wrote that long article about him and you still don't believe me?"

"I'm not paid to believe. I'm paid to report what I unearth. I threw a lot of allegedlys into my article. My editor didn't insist. Any way it comes out, there'll be a story people think they need to hear. And probably a sequel. These cases always go to the next stage."

"What convinced you to lean on the guilty side of the scales?" I said.

"You get a feel for the way a trial plays out. The prosecutor laid out a strong case, and the defence fumbled the rebuttal. Crown made chopped suey out of your theory about a second murder suspect and planted evidence. You came across as irrational and obsessive."

"I can be both."

"Then there was that hilarious Darryl, the important witness you'd touted. The defence showed him a picture of Melody, and he dutifully identified her as the woman he saw at Davenport's. But he'd barely glanced at it. During the cross, the prosecutor showed him a line-up of pictures and he couldn't pick Melody out. He had to admit he didn't look at her face, and why. We're still laughing about that."

I'd heard the same story from Lauren, who'd exclaimed, "What a pig!"

"I gather Gould came across as equally unbelievable?"

"The prosecutor wore a chest full of ribbons after Corporal Smith took the stand and described Gould's *volt-faces*. He must have fallen for every interrogation blunder in the book. Once you change one story and then backtrack on it, nothing you say is credible. But Gould guaranteed his own conviction when he took the stand."

"He'd insist on giving his side," I said dryly.

"He desperately wanted to, despite his lawyer's advice. By then, the prosecutor had primed the jury not to believe a word he said. Gould pleaded with them, broke down, said he deeply loved the daughter he had abandoned and only just met, that he had reformed his life and wished he could share it with her, yadda yadda. It was incredible, in the actual meaning of the word."

"And, by testifying, he opened himself to cross examination," I said.

"It was brutal. The fact the victim was the accused's daughter shocked the jury when they learned about the connection."

"Lauren wanted to leave that out to protect Morgan."

"Not a chance. It headlines all three of my versions," Slim said.

"Then the forensics experts piled on the hard evidence," I said.

"Juries find it irresistible. Like Gould's foot. It had a fresh sore exactly above the nail coming though the bloody hunting boot. He'd recently worn it."

"Technical evidence is a lot more complicated than it's made to sound."

"The jury sits there and their eyes glaze over while the experts disagree over their different, but absolutely scientific, results. The same for the lie detector test. What's the jury supposed to think?"

I frowned. "Wouldn't disagreeing experts lead to reasonable doubt?"

"The jury wants to believe someone. In this trial, it was the judge."

"There's a rumour he wasn't the neutral arbiter he's supposed to be."

Slim gave a shrug. "The jury already loved him for his unctuous concern for their comfort. In his instructions, he focused on the reliability of the prosecutor's expert witnesses and said they should believe what the physical evidence has shown to be factual. He singled out the blood as a stand-in for the victim's body. You didn't have to be an Amazing Kreskin to read the bias in his mind."

"It sounds like the judge was trying his damnedest to join the legion of Canadian miscarriers of justice," I said.

"All of these errors have come up before. But the point is, the evidence in this case was convincing. Motive, opportunity, forensics, the whole thing. Your girlfriend was clear and concise, strictly professional."

Slim turned his head to look directly at me. "I'd sure like to overhear the pillow-talk between you two when this case comes up. It can't make for pleasant evenings."

"We try to appreciate each other's point of view."

"Good luck with that."

"Sounds like I should start polishing my coin."

"You haven't done that already?"

We sat in silence while Slim began taking notes about the mood in the courtroom. No doubt he'd already included the description in all three versions, saying it matched the weather.

Light rain had made for an especially gloomy drive from Halstead. The rain, drizzle, and fog pattern was stodged in for days on the South Shore. The miserable weather provided a fitting but entirely random metaphor for the trial.

Finally, with the judge seated in place, twelve of Gould's so-called peers filed sombrely into the jury box. I retained the slimmest of faint hope clauses for my fifty-cent piece and the much heftier denomination Gould had at stake. The defence lawyer's summation would have stressed the meaning of reasonable doubt, a cornerstone of justice. Even so, the prosecutor speaks last, which can tip the scales in favour of the Crown.

When the foreman pronounced the jury's verdict, the gasps from the assemblage were difficult to gauge. They had found Gould guilty of manslaughter.

The judge scheduled a sentencing hearing for a week's time. He would hear submissions as to sentence, including victim-impact statements, all premised on Gould's now factual and certified guilt of manslaughter.

Gould hung his head and visibly shrivelled as he was led out the back door to the county lockup.

Slim pushed his way out, heading for the foyer pay phone to file story draft B. But not before he pocketed my fifty-cent piece.

Almost no one in the courtroom seemed pleased with the outcome, including the throng from Halstead who had come down to witness a legal lynching. Guilty of murder would have made a more just-deserts verdict for the bloodthirsty. Morgan was shaken with sobs and needed Lauren's consolation. Georgina and Mrs. Gould were also in tears. No one comforted them.

Philip Lockhart sat, stone-faced and unmoved by his wife's emotional outburst. He'd remember the weather as having been clear and sunny.

The courtroom cleared quickly. I followed the disgruntled crowd to the front steps, where reporters waited to snatch a soundbite from any of the principals they could ambush. The prosecutor recited a short, set speech about justice being served. The defence lawyer promised her client would be considering grounds for an appeal. She meant she would be.

It wasn't only the verdict or the prosecutor's circumstantial case or my failure on the stand that left me feeling drained. The enactment of formal justice leaves me cold and discouraged. The simplistic verdict of guilty or not guilty seldom fits the complex context of a case. Finding the whole truth and compressing it into one or two words is beyond the possible.

So many contingent and random factors converge at the individual level that doubt shrouds plausability. In science, a fact is only a probability, even when the likelihood is so high it seems absolute, like the inevitability of the sun rising every morning. Until one day it doesn't because it no longer exists.

I looked for Lauren in the melee. She was trying to shepherd Morgan and her parents away from the mics and gawkers. After she manoeuvred Georgina and Philip into her car, we had a brief chance to talk.

"How's Morgan taking the verdict?"

"She's even more sure she wants to talk to Gould. How do you feel?"

"At least the verdict is recompense for Morgan's rape, which Gould has never acknowledged. How about you?"

Lauren reached out and touched my hand sympathetically. "I don't feel vindicated." Then she hurried the Lockharts away.

I felt empathy for Morgan's loss. Nothing that had happened in the last eighteen months had given me any closure, either. Not only had the murderer escaped, but Gould had been wrongfully convicted in his stead. Picturing my upcoming weekend with Lauren kept me from feeling hollow and defeated.

30: Choices

For the next two weeks, fall semester classes and noon hour basketball gave a semblance of order to the irregular pace of my life. Then a couple of developments brought the Melody Lockhart case to the forefront of my sloping head.

On Tuesday, while eating a take-to-work lunch of Massaman curry and home made, fried roti bread, I received a call from a lawyer in Toronto. He had read Slim's articles about the Gould trial in the *Toronto Star*. At this stage, he said, he was collecting more information and sought my opinion on the verdict. I gave him an earful about the competence of the judge and Gould's lawyer. He intended to examine the court transcript when it was available. He'd worked with Innocence Canada but wanted to avoid raising false hopes and hadn't suggested Gould may be innocent.

"You can be wrongfully convicted if the trial is patently unfair," he said, "even if you actually did it. I'll offer to do some *pro bono* work on his appeal."

Gould's dangerous new world was behind the walls of the Atlantic Institution, the regional maximum-security penitentiary near Miramichi, New Brunswick. He was suffering the dull, punishing boredom of long-term confinement. I pictured him pacing back and forth in his cage, trying to keep the bottoms of his feet from over-heating. The judge had sentenced him to nine years, three fewer than the prosecutor had recommended. He'd been awarded reduced time to compensate for his pre-trial remand when he was still officially innocent.

I had some ambivalent sympathy for Gould, since he'd been convicted for an act he hadn't committed. Assuming he knew how to manage the parole hearing, he'd be let out on full parole in three years. The Board would expect an admission of guilt as a sign of his remorse. If Gould refused, he'd stay inside for three more before being released on mandatory. I thought he'd have better luck with an appeal and would bet a silver dollar on a positive outcome.

The following morning, I went to retrieve my college-destination mail from my box in the A&A building. The bulk of it usually consisted of inter-departmental envelopes with notices, agendas, and minutes from the tedious work required for what is left of faculty self-governance. On good days, I would find a copy of a journal. Today, only a single postcard lay on the bottom of the shelf. I pulled it out and stared at a picture of the gaudy Venetian casino on the Vegas Boulevard. It looked like it belonged in a Disney amusement park. Maybe that's where it was.

Flipping the card over, I saw at the bottom the initials XOX with a diaeresis above the O. I recognized the green ink and the feminine handwriting from June's card to Mary. This one had been mailed five days after the Gould trial ended and was postmarked Macao, a gambling haunt on the other side of the world. The hand-written note filled the space on the left of the card and spilled over under the address:

> Dear Ian
> I'm glad to hear that the case of poor Melody Lockhart has finally been resolved, although I doubt you have any satisfaction in these just deserts. I hear you're still prying into my affairs. You were wrong about the Rolex. It's genuine. And you still believe you're right about so much. My companion and I are enjoying life here immensely. I've had everything I could wish, except for a happier outcome from our last chat at the lake. Better luck next time?

The card reeked of Davenport; and now, so did Mary's card.

Selecting a reusable college envelope from the pile stacked by the outgoing mail slot, I dropped the postcard inside and took it to the detachment to show to Lauren. Even though the receptionist behind the security barrier knew me, I had to identity myself and tell her whom I expected to see. Constable Martin was in, as I had seen, spying through the glass into the main room.

Lauren perused the card and let out a thoughtful "Hmmn," like an annoying physician keeping his conclusion to himself. "Sergeant Young should see it," she said.

"That's the second reason I'm here."

She placed the card in a clear plastic evidence bag and knocked on

Young's open door. He was busy and said to wait. After a token ten minutes, he invited us into his office, making a vague excuse about paperwork, and made a show of examining the postcard.

"The green ink, the handwriting, and the little flourish at the end on this card match what's on the one June Davenport supposedly sent to Mary. Davenport sent them both."

"If you're right, now we know two places we won't find him," Young said. "I'll want to keep this."

"He probably spends time in both places, financing his lifestyle through gambling."

"He's smart enough to beat the odds," Young said. "Everyone I know who tries their luck in Vegas calls it Lost Wages."

"Macao is a former Portuguese colony," Lauren said. "But it's small and hard to hide in. Davenport might be somewhere in Indonesia. That was Dutch, like South Africa."

"Well, that narrows things down," Young said sarcastically.

He sat back in his chair, read the card, then re-read. He flicked it with his index finger twice. "To be clear, this card doesn't corroborate anything you said about the Lockhart case. We are still some distance apart on that."

"That's not the way I see it. It's his confession, only for two victims. But that implied threat at the end is hollow. He'll never come back here."

"I don't see Lockhart in this message. Once you get a fixed idea, you twist everything to make it fit," Young said, using an accusation I recognized. "But I'll need to see the first postcard and have both analyzed and fingerprinted. If they do appear identical, I'll open a quiet investigation into June Davenport as a missing person."

After Young's begrudging acknowledgement, I had to struggle to rein in my feeling of vindication. "Mary Tanner has the first card. She lives in Tedburn."

"It won't be easy to find June," Lauren said. "If she vanished on her own nickel, she'll be using an alias."

"Looking for her is work for a private investigator, with real police experience," Young said, not willing to commit any further.

I accompanied Lauren back to her desk and pulled over a seat from an empty cubicle. I sat at the side, angled towards her.

"It feels like I've just come out of a cock fight in Mexico," Lauren said. "Between two stubborn, male egos."

"I'm right about Davenport."

"Thanks for demonstrating my point."

"You don't agree?" I said, feigning surprise.

"No, but not for the reason you think. I startled myself awake about three o'clock this morning and said aloud, *Melody isn't dead*. I've been thinking it through ever since."

Her claim stunned me. "What? I understand Morgan clinging to a final hope, but not you."

"Davenport meant Melody when he wrote 'my companion.'"

"Surely not. He's been stringing different women along for years. I'm the one he sent the postcard to. It's some chest-pounding about his latest conquest."

"Men view the world from the point of view of the sun. Everything revolves around them."

"Are you sure self-centredness is sex specific?"

"We've been presuming Melody Lockhart is the innocent victim of some evil man," Lauren continued, ignoring my rebuttal.

"Evil men. It started with her adoptive father and ended with Davenport, and I mean ended with."

"There are some things that don't add up in your version of things."

"Like for instance?" I said testily.

"The motive you gave Davenport for killing Melody has always seemed iffy to me," Lauren said.

"Motives, you mean. He's a white supremacist. Seeing her as non-white diminished her as a person. And he had to protect his dangerous secrets. Just as he destroyed his history in Nova Scotia, he extinguished Melody as part of it."

"White men have assaulted women of colour for centuries. Don't assume Melody's apparent race reduced Davenport's attraction. He believed the *Birth of a Nation* fable about bi-racial offspring being congenitally cunning and sexualized. He wanted to exploit the idea, not extinguish it."

"Maybe," I said, trying to remember what he'd told me. "He didn't confess because planting false evidence implicating Gould made a cleaner get-away."

"That fits with my reasoning. But making Gould look guilty was also Melody's revenge for her mother's rape. She'd hugged her mother so tightly their last time together partly out of sympathy for what she'd gone through. But she was also saying good-bye."

"Wouldn't it devastate Morgan to believe her daughter was dead?"

"She was the only one that Melody was concerned about. I think she made that hard choice. Morgan says she doesn't believe it."

"That's self-protection." A rock-hard image was working its way into my shoe. "Why would Davenport take his boat into the bay in the day before he left except to dispose of Melody's body?"

"His boat hadn't been in the water since the fall, and he needed a trial run."

"She knew secrets he wanted to protect," I said.

"I agree with you that Melody discovered something about Davenport's past, or he revealed it to her. I think that strengthened their bond rather than making her a threat."

"I saw in her binder diary that her personality was morphing. Aren't you making the transformation too extreme?"

"Not if she has a predilection to extremes, like her father," she said. "Davenport's lifestyle was privileged, but he wasn't just a good catch. Melody saw him as exciting, edgy, daring. Some women are drawn irresistibly to dangerous men."

"Okay, but you're describing the Melody before Morgan came out as her mother and before she discovered Gould was her father. That's when her relationship with Davenport unravelled."

"I don't think so. Melody believed what her mother told her about Gould. He wasn't any father saying how much she looked like her pretty mother. Melody told Morgan he was checking her out. Seeing through Gould strengthened her ties with Davenport."

"Okay. The new-skin Melody was drawn romantically to him. You're suggesting his attraction to her was mutual and not opportunistic."

"Thinking about Davenport," Lauren said, as though she were painstakingly developing the idea in the dark room of her mind, "the repressed Melody posed no challenge. He was attracted to her because he saw something more than an abused and timid young woman he could exploit. She had sparks of independence and autonomy. During their passionate affair, he helped her emerge from her chrysalis. And when she did, he found she was more than his creation."

"My eyewitness didn't glimpse an in-command, assertive Melody at Davenport's house, only a drugged, almost comatose one."

'Unless it was self-inflicted, part of some risky and intense infusion of drug-induced dopamine."

"If Davenport is drawn to independent women, it's to impose his will and break them. We've learned about the ways women are victimized by the men in their lives."

"Power dynamics are crucial," Lauren agreed.

"But Melody wasn't your classic victim, locked in a basement waiting for Detective Charming," I said.

Lauren crinkled her eyes as though she'd suppressed an amusing comeback. "Or freeing herself through her own initiative. Seeing women only as victims is one-sided. Women are also independent agents who act on their choices."

I could complete the picture Lauren was fashioning. Sex, so vital to humans, can be a paradox of opposites, a weapon of total power or a gentle caress laced with passion. "Sex is an enigma that may have nothing to do with love. It can be a tactic of the dominant or of the powerless to assert some control."

"He'd awakened her will to power as well as her libido," Lauren said. "But sexuality isn't the only power women have."

"I can see that, looking at you."

"Are you coming around to my point of view? The simplest explanation is best."

"It's troublesome. Your story makes Andy's explanation spot-on. Melody ran away with her boyfriend. It also means Young was right about me being blinded by tunnel vision."

"The problem I have is that mine is too much like yours: held together by thought more than facts. And it makes Melody a criminal for planting evidence and obstructing justice, not to mention the frauds she'll have to pull off to sustain a new identity."

"If you're right, Melody will soon learn the man she's attracted to will bring her nothing but grief."

"That worries me, too," Lauren confided quietly. "I hope it's Davenport who's taken on more than he can handle. I feel confident about our new Melody."

"Our new Judith, assuming she's using her Biblical first name."

Lauren looked beyond me towards the window and the wider world. "I hope it's prophetic."

"I love your out-of-the-box thinking, Lauren, and especially your wilful optimism. I'm mired in the pessimism of intellect."

I wasn't convinced she was right. Davenport wasn't merely capable of murder. He had no proverbial ethical ballast, no moral scruples. For him, only the end mattered. Killing me would have been an inconvenience. Melody had become a liability he had to bury before he returned from limbo. He lacked the sentimentality to think the way Lauren did, let alone act on the impulse.

I went back to my regular work feeling humbled instead of vindicated. Lauren and I have shared many experiences and interpreted some of them in different ways, but in our relationship, we lived a common reality. I hoped this feeling of oneness would continue as we lived together separately.

Leaning back in my chair, I reflected on the diversity of truths and each person's understanding of reality, on the difference between knowing and believing. People don't perceive reality or interpret things the same way. And what we assert as truth is never simply the outcome of rational thought. I had doubts about all three versions of Melody's fate. Applying our beliefs to a narrative creates a new reality, changing our way of perceiving it and transforming its appearance.

Keats may be right that truth and beauty are one and the same. Then truth must also be in the eye of the beholder. If truth isn't an illusion but a matter of belief, is one person's version of truth more valid than another's?

I pictured myself searching for the answer in Tennessee Williams' dark, bottomless well. Maybe that kind of truth is unfathomable. Truth is what we believe, regardless of why. You can always find evidence to support any theory.

But a world of complete relativism can't exist. Daily life is impossible unless we act on the assumption that the well has a palpable bottom, the way we trust in the existence of the atom, a thing so small we can't see it. I live with ambiguity, but my faith is in the means, not the end—the rational and just search for transient truths, big and small.

Survival requires some common realities, although constructing them seems inconceivable in this increasingly polarized world. Relationships can bring anguish to our lives, but they are also the salve that softens the relentless desire for truth and ideals, and relieves, however temporarily, the bleak aloneness.

The End

Tony Thomson

Acknowledgements

This book is the result of a collaboration with many people, and I owe many debts of gratitude to them. Foremost, I offer my heartfelt thanks to my wife and partner of fifty years, Heather Frenette. From the book's first conception, she supported and encouraged me to tackle fiction, an entirely new venture for me after the academic tomes that preceded it. She focused her critical, poetic, wordsmith, and editorial skills to sharpen the writing, to have it say what I had intended, and to save it from some big and small blunders—we shared many laughs over them. Heather, I could not have written it without your inspiration and our spirited dialogue.

We owe a special thanks to our son, Devon Thomson, who created the cover art. We are proud of his work and impressed with how well he incorporated thematic elements of the book into his artistic vision. We want to express our heartfelt thanks to our daughter, Julia Barnes, who witnessed the process of writing and editing over several months while we enjoyed her hospitality and spent time with family in Medicine Hat, Alberta.

I have had the privilege, over the years, of working with many talented editors. At Moose House, I could not wish for a more collaborative and supportive relationship than the one I enjoyed with Andrew Wetmore. Even after many years, I am still amazed how an editor can improve sentences I thought were fine, suggest the perfect word, shock me with background error checks, and discover misplaced modifiers and other gaffes, always with an equally keen sense of humour. I am a slow pupil. He must have chafed every time he had to point out the creative ways I tried to use the passive voice. He probably thought I was writing a lab report.

Lyn Thomson read the earliest iteration of the book in chapter-by-chapter instalments as they rolled out of my computer. Thank you, Lyn, for your encouragement and for your insight and commentary. Among other things, she tried valiantly to rid the book of unnecessary 'that's and 'up's. Some have crept back in.

Many other people had a hand in reading all or parts of the manuscript and offering valuable help. Once the manuscript had reached what I thought erroneously was a final draft, I sought readers who, I hoped, would find the book promising and offer critical help. I want to offer them my humble thanks for their time and support.

In addition to her long list of errata, Rhianna Trillo reminded me that carbon monoxide is odourless. Susan Haley asked some relevant questions about parts I had handled inadequately, told me to keep my names straight, and pointed out the importance of motivation. It was so good to hear her say I 'had something.' In addition to pointing out the coniferous hackmatack loses its needles in the fall, not the spring, Ann Manicom hinted broadly about the danger of writing too fancily. Bernard Delpêche tried twice to improve my first-year French. I'm grateful for his efforts.

Chris McCormick liked the manuscript enough to discuss who, in New Brunswick, might be interested in publishing it. Herbert Gamberg couldn't believe I dared to write fiction. Tony Gamberg was shocked to discover some of the dialogue was quite acceptable, and he recapped for me the necessity of following a classic story arc. I had never intended to follow all the blueprint, but he tried.

I am indebted to James Lawther, who is busily compiling an encyclopedia of crime fiction. He agreed to post my appeal for manuscript readers on his Twitter account. With his help, several brave volunteers from three countries offered their help. Nic Perrins read a second draft of the manuscript that opened with a prologue, drawn from later in the book. She asked, if I ever thought to publish the book without it, to let her know and she would talk me out of it. In addition to thanking her for her assistance, I apologize for not getting in touch about plunging into the story unprologued. Janaki Brolin swapped stories with me and found places where my story lagged. I read her "Tukul Story" about European physicians practising in West Africa with great interest. I want to thank Kylie Wells for her offer to edit the book when it was still in a raw state. I was pleased with her reaction to the ending and hope to have at least one reader of the final version down under.

Bianca Marais hosts a regular podcast called "The Shit No One Tells You About Writing." She linked many of her numerous contacts into small writers' groups, based on shared interests, to exchange their writing and comment on other members' work. My group consisted of four other aspiring or practising mystery/thriller writers, all American. I am grateful for the critiques of Dyan Fox, Cindi Pauwels, Phoebe Rowe, and Linda

Koeniguer. Unlike my book, in which the narrative voice belongs to an investigator with no personal connection to the victim, the first-person protagonist in each of their works was someone intimately connected with the crime.

I am responsible for any remaining errors in the book, which have stubbornly persisted despite the best efforts of all the above editors, reviewers and early readers.

Tony Thomson

About the author

Tony Thomson was born in the Hydrostone District of Halifax and spent much of his youth on Lawrencetown Beach, where his parents had a cottage and later built a permanent home. He graduated from Graham Creighton High School and studied at Dalhousie and the University of Cambridge, where he completed a doctorate in social and political science. He enjoyed a long career teaching sociology at Acadia University, and still teaches part-time.

He and his wife, Heather Frenette, worked on restoring a century home in Canning, where they raised two children, Julia and Devon. They now also enjoy their two grandchildren.

In addition to articles, book chapters, and two co-authored books, Tony has written two volumes on the history of social thought, published by Oxford University Press: *The Making of Social Theory: order, reason, and desire* and *Modern Social Thought: an introduction*.

About Face is his first work of fiction.

CPSIA information can be obtained
at www.ICGtesting.com
Printed in the USA
BVHW092050110822
644329BV00003B/11